"Pardon?" Alyss's voice came in a whisper, but he seemed to hear well enough.

"I said your brother wished us to wed."

The sound of a million crickets chirruped in her ears. His lips continued to move, but she heard nothing as her bottom hit stone and she collapsed onto a step. Her eyes saw only him.

He loomed over her, fists propped on hips, dark hair brushing those broad shoulders. She raised her brows in a level gaze—and inhaled sharply. Hazel eyes, sprinkled with green and gold chips, gleamed back. Luring. With effort, she recalled his recent words, and her thoughts focused.

She shot to her feet. "You must be mad. I have no intention of wedding a stranger who appears at my gate with some imaginary story of my brother's last commands. I remind you, sir, you are a guest. In fact, I must ask you to leave. Your behavior is intolerable."

His big hands closed around her shoulders. They were warm. Firm but gentle. She shook them off.

"I'm afraid I can't do that, my lady," he murmured.

For This Knight Only

by

Barbara Bettis

Knights of Destiny

This is a work of fiction. Names, characters, places, and incidents are either the product of the author's imagination or are used fictitiously, and any resemblance to actual persons living or dead, business establishments, events, or locales, is entirely coincidental.

For This Knight Only

Cover Art by *Debbie Taylor*

The Wild Rose Press, Inc.
PO Box 708
Adams Basin, NY 14410-0708
Visit us at www.thewildrosepress.com

Publishing History
First Tea Rose Edition, 2019
Print ISBN 978-1-5092-2547-7
Digital ISBN 978-1-5092-2548-4

Knights of Destiny
Published in the United States of America

Dedication

Thanks to the wonderful critique partners
who were part of Roark and Alyss's long journey:
Diana, Jean, Kaye, Angela, Jenn, Sara Ann, Marci,
Kayla, Lisa, the Critters,
and beta readers Samanthya and Lane;
and to my patient and supportive editor, Allison Byers.
I appreciate you all tremendously.

Chapter One

Chauvere Castle, Nottinghamshire, England
January 1194

Alyss of Chauvere winced at the grating thud of stone against stone. Another catapult strike. She clinched her teeth and frowned. Blast and bedamned to Sir Jasper of Windom for attacking her home. The land-greedy wretch. Another jolting crash sent her thirteen-year-old sister, Evelynn, into Alyss's arms. The girl's stiff form trembled, and Alyss knew she fought back tears.

Hovering just inside the solar, Chauvere's priest braced himself.

"Have mercy on these your children, O Lord." Father Eudo closed his eyes and raised his pinched face piously in the direction of heaven, but his thin hands never loosened their grip on the door jamb.

Alyss slanted a glance at Evie, whose face pressed against Alyss's shoulder. "If God had mercy, he'd direct a bolt of lightning at Sir Jasper's black heart. Although He probably couldn't find it."

Evie choked out a laugh, and her tense muscles eased under Alyss's fingers.

The priest leveled his unamused gaze at the two.

Oh, dear. Alyss sighed. He had his women-are-the-spawn-of-Satan look. If he began his speech about

1

females understanding their place in God's plan, he'd be impossible to divert.

"Father, are you certain you can get Evie away unseen?" Alyss hoped the question turned his thoughts away from his impending lecture and back to the upcoming journey. For good measure, she added, "I can always send one of the guards."

The maneuver worked.

"I am the best one to escort Lady Evelynn to the convent." Father Eudo's tone lost its sanctimonious lilt when he added, "From the sounds of the army outside the gates, all our soldiers are needed here."

His expression managed to convey both indignation and scorn—indignation at the thought of sending another in his place and scorn that Alyss resisted the siege.

Alyss gave Evie a hug and stepped away, hands clasped at her waist. "I trust no one more than you with my sister's safety. I'm certain Sir Jasper's attack will end soon. No knight would intentionally destroy a holding he wants as his own."

If only that were true. She didn't trust Windom's lord to behave reasonably; experience proved him a lying schemer.

Father Eudo's mouth twisted in disdain. "Perhaps if you had accepted his offer of marriage—but I've said all I can on that matter." He released his hold on the doorframe and made for the corridor. "I will be in the chapel, praying for our journey. Have your sister ready to leave following compline."

After he disappeared, Evie raced to drop the bar across the door and whirled to Alyss. "If Sir Jasper won't do more damage, there's no reason for me to go.

And Papa will be better soon. Things will change."

Her voice brimmed with such confidence, such faith. Alyss recalled a time when she'd possessed a similar trust in the world. Long ago, it seemed. Now she knew better, and she'd do everything in her power to postpone the hard awakening destined for her sister.

Evie had to leave. The outer bailey defense had weakened, and if Sir Jasper and his soldiers breached it with their infernal catapult, who knew how long the inner bailey wall could stand? A chill skittered down Alyss's arms at the thought of what might happen to her sister then.

But worst of all, Papa would never be better. Not in this life.

She must not allow Evie to suspect. Alyss swallowed against a burning tingle in her throat. This was no time to break down. And frankly, she couldn't do what she must with her sister close by. The danger was too great.

"You know it is for the best, love." Alyss tucked a glossy brown curl under the cap covering Evie's hair. The rough black wool was part of the clothing Alyss had borrowed from the cook's son. Father Eudo had been horrified when Alyss suggested it. But enemy soldiers took no notice of a boy.

"Papa will feel easier when you're not in danger. Visiting at St. Ursula's is wise, just until this dispute with our neighbor is settled."

"Come with me, then," Evie begged, her voice edged with panic. "I don't want to leave you alone."

"Until Papa is better, I am needed here. But if things get too bad, I'll join you at the convent." God forgive her for the lie. Alyss would not be leaving

3

Chauvere.

As long as no one knew the seriousness of Papa's condition, the castle would be safe. Provided the garrison withstood this latest threat. Sir Jasper had proved disgustingly persistent since she'd rejected his last offer.

"If I go, do you vow not to marry Sir Jasper?" Evie whispered. "I'm afraid of what will happen."

"You have my pledge. Nothing could force me to wed that snake." He cared not a whit about her. He wanted access to Chauvere's extensive land and tenants. With her brother away and her father's health failing, Sir Jasper intended to take advantage. If she wouldn't marry him, he'd try to find another way to usurp control of the castle.

He'd underestimated his opponent. She'd never relent. And with Evie safely away, he'd have no means to compel her.

Evie half-heartedly stuffed a comb into her pack, then knotted the top. "When do you think Henry will return? If he were here, no one would dare attack us."

When indeed? Their brother needed to be home now, not gallivanting in another land, awaiting the convenience of the kidnapped King Richard. "The king's ransom is being delivered, and he's bound to be released soon. Henry will accompany him back to England."

Evie studied the satchel. "What if he doesn't arrive in time?"

Alyss hugged her. "Stop fretting. Sir Jasper will go home, like before. He doesn't really want to destroy the castle. We will be fine. Now, while you say goodbye to everyone, I'll make certain enough guards are posted for the night. Listen. You hear? The barrage has stopped."

Striding along the corridor toward the great hall, Alyss prayed the decision to send Evie away tonight had been the right one. Even if Sir Jasper resumed attack come dawn, the night promised cover enough for two people to slip through the secret tunnel. Once in the village, Father Eudo and Evie would gather horses and be off to St. Ursula Convent. It lay close enough for the priest to return by first light.

The evening passed in a fog of unreality. Alyss bid farewell to Evie and Father Eudo, then returned to the keep where she prepared a tray for Papa. Perhaps this night he'd awaken and wish for soup. Or at least some ale. He did like his ale.

When she slipped into her father's bedchamber, his still figure lay in the same position it had when she left hours ago. Alyss placed the tray on a table, added a few lumps of charcoal to the brazier, then pulled her father's carved-back chair close to the bed. As she had last night and the night before, she wrapped a fur around her shoulders and prepared to keep vigil.

Placing a hand lightly on his chest, she kissed his forehead. "I'm here, Papa. Please come back to us. If you can't, then know we love you. And give Mama our love when you see her."

****

Alyss awoke abruptly, as if she'd been prodded. Silence. A weak flame from the night candle winked in the darkness. Chill enveloped the room. Around the edges of the window covering trickled the faint light of dawn.

She rose and touched her father. Beneath the furs

that covered him, his hands were cold. She lifted one to her lips. The skin held an odd quality, apart from the temperature of the bedchamber. She knew this chill. Her mother's skin had the same feel after the fever claimed her.

Alyss collapsed onto the chair. He was gone. Her strong, courageous, warrior of a father. At three-score and ten years, he'd lived a long life, filled with glory in battle, and love for his wife, his children, and his people. And they all had loved him in return. The knowledge didn't lessen the pain in Alyss's chest. She'd need to notify Sir Baldwin and the others. Head bowed, her father's hand clutched between both of hers, she wept.

Suddenly, the grinding crash of rocks penetrated her grief. Startled voices mingled with the grating, shuddering thuds that echoed in the too-still bedchamber.

Alyss leaped to her feet, laying her father's hand on his chest. Sir Jasper had used the catapult again. *Jesu.* She raced to the window, pulled aside the thick linen covering, and opened the wooden shutter. Cold dampness bathed her cheeks as she peered into the fog-drenched darkness. Heart thudding, she listened.

Nothing. Perhaps he'd thrown one last, bitter volley as a farewell. Now he'd pack up and leave, as he had the last time. He'd likely be back, as happened before, but she'd face that problem when it came.

Then another thud...and the sound of crumbling rock rumbled. Shouts floated upward. She stood on her toes to see what had happened, and... Her breath caught in her throat. The outer bailey! Whether or not he'd intended to bring down the curtain wall, it had collapsed.

Chauvere's emergency plan called for the men to retreat to the inner bailey where they'd take up pre-assigned posts. The wall there was strong, as was the gate. Still, Sir Jasper gained an unexpected advantage. Knowledge that the enemy had breached a part of the perimeter was bound to affect the people's confidence. She needed to reassure them.

First, however, she returned to the bed, gently smoothed the arm of her father's shirt. He was pain-free at last. She should thank the Holy Mother for that. But she wasn't grateful, she was sad—and angry. Her rock of a father gone—it seemed impossible. And how could his people grieve him properly when they must battle a heedless enemy?

For the last sennight, after Sir Jasper brought his army to camp in the clearing outside the castle, the soldiers had displayed little aggression. They much preferred to relax in their tents and devour food confiscated from the villagers.

Why attack now? It was as if Sir Jasper learned her father's health had suddenly worsened. But only Sir Baldwin and Father Eudo knew. Alyss had asked that no one else in the castle or village be told. They'd enough to worry over without fearing for their lord's life.

Even Sir Godfrey had left for Mainz immediately after her father had collapsed days earlier, before this last decline. How long would it take him to bring back Henry, along with the men of the garrison who'd gone with her brother to fetch the king?

Alyss couldn't deny Sir Baldwin's devotion, but battle days were long over for the old knight who took

Sir Godfrey's place as captain. At least she'd been able to help plan the defense.

Someone pounded at the door. "Lord Ulrich. Lady Alyss. He's gained the keep."

Impossible! Sir Jasper's soldiers couldn't have overrun the inner bailey so quickly. Brushing back a strand of hair, she dashed to the window again.

A glow of weak morning light revealed a lifting of the fog—and Windom's army, just clambering over sections of the outer bailey wall where the rocks had given way. Nowhere near the castle. Who was inside?

Clashing metal sounded right outside the door. Heart at the back of her throat, Alyss raced to the bed. She grabbed her father's prized dagger, always at his side since the old King Henry bestowed it, and tucked her hand behind her. Pressing her other palm against her stomach to quell the trembling, she sucked in a breath and waited. If her life had come to this, so be it. At least Evie was safe.

The knife handle lay warm and smooth beneath her fingers as she maneuvered the grip in readiness. She'd never surrender. If Sir Baldwin could not come to her aid—well then, she would see how well his lessons had prepared her.

Alyss heard a grunt followed by a thud. The door shook. It burst open under a heavy boot and hit the stone wall behind.

Sir Jasper of Windom ducked his head and barreled through the opening, his sword lifted to catch the expected blow that never came. He stopped. He looked at the still figure of Sir Ulrich, then at her. He smirked.

"I heard your father was ill," he said, lowering his sword. "Pity."

He stalked toward the bed. "I had hoped to settle this today."

He stopped, sweat dripping onto his gray, bristly chin, moisture from his blue-veined nose coating the hair around his upper lip. The smell of horse, sweat, and unbathed man surrounded him. Alyss swallowed a gag.

"Ah, well. I still can." In what seemed like slow motion, he lifted his sword and plunged it into her father's chest.

She raised a horrified gaze to Sir Jasper. Her heart pounded, and she couldn't draw breath.

He laughed and strode toward her.

Alyss clutched her father's dagger and waited.

Chapter Two

On the road to Cologne
Early February 1194

He couldn't breathe.

Sir Roark of Stoddard struggled to free the twisted metal pressed against his nose. Finally it dislodged. He ripped off his bent helm and gulped in lungsful of air while his destrier, Cin, stood, head bowed. The battle raged nearby.

The king. Roark flung the helmet to the ground and surveyed the area. At the edge of a small clearing, Richard remained mounted, circled by his cadre of personal guards. Roark squinted toward a haze of dust disappearing down the road. Most of the soldiers chased the retreating outlaws.

Safe, then. He settled back and allowed himself a moment of ease. His left arm braced on the edge of the saddle, and his right arm rested along his thigh. In his hand drooped his sword, a pregnant drop of congealing blood trembling near its tip.

A sweet-metallic smell mixed with a sour stench clogged his throat. He'd nearly forgotten the murk of death surrounding a battle—odors of cooling blood, the bowels of men and horses, loosened in death. He had hoped never to experience it again.

He should have known better.

And just where in Hades had the band of outlaws come from? Surely they knew whom they attacked. Richard always traveled in ostentatious style. Which meant they hadn't been common thieves, to set upon a royal party bristling with guards.

A movement at his right brought his head around. Sir Alain reined in his horse and nodded toward the disappearing figures. "They were routed mighty quick."

"So they were," Roark muttered, then straightened. "I must find Lord Martin."

His liege lord had disappeared at first sign of attack, undoubtedly to aid King Richard. Roark prayed so. Martin of Cantleigh had been acting mighty odd the last days before Richard's release. Secret meetings, new mercenaries added to the troop, all with no word to Roark, captain of Cantleigh's guard.

"Where did he go?" Alain asked. "When I chanced to look, he'd disappeared."

Roark didn't answer. He rose in his stirrups to gaze again at the small clot of knights surrounding the king.

There. He picked out Cantleigh's wine-colored surcoat. His lord led a trio of horsemen approaching the royal circle.

Suddenly, a second band of riders burst from a clutch of thick brush and trees behind the king. *Satan's balls.* They must have waited while the others lured the bulk of the soldiers away, leaving the king vulnerable.

Roark touched his mount's flanks and raced forward. From the corner of his eye, he saw Alain alongside. Ahead, Richard's personal guard turned to meet the new onslaught. They were outnumbered.

The tight ring of warriors shielded the king. But damn. There went Richard, around the side with his sword drawn. Did he have no sense at all? That left his back unprotected.

Roark had almost reached the battle when he saw help approach the beleaguered group. Cantleigh and his three soldiers circled behind. But—

They didn't turn to ward off the enemy.

Roark froze with an icy sense of inevitability. Just what he'd feared. Damn all greedy nobles to fiery hell. Bile churned in his gut as he watched Cantleigh raise his weapon. Point it at the king's back.

The scene moved slowly before Roak's eyes, as if the action struggled through cold honey. Yet his thoughts raced to the decision he must make.

His liege lord or his king?

The man who rescued a miller's son from a burned cottage and set him on the path to knighthood, or the ruler to whom Roark pledged his life?

Before he was conscious of deciding, he roared, "'Ware, Richard. 'Ware the king."

The words scarcely left his lips when one of the guards broke away. Someone had heard, praise God. Turning, the knight met Cantleigh's attack.

The remaining guards hacked their way forward, pushing back the assassins. For the moment. But the odds were not favorable. Unless the absent soldiers gave up pursuit of the original outlaws and returned, the king's men would fail.

But by God's heart, they'd try. He'd try. The knowledge that his own lord turned traitor threatened Roark's concentration. He pushed the distraction aside. He'd deal with it later.

For now, he guided his horse to the right, behind the last of Cantleigh's men. Roark recognized Jenkins, the latest hire, from the man's studded shield and stained brown tunic.

The knight heard Roark's approach and turned, sword lifted. Roark blocked the blow, and the momentum of the move brought the other man around. They hacked at each other, both searching for an opening.

Roark slashed his sword time and again on the mercenary's right side where the man's guard proved weak. The repeated blows loosened links of his opponent's mail. If he could get close enough to act on that opening…

Then Cin proved his worth as a war horse and nipped the neck of the other mount. It swerved, bringing Roark close enough to thrust his sword through the damaged mail. He jerked the weapon free in a spurt of blood.

The mercenary swung his own sword as he fell, and a sharp pain pierced Roark's leg, a hand-span above his knee. He ignored the blow as the other man plunged to the ground, one foot caught in a stirrup. Wild-eyed, the man's horse lurched back then galloped off, dragging the body alongside.

Through the ringing in his ears, Roark distinguished shouts and the thunder of hooves. The rest of the contingent had returned. As he prepared to join them, he heard a bellow and saw a pair of fighters to his left.

His liege lord still faced one of the king's personal guard, the one who'd broken around at Roark's earlier warning. Roark watched the man who'd fostered him, knighted him, bound him with promises of land. Cantleigh was a skilled—and devious—fighter. But he'd met his match in this opponent.

Cantleigh swung; his blade connected. The knight flinched. The movements brought the horses close, and when Cantleigh shifted for another thrust, Richard's man found an opening. A flick of the sword severed the leather fastening of Cantleigh's neck guard, and the linked covering sagged. In a few more moves, the knight struck. The tip of his sword caught the other high in the throat, just beneath the chin. Blood spurted as Cantleigh tumbled to the earth.

The victor peered across the short distance at Roark. He lifted his sword in salute before surging back toward King Richard and the remnants of the battle.

"You know him?" Alain appeared at Roark's side, his horse blowing.

"Sir Henry of Chauvere." The knight was one of Richard's close-knit team of former Crusaders. Occasionally, Roark had overheard Sir Henry and his cronies joking, reminiscing of home as they all whiled away the weeks before Richard's release.

He'd never been a part of that elite group. But he'd had enough to do, keeping his own men in order during the long, cold days of waiting.

"Did he recognize *you* is the question?" Alain's voice took on an edge.

At this point, it didn't matter if Sir Henry had identified him. Roark shrugged and nudged his mount toward his fallen lord.

"Why do you suppose Cantleigh did it?" Alain sounded tired, resigned.

"God knows. He had riches, a large demesne, a beautiful lady, and a promising son." Yet he'd never been satisfied. Always fomenting some plan to oust a neighbor, claim the land. Although Roark shouldn't complain. One of those pieces of land had been promised to him as soon as they'd returned to England.

"More power?" he continued at last. "Why else would he plot against the king?"

"Then he was a fool," Alain said. "Who encouraged him, do you think?"

"Only one man could grant that kind of power." Prince John, Richard's far-from-loving brother. The man who would be king the day Richard died.

Today was not that day.

Roark stared at the body. His own dream lay just as dead as the figure before him. He fought the compulsion to howl in frustration. Everything he'd worked for, planned for, gone. Nearly twenty years of effort, destroyed the moment Martin of Cantleigh pointed a sword at the king's back.

"Who else of our men fought with him, could you tell?" Alain's voice brought Roark's thoughts back to the present.

"Findley, Morgan. And Jenkins."

"The mercenaries from Rouen?" Alain considered that piece of information. "Only the new men. None of our own company. Interesting."

"Isn't it?" Roark straightened at last and winced. Damned leg. But he'd suffered worse, and he had bigger problems right now. "Best find the priest...what's his name? Father Francis. He'll know what to do. And tell the other men."

Alain turned. "Are you coming?"

Roark shook his head. "Not now." He dismounted, but when his left foot hit the ground, his leg collapsed. Forehead beading with sweat, he caught the saddle with his left hand. His right still clutched the bloody sword. Blast, he hated to lose control like this.

"You're hurt." Alain slid to the ground. He checked the leg where blood welled sluggishly around metal links embedded in flesh, prodding until Roark hissed. "That's quite a gash. We need to get it tended."

"Not now," Roark repeated. "I'll be fine." He steadied himself, pushed away from Cin, and with determination limped forward. He paused beside Cantleigh's still figure for a moment, started to bend, then thought better of it. *Damned leg.*

He motioned to Alain. "See if he carries anything."

Alain went to one knee. Getting beneath the hauberk was nearly impossible, but Roark suspected a secret pocket in the gambeson. Alain pushed aside the mail neck guard and ran his fingers along the side of Cantleigh's throat, grimacing when he encountered cooling, sticky gore. He tipped the body to reach the other side.

"There is something." Sitting back on his heels, he grunted. Working his hand back and forth, he pulled free a cord. A bit more tugging brought forth a small, flat, leather packet.

"Here, use this." Roark handed him a dagger, and Alain cut one side of the cord, dragging it and the bag free. He held them up.

Roark opened the packet and peered inside. No use taking the parchment out; neither of them could read.

"Would he keep evidence that could convict him?" Alain asked.

Roark pursed his lips. "He would keep proof of promises made. He trusted no one. Hold on to this for now." He handed the pouch to Alain and limped toward his horse. A sharp pain made him clench his lips. Satan's backside. He didn't have time for this inconvenience. "There's a village just ahead, Cantleigh said last night. Meet me there after you've notified everyone. Tell Bernard he's in charge."

"Wait," Alain called. "What are you going to do?"

"The king's keepers won't notice one less sword. I need to think."

Roark pulled himself into the saddle, then urged Cin into a walk. The pain burning in his leg was manageable. The pain squeezing his chest for the life he would never have? Not so bearable.

All he ever wanted was a place to call his own. A small manor tucked away somewhere. For him the dream had an added incentive—the chance to rise above his birth. Eighteen years before, Martin of Cantleigh had given a ten-year-old boy that dream.

He'd worked tirelessly to prove himself loyal. Yet he'd been kept ignorant of today's plan. Little good that ignorance did him now. No one would offer a place to the captain of a traitor's guard. Provided he escaped being branded a conspirator, himself. Lifting the reins, he set out.

Cold dampness made the ride miserable, but as the morning progressed, the throb in his leg eased. He'd nearly decided he had taken a wrong turn and missed the village when a drift of gray appeared against the anemic blue sky. Fire. Warmth. God's legs, he could use some.

At the tiny inn, he eased down on a rough plank bench behind a table at the back. A half-dozen villagers dotted the dim enclosure filled with the comfortable odor of warm ale, stale smoke, and old grease. Luck was with him. None of the king's party had landed in this nondescript settlement. The entourage likely had moved on to Bonn.

He waved at a serving maid for a cup of ale, then giving a sigh, leaned against the wattle and daub wall. His bedamned leg throbbed again. Three refills of ale later, he closed his eyes to wait for Alain.

And to wonder. *Where do I go to start over?*

Chapter Three

Roark's eyes jerked wide, and his body tensed. Where the hell was he?

Then he recalled. The battle. The betrayal. The loss.

The disheartened ride to this village inn.

Alain should be here soon. He planted his elbows on the scarred wooden tabletop. Blasted head felt stuffed with wool. Mouth too. He ran his tongue around his lips. Dry. Must have downed too many mugs of ale.

He started to push to his feet but stumbled back at a searing jab in his leg. He sat heavily. Not only did his leg burn, his whole body throbbed. Satan's teeth! Felt like a team of oxen had done a fine job of trampling him. He set his jaw then gazed around.

Through a crack in the wall, a ray of light fought its way into the now-crowded room, catching dust motes in its watery beam before falling across a figure hunched at the end of the table.

An old knight with gray streaked through his thin brown hair wore a likewise-old chain mail hauberk in need of polishing but unbattered. He hadn't fought this day.

The man caught Roark's gaze, then pointed to the wound with his chin. "You get that riding with the king?"

Roark grunted.

19

"My lord's son was in that battle," he said. "I met the king's troops on the road. They're sayin' he died, but they didn't find his body. Nobody even looked, what with gettin' the king away safe." The harried serving maid brought a pitcher to replenish the oldster's drink. Seeing Roark awake, she refilled his cup.

"Don't know how I'll tell Lord Ulrich his boy's dead. If he's still alive hisself." The man downed a good bit of the fresh cup of ale. "Trouble 't home. Maybe more since I left."

He stared at the cup's remaining contents, sighed, and his elbow slipped off the edge of the table. Ale sloshed on the floor. He carefully placed his elbow back onto the plank top. "Sir Henry's needed there. And the men. If there's no help, the next siege'll end us."

Roark shook his head to clear the ringing in his ears. It didn't. "Your lord is under siege?"

"Not last I knew, but that'll change. Devil's spawn Jasper of Windom went away, but he wants our land and our lady. He'll be back."

The old man slammed down his cup. "If he learns Lord Ulrich's bad off again, he'll come like afore, and this time he won't leave."

"Jasper of Windom plans a siege against your lord?" Roark couldn't seem to get the story straight.

The knight nodded and leaned in, his voice becoming softer. "That Satan's backside thinks he'll take the castle and Lady Alyss. And her all worried about little Lady Evie."

The old one's voice sounded distant, but Roark was too tired to move closer. A little sword nick shouldn't wear him out like this. The pain seemed less now. Another drink might help. Roark waved the serving maid over while the old man continued to mutter.

"What about your lord?" Roark managed.

"Healer says he won't recover. Now our boy's dead. Lady Alyss'll be defenseless. First knight t' come along could marry her and take all. She deserves better."

The ringing in Roark's ears eased. *A lady alone.* That should be important to him, but he couldn't recall why. "Who is your lord?"

"Ulrich of Chauvere."

Roark's pain receded as memory fought to the surface. "Sir Henry's sire?" he ventured, breath held.

"Said so." Thick gray-brown eyebrows lifted in surprise. "Friend of the king, he is. Did you know our boy?"

Another wave of dizziness hit, and Roark struggled to look alert. He *would* focus, by God. "A good man. A warrior. Saw him just this morn, fighting alongside Richard."

He searched his memory for a name, any name he'd overheard Henry and his cohorts throw about in drinking sessions. One floated up from the depth of his mind.

"Would you be Sir Baldwin? Henry talked of you often." He wanted to set his cup down, but he wasn't sure of a steady hand, so he clutched it.

The man's faded gray eyes widened. "No," he rasped. "I'm Sir Godfrey. Sir Baldwin's captain of the guard, now. He's home, protectin' our ladies."

Godfrey…had Sir Henry ever mentioned him? Given the oldster's age, Roark took a chance.

"Ah, yes. You and Sir Baldwin, fighting friends of his father's." Guilt should have stopped him when he

21

saw the look of happiness on the lined face. He pushed it aside. Surely God understood. "Sir Henry was a good knight and a good friend. Pity if he's gone."

Roark blinked away two Sir Godfreys. Then the table seemed to move, and he nearly tumbled off the bench. He grasped the edge and lifted his head to see the old man come around to his side. The figure swayed back and forth.

Hands grasped his shoulders and leaned him against the wall. "Get yourself looked after now," he heard through the roar in his ears. "I'm goin' back to find Sir Henry."

****

A tug came to Roark's hand. *What?* Roark intended to speak, but the word echoed in his mind. Faded in the dark abyss of sleep. Why was he sleeping? A blunt force buffeted his shoulder, and his body slid to the side until the pressure on his stomach made him gasp and lift his eyelids. Try to lift them. Through their heavy, narrow slits, he recognized Alain.

His friend knelt in front of him. What in Hades was he do... Pain stabbed Roark's leg. "*Merde!*" The word burst from his throat in a near-whisper.

"*Jesu.* You didn't see to it."

"Waiting for you." Odd, the words were clear in his mind but garbled when they left his mouth.

Alain shoved him straight again. "Your leg. Needs to be cleaned."

That's right. He had a gash above his knee... The attack on the king.

"Let's get you back to camp." Alain grabbed his arm and tugged.

Roark wobbled to his feet. "No camp. No time."

Why? Why did he feel such urgency?

"Just as well," Alain muttered. "We probably couldn't make it that far in your condition."

Roark jerked his head and opened his eyes. "Need to tell you—" What? Something was hiding in a corner of his mind. What was it? Ah. About England. Something the old man said.

"We find a room, then talk," Alain insisted.

"Good. Bring the old soldier. He'll give us directions home."

"We'll see to this before we head home. You don't want to fall ill from your wound."

"I'm never sick," Roark said.

But Alain wouldn't stop, all but dragging him along to the front of the inn.

That's what I get for knighting my squire. Doesn't listen any more. "Wait," he insisted. "Got to remember... The old man at the table."

"There's no one else at the table."

The serving maid came toward them, and Alain said something to her. She shrugged and frowned, then Alain motioned toward Roark. What...? Oh yes. Language differences. Didn't matter. All Roark wanted right now was to sleep.

He didn't get his wish. By the time Alain and the girl helped him to a dingy storage shack at the back of the inn, he was wide awake. The place contained no cot, but propped against a wall was an old work table with a leg broken off. An empty wooden crate lay to the side. With his foot, Alain pushed it around, then pulled down the table. The edges failed to meet, and the flat surface trembled up and down.

"It'll have to do." Alain leaned against the edge.

"Roark? Here, sit."

Roark lowered himself to the makeshift bed, and the next several breaths came in grunts as his friend struggled to remove the damaged chausses. Finally, Alain dumped the mail to the side of the space, and Roark saw the wound in the wavering light of the lantern the girl held.

It looked like the devil's work. The force of blows had driven broken links into his flesh along the edges of a gash. Alain pulled his dagger and went to work loosening what he could, cutting away Roark's hose.

As the bloody material revealed the wound, the serving maid set down the lantern and pressed her hands against her mouth. Alain tugged at the dried fabric, re-opening the injury. Blood welled bright, trickling over the crusted remnants of earlier bleeds. She dashed for the door.

"So much for help," Alain muttered. "I'll need to dig out the embedded metal. We need rags and water, and something to bind this."

"Whole damned river out there," Roark gritted out.

"If only it was closer." Alain snorted. "This should be stitched."

Roark gave a strained chuckle. "Looks like we'll see if you've learned to thread a needle." The two of them had laughed once, during his squire's training, at the thought of Alain the smith's son trying to poke thread through the eye of a needle.

A scraping sound brought Roark's gaze to the door. The maid slid into the small, dim space and held out a wooden mazer filled with something.

Not water, he could smell that much. She pointed from the contents—was it ale of some kind?—to his leg. She wanted Alain to wash the wound in that? Eyebrows raised, she set the container on the ground.

Alain nodded thanks, then gestured as if he were sewing. She jerked her head and left.

"I could see better if you'd get your body out of the light," Alain grumbled. "Lie back."

"Mighty free with your orders," Roark muttered. "But under the circumstances, I agree." He lay, holding his jaw tight against any more sounds of discomfort. Self-pity had already made him drink too much earlier, and he hated to lose control. He refused to admit this puny cut might affect his stamina.

Cleaning out the gash was slow going and uncomfortable; perspiration trickled along Roark's forehead and down the side of his face, causing him to twitch his head. Alain growled at the movement. He'd finished when the girl finally appeared with a needle. God bless her, it was threaded.

Roark jerked at the first stitch. He longed to close his eyes and imagine his dream manor as his friend worked, but he forced himself to watch. Guided by the light of a sputtering stub of tallow candle in the old lantern, Alain pierced the ragged flesh carefully. Except for that first flinch, Roark didn't move. At some point, he must have closed his eyes, because the next he knew, a beam of sun woke him.

****

Roark disliked recovering from an injury. It forced him to sit still, and he hated inactivity. So by the next evening when Alain returned from the main camp, Roark had managed to pull himself up to sit on the side of the table. Injured leg straight out, he sipped a hearty, strongly fragranced soup of fish, onions, and cheese the maid had provided.

"You don't need to be up yet. You were lucky to have avoided the fever. Rest." Alain stepped into the cramped area, closed the door, and dropped a canvas bag. "And don't tear out those stitches. I refuse to do them again."

"You sound like your granny." Roark set aside the wooden bowl and looked down at the wound. The stiches lay straight and tight—damned good job. But Alain wouldn't like it if he said so. "You're right. You won't sew me again. I've never seen such sloppy work. Any lady in her right mind would make you tear those out and do them over."

Alain made a rude sound with his mouth, then grabbed a ragged blanket from the makeshift bed and wrapped it around his shoulders. Shivering, he picked up his own bowl of stew the girl left.

"What news?" Roark had spent the long hours of the day restless with worry over his men. He glanced at his friend, then gingerly tried to stand. After one tentative step, he tried a second.

"The king's party went on, but Richard was shaken by the surprise attack. There's talk he'll stop for a while in Cologne. The bishop invited him."

"How about our troop? Did we lose anyone?"

"The three with Sir Martin, of course. Two men-at-arms. Father Francis said he'll notify their families."

"God's bones." Roark's fist hit the table in frustration. He needed to be with his men. "What's happening with the others?"

"They're returning to Cantleigh with the priest, although the king asked them to stay." Alain's voice was nonchalant, but his blue eyes sparkled. "Sir Martin died protecting the king, after all."

Roark's head came up, and he winced as his leg jerked.

Alain nodded. "That's the story. Oh. And you're missing," he continued in a mournful tone Roark recognized as jesting. "Lost amidst the carnage."

Missing, am I? Perhaps it's for the best. He eased himself backward, balancing on his right leg again. "Tell the men..."

What? What could he say to the handful of warriors who had made the last years bearable? "Tell them I'll send word when I'm settled. Tell them thanks. And tell Bernard I'll collect my belongings as soon as I'm able.'"

Noticing his former squire's cold-pinched face, Roark added, "When you ride, carry along that blanket you're wearing. At least I'm in out of the weather."

Not until Alain left did Roark ease back onto his rickety bed, a grunt becoming a moan, pain pulling at his mouth. His fingers brushed dry, cracked lips and came away bloody. A flick of his tongue dampened them once more, the metallic taste bitter. He sighed. The sound was lost amidst the whistle of February wind nudging the drafty shed's rickety boards.

What a damnable pass his life had come to. Eighteen years of loyalty to a lord who didn't deserve it, and for what? He couldn't return to Cantleigh, knowing what he knew. *Sir Martin died defending the king, my arse.*

He could hire out his sword as a mercenary, but the chance of gaining property now was as likely as Prince John's giving up women. Even so, Roark was tired of battling for other men's holdings.

There was always the chance the king's men would realize the truth about Sir Martin, then seek others involved in the conspiracy. Suspicion would fall on Roark as Cantleigh's captain. No one would believe him innocent, even if he *had* warned the king.

Only Sir Henry knew that fact, and he'd died. Sir Henry. The name swam in his mind. Something about…he couldn't recall. It didn't matter.

Roark's future looked as bright as the inside of this dirty little room. He had no position, no home, no nothing. He snorted. *I'm thinking like some damned minstrel, milking false sentiment from over-emotional words.*

Of course he had something. He had hope. He had determination.

He had to piss, actually. Groaning softly, he rolled over and eased onto an elbow. The bucket seemed a long way off. His stumbled trek across the narrow, hard-packed dirt floor disgusted him. He needed to gain strength. He'd start by walking.

On his third limping round of the lean-to, fragments of conversation wafted through his mind. Of his hours at the inn. Of an aged knight from England who said Sir Henry had died. Bit by bit, the story returned. Something about a castle and a lady, alone for the taking, all her family now dead.

Vulnerable to the first knight who came along.

Roark had heard of brides kidnapped and wed for their land, long ago. It was not common practice these days, but it happened.

It happened.

Roark stopped, eyes narrowed. If it were going to happen…

Damn, where is Alain? We've got to find that old man.

Chapter Four

Paris
February 1194

In a crisp, star-crinkled midnight sky, haloed by a ring of clouds, the late-winter moon hung low. Shadows spiked across the courtyard, ghostly reminders of the dormant trees from which they slipped. A smaller shadow flicked between them, moving silently toward the castle's black bulk.

The snap of heel against rock was deadened in the closeness of the cold air, yet it rang in Sir Paxton of Corbeau's ears. He flattened against the stone wall, then eased to the edge and carefully peered around the corner. No one in sight.

Why the hell am I trying to hide? He was a knight returned from a dangerous mission and should be welcomed. No doubt he would be, soon.

He moved quietly in the darkness, nonetheless. Prince John likely had heard of the battle's outcome by now. The would-be king would want to know why Paxton delayed in reporting.

He'll have his royal prick in a knot. Well, Hades. I couldn't travel fast with a slashed arm, could I?

He scratched on the wooden panel, an entry he'd used before, counted to four, then scratched again. After he waited what seemed an eternity, the door opened a sliver, and he pushed his way in. When he saw whom he'd shoved aside—*shite*. He dropped to one knee.

"My lord." He wasted no words. "The king lives."

Eyelids lowered to a slit, John watched him. "So I learned not two days past," he at last said, softly. "Why?"

"I was wounded, my lord, and I—"

"Did I ask about your health? I referred to the outcome of the attack."

Paxton shook his head. He eased his aching arm to rest on his bent knee. "God knows.

"The plan should have worked. The king's party was separated from the rest of the group. The fools actually went hunting. When we attacked, Cantleigh moved his men in from behind as planned. Then something happened. A noise—a shout. It alerted the king's guard."

Prince John turned away and walked toward the center of the bedchamber. Candlelight muted the purple and gold of his robe and etched his features, making the nose seem sharper, the intelligent eyes more menacing. He gestured. Paxton rose and followed.

The chamber was empty but for the two of them. No woman. Surprising for this time of night. John must have been expecting him.

Flickering light cast the men's shadows long and narrow against the far wall. Paxton watched as those dark forms undulated in the silence. He caught smells of candle wax and heady perfume, underscored by a trace of body odor and woman's musk. *So the royal cock hasn't been alone. No wonder he made me wait so long at the door.*

31

Waiting for the king's brother seemed to be Paxton's lot in life. And waiting for him to speak now rated worse than facing a trio of soldiers on the battlefield. He could at least defend himself there.

"Did any of Cantleigh's men survive?" The sudden sound of the prince's voice made him start.

"None of those with him."

"Jenkins as well?"

"Dead."

Prince John's pacing ended in front of Paxton, who wove slightly in pain and exhaustion.

The prince pointed to a bench near the hearth. "Sit before you fall."

His mouth pursed, John stared at him. "And what does the king say of the matter?"

"In the confusion of fighting, he couldn't see the attackers clearly. I suggested someone may have followed from Mainz, people unhappy with the terms of his ransom. The dead carried no identification, just as instructed. Richard is convinced they were outlaws on the prowl for rich travelers."

Looking smug, Paxton added, "As for Sir Martin and his three, the king believes they died defending him. I, myself, am recovering from wounds at a snug little farmhouse with excellent ale stocked by a charming widow."

John nodded once. "That is the story, then. Go home. Clean yourself up and rest."

Paxton had turned when he heard, "You identified Cantleigh?" At a nod, John drawled, "Was anything found on him?"

Incriminating evidence, perhaps? Are you becoming careless in your panic?

"Nothing." Paxton hesitated. He dreaded to relate this part, but he didn't dare omit it. "Two of his knights were before me when I found the body. One held something. It may have come from Sir Martin."

"And this something was…?"

"A leather packet? I couldn't see clearly. I hid until they left."

"Did you know them?"

"Only Sir Roark, Cantleigh's captain. Has a reputation as a fighter. The plan didn't include him. Cantleigh said the man had a peasant streak of morality. But I heard he's died of his wounds."

He paused, eyeing John. He knew that stare, had seen it countless times in the four years he'd served the king's brother. It made even Paxton edgy. John sat, leaned back in an ornately carved wooden chair, his fingers tented before his lips. For a moment he did not speak, he did not blink, and—Paxton could swear—he did not breathe.

The silence drew out until John murmured, "Pity you were so careless as to be injured. Such an inconvenience. Still, report after the midday meal. I have a different commission for you. There's a holding near Nottingham I want secured before Richard returns to England. The knight who owned it recently died. Marry its lady if you want. Less trouble that way. You'll receive details tomorrow.

"Don't disappoint me."

Paxton had no intention of disappointing the man. After all he'd done in his service? *Time for my reward, Johnny. Oh—so sorry my royal arsehole, 'Prince' John.*

Time for a promise to be fulfilled.

Chapter Five

Chauvere Castle
Mid-March 1194

"Lady Alyss, Lady..."

"Here, Will." Alyss placed a small stoppered jar on a shelf in the spice chest and inhaled. Images of mysterious Eastern lands trailed the piquant odors. She'd just doled out a measure of precious cinnamon to flavor the beef for the midday meal. Chauvere had been lucky with stores this winter; the meat had kept well.

And Martha the cook was experimenting with her own recipe for dried apple pasties that called for honey and cinnamon. Alyss couldn't imagine such a thing. But she was willing to trust her old friend with the expensive seasoning.

She locked the chest and walked to the kitchen door, tucking an errant strand of gold-brown hair behind her left ear. The stable boy nearly collided with her as he swooshed in. She grasped his shoulders. "Steady."

"Someone's comin'," he shouted. "They're far away. We can't see who they are."

"My hearing is fine, Will," she said when he drew a breath.

"Two men, knights I think—" He paused as her words appeared to sink in. His voice dropped, and he peered at her through the black curls bobbing around his pert nose.

"Sorry, m'lady. Sir Baldwin sent me to tell you someone's comin'." His voice had calmed, but still he bounced on his toes. "They're alone. No army with 'em, so they must be friendly."

The lad's voice rose again. "Maybe it's Sir Henry, come home. Could it be Sir Henry, lady?"

Alyss's heart gave a happy lurch at the thought, but she forced herself to remain calm. "Tell Sir Baldwin I'm on my way."

When Will dashed out, she glanced at Martha. "He's certainly excited if he didn't stop to plague you for a treat."

"Must be the first time since he learned to walk, milady," the cook said. "Could it be Sir Henry?"

"Perhaps. If Sir Godfrey located him, and the king allowed him to leave. We shall see."

More likely another ambitious knight looking to wed. Alyss stepped outside and sucked in a deep, shaking breath. She pressed her hand on her stomach. Mary's tears, let it be Henry. She couldn't tolerate one more demand of marriage. Over the last weeks, she deflected two offers that amounted to threats. Both lords had the mistaken belief that her brother was dead. He wasn't. He couldn't be.

At least no one had attacked yet, not after Jasper's fate became known. None doubted the ferocity of Chauvere's garrison. She allowed herself a smile. Fortunately, all those demands to wed were met at the gates, and no one had ventured inside. Her secret, along with that of the castle's unrepaired wall, remained safe. The outer stones had been replaced, and all looked normal, although she feared a strong wind might send them rolling.

Straightening her shoulders, Alyss started for the outer bailey. She would show her people she was up to this challenge, as she had been to all the others. And if neither traveler was Henry, well, she would continue to hold the castle until he arrived.

Her firm stride took her toward the guard tower at the gates. She fought to maintain an air of composure as she climbed the stone steps. The appearance was deceiving. Clasped hands showed red fingers and white knuckles. Air fought for a path through her lungs, and her stomach clenched as tightly as her fists.

She longed to lift her hems and race to the top of the battlement. She wouldn't, of course. The young and impulsive Lady Alyss had matured into a self-controlled woman whose quiet command kept Chauvere secure. At least she hoped people thought so. Days like today she feared her confidence was all for show.

Pray God it is Henry. Some things she could handle adeptly. She'd managed the household since her mother's death from fever three years earlier. She'd managed the business of the castle and holdings since her father's first seizure shortly after her mother's death. Someone had to, with Henry away so often.

And Alyss could fight a little. She discovered that a few weeks ago, when Jasper of Windom attacked. Even more surprisingly, she knew how to organize a defense.

What she could not do was lead the knights and men-at-arms. Baldwin, bless him, drilled their few numbers every day, but his age slowed him. Chauvere's force needed a strong leader when the battle came.

In her heart, she knew it would come. Yesterday, friends at Windom sent word that Jasper's replacement had arrived. Immediately, he'd asked about the lady at Chauvere. A Lord Paxton. Hah. Another favorite from John Lackland.

She *must* hold out until King Richard returned to rein in his younger brother's greed.

At the top of the stairs she paused and inhaled. Sharp air eased the tightness across her chest. A gust nipped through her warm woolen gown and linen smock, reminding her winter hadn't faded. She caught her lower lip between her teeth and faced facts.

If only two knights approached the castle, they were not Henry and Godfrey. Her brother would never return without his men. No, these were strangers. She pressed her palms together to ease the tingling that always signaled nervousness.

The pair of travelers must mean bad news. Perhaps someone discovered how Jasper really died. An icy tingle shot through her body. She shivered. Impossible. No one else knew, just she and Baldwin.

Sir Baldwin moved to one side, and they watched. Several horses made up the cortege nearing the castle. Some contained packs but only two contained riders, who appeared to be knights. Wait. Alyss blinked several times. A slight figure sat atop one mount. A young squire, perhaps. No, two—she could see the other, smaller one, now. And behind them plodded a pair of huge animals. War horses. Surely these few didn't travel alone. Yet she saw no trace of others.

"Is it Sir Henry do you think, milady?" Sir Baldwin asked, leaning forward and squinting. "It's not Sir Godfrey. Both too big."

"No." Disappointment tasted bitter in her throat. "I can tell the way they sit their horses. Neither is Henry."

Her brother rode taller than either of those two, lighter in the saddle, as if he couldn't wait to leap to the ground. And Henry would never move in such a dawdling fashion so near home. He'd gallop.

"They're not carryin' a standard," Sir Baldwin said. "I don't like it. We see only two, but they may have more men, I'm thinkin'."

The approach to the castle had been cleared of cover. The woods, still winter-naked, lay in the opposite direction and too far away for troops to hide. But the past few weeks had taught her caution.

Sir Baldwin turned and called to the guards, "Don't raise the portcullis 'til I say so."

Alyss narrowed her gaze. This might be the newest lord from Windom come courting. If so, he was doomed to failure. Nothing could persuade her to marry him, or anyone else for that matter.

Surely the humiliation of being jilted entitled her to choose her own future. The only one who could force her to wed and leave Chauvere was Henry. And he'd promised never to do that.

She and Baldwin observed silently for the time it took the small entourage to reach the gates. Finally, they halted. The leader urged his mount a few steps forward and pushed the mail coif off his head to settle at the back of his neck. A breeze lifted dark hair from his broad forehead. Even from the battlement near the guard tower, the knight's hawk-like nose and square jaw were evident. This was a man used to command, Alyss could tell from the set of his shoulders, the tilt of his chin. An unfamiliar frisson of excitement moved across her shoulders.

"Sir Roark of Stoddard requests entry to speak with Lord Ulrich of Chauvere."

His voice was rich and deep; the words carried easily to the top of the tower.

Sir Baldwin leaned around a merlon. "What brings Sir Roark of Stoddard to Chauvere?"

Before an answer could be given, one of the boys waved. "Sir Baldwin," he shouted. "Hello, Sir Baldwin. It's me, James."

The old captain looked at Alyss. "James was the page Sir Henry took with him this last trip, wasn't he?" Alyss nodded. "Can you make out if that's him?"

"I think he is our James." She lifted her voice, "Where is your lord, James?

"Where is Sir Henry?"

"Lady Alyss?" The youth slid off his horse and ran to the rider who led them. His words drifted up. "It's Lady Alyss, sir. Sir Henry's sister."

The knight spoke to James, and the youth ducked his head. He was being reprimanded. Well. She would halt such presumption. The stranger had no right to utter sharp words to one of Chauvere's youths.

"Are you all right, James?" she called. "Are these men forcing you to stay with them? Where is Sir Henry? Where are Sir Godfrey and the rest of our men?"

The page looked up at her. "Oh no, my lady. These knights have brought me home. May we come in, please?"

Alyss watched the small group for a moment, her lips caught between her teeth, then nodded. "Let them in."

"I don't say I like it, milady, but I agree," Baldwin said. "We'll keep an eye on 'em, you can be sure." He ordered the portcullis raised, and the gate opened while Alyss observed the scene below.

James appeared to frown at something the knight said, but he returned to his horse. There he stood, unable to mount because of the distance between his short legs and the tall stirrups. He grasped the saddle and jumped, but the sturdy chestnut mare sidestepped, and he fell to his knees. The other knight said something, then walked his large gray gelding to the boy and hoisted James up before him.

Her brother would never send his charge off with strangers. She feared what that must mean. She swallowed a lump in her throat and started down the stairs. No tears. She would not cry in front of everyone. When the group rode through the gates a few moments later, she waited, chin high.

The two knights reined in their horses. James slid from this perch and raced, chattering, to Sir Baldwin. Her attention focused on the man astride the huge black gelding. The one who called himself Sir Roark.

She didn't like the determined set of his mouth or the way one dark brow rose while the other remained straight, as if pinned in place by the slash that separated it. Too arrogant. When his eyes looked into hers, Alyss shivered; a cold wind must have swept through the bailey. Anticipation squiggled in her chest. For a moment, she could only stare at him. Behind the stubble of beard that darkened his face, energy fairly popped.

Danger.

Drowning the whisper in her mind, Alyss

demanded, "What have you done with my brother? If you have harmed him, you will not leave here alive."

Chapter Six

Roark propped his hands on the saddle, leaned forward to stretch the tired muscles of his back and neck. His gaze swept the outer bailey, stopped at the entrance to the inner bailey. Closed. Did an enemy lurk within? He'd seen no trace of an occupying force, no evidence of battle.

Perhaps the threat of siege Sir Godfrey spoke of had ended amiably. Or perhaps the old knight mistook the urgency of the situation. If so, this peaceful gathering represented Roark's first fortunate circumstance in two fortnights.

He straightened and considered the woman confronting him. This was the one on the tower earlier. He could tell by her fly-away hair and the rust color of her gown.

Lady Alyss, James had said. Lord Ulrich's daughter, Sir Henry's sister, and his—Roark's—bride to be.

If she but knew it.

The nippy breeze had picked up and sent a thick strand of tawny hair across her face. She caught it and tucked it firmly behind an ear. Hard to tell if the lady had beauty, with her brow crunched in a frown and her lips clenched between her teeth. Ah, well. Beauty mattered little.

Time to begin.

"You are Lady Alyss," Roark said. "I recognize you from Sir Henry's description. He mentioned you fondly."

Her eyes narrowed. Blue eyes? Gray? He couldn't tell.

"You know my brother? Where is he?" She stepped forward. "Do you have word from him? Is he following you?"

When she spoke, her clenched lips eased into fullness. Her tension-tight voice warmed with unexpected sweetness.

An older knight moved to Lady Alyss's side, hand hovering near his sword hilt. His sun-browned, wrinkled brow creased. This must be the captain. "And you are Sir Baldwin."

The man looked at Roark suspiciously. "I suppose Sir Henry spoke fondly of me too?"

"No. Sir Godfrey," Roark answered, his tone hard. He was tired of travel, and now he was tired of talk. He swung up in the stirrups and dismounted. It took every bit of determination not to stumble. Damn, his healed leg had stiffened. He stood straight, weight unobtrusively on his right side. Time to see if the lord yet lived. "Take me to Lord Ulrich. I have news of his son."

Alain stood beside Roark, hands on hips, as they waited. James and Ralf, Roark's squire, headed for the stables with the horses, James showing the way. Another youth emerged from the group gathered to watch and ran toward them.

"Ho, Will," James called to the lad. "I was nearly in a battle, and I fell out of a tree. You want to see my scar?"

As others took charge of the remaining horses, Lady Alyss murmured to Sir Baldwin. Then she looked at Roark. "My father is unavailable," she told him. "You may give me the message. I will deliver it."

Not good enough. "I'll wait until he *is* available."

Despite weariness, he folded his arms across his chest and caught her glance. *Blue-gray eyes.*

"Impossible." Her chin lifted higher, and she refused to look away.

"Take me to him," he demanded in a tone his men would not have ignored.

A tiny smile lifted a corner of her lips. "If only I could."

He uncrossed his arms and nodded toward the audience gathered around them. "Very well, my lady. Shall I announce the news here?"

That gave her a start.

"Of course not," she answered. "You will come inside."

She turned toward the hall. "You and your companion are welcome to bread and ale. Afterward, Sir Baldwin will find you a place in the barracks. You undoubtedly will want to rest before you continue your journey after the midday meal."

Roark was not about to leave. In fact, he had nowhere else to go.

Alain nodded at him, eyes sparking with humor. "We eat," he whispered.

Roark shook his head once, and together they followed Lady Alyss across the bailey. The errant strand of hair, still tucked behind her ear, had worked loose from a single braid that hung below her waist. What an ugly gown she wore—more fitted to a servant.

Perhaps she had been working today. Sir Godfrey had said she was a right one for pitching in.

He glanced around. A few tumbled stones lay along one section of wall that showed recent signs of rebuilding. The repair wasn't complete on the interior, but the outer defense looked solid. Either the damage had been inflicted recently, or there were too few men to set it to rights quickly.

So there *had* been an attack. Unsuccessful, by the look of it. The garrison had fought off the intruders, then, as Sir Godfrey predicted. But Roark had yet to see evidence of Chauvere's soldiers. Not a hint of armed opposition anywhere.

The only resistance strode in front of him, hands clasped at her waist. She had a determined, no-nonsense walk. Not at all like the languid movement of the ladies he usually met. Still, the sight of her swaying hips tightened the only muscle Roark hadn't exercised lately.

A breeze stirred her long skirts and coaxed the lock from behind her ear, across her face. She turned her head, and he could see the strand caught on her moist lips. Morning sun turned the hair to honey gold. An odd urge made him long to loosen the rest of the braid, to wrap his hands in the length of it. To lift it away from her beautiful lips. Her hair would be soft and sweet-smelling, her mouth welcoming wherever it went.

The errant muscle between his legs tightened further, and he growled in frustration. This was not the time to indulge in fantasy. Too much depended on the next few hours. Besides, his bride's looks didn't matter. He'd keep telling himself that.

As the little group made its way across the open

ground, Roark's initial opinion of the castle was borne out. When it first came into view, it had appeared modern in construction, made of stone, unlike many of the older wooden structures. Up close, he saw the design was modern, as well.

The bottom floor for storage set partly into the ground, leaving the first-floor hall approached by wide steps. Not so high as in most castles—easily breached from outside. The warrior in Roark disliked the arrangement—too weak. But something within him responded to its welcoming feel of openness and comfort.

Inside, the great hall gave an overall impression of cleanliness and brightness. Windows, slightly wider than normal arrow loops, were built into the stone, allowing the sun's strengthening rays to slash across the room.

Dotting the walls were tapestries worked in hues of blues, greens—even reds and yellows. Some funds expended there. At other places whitewashed surfaces gleamed through, adding to the chamber's feeling of light.

A stairway at one side of the back wall led upward. Along one end of the huge room was a fireplace, big enough to roast an ox. The floors were covered with rushes—clean and fragrant. He nodded in satisfaction. His new wife was a good housekeeper.

Near the fireplace on the right was the dais that contained the lord's table, bare of cloth now, but gleaming clean and holding candlesticks. Two maids stopped work at the hearth to watch.

They had scarcely entered when a priest came hieing it from behind a side partition. Of medium height and slight build, dressed in a brown robe that looked new, he held a chunk of bread.

"My lady, I hear there are visitors," he called. "What word of Sir Henry?"

"Father Eudo, these knights were sent by Sir Godfrey and will tell us their business in good time," Lady Alyss said. "For now, they're hungry. Annie, please bring some bread, cheese, and pitchers of ale." One of the maids disappeared behind the partition.

The priest popped the rest of the bread into his mouth and wiped his hand on his robe. He chewed quickly then gulped, frowning and shaking his head the entire time.

"Why did you not call me before you opened the gates, my lady?" He didn't look at Alyss but directed his words to Roark and Alain. "I must apologize for Lady Alyss. As priest, I should have been present to greet you with our Lord's mercy. Come and sit; tell us your news."

"It is not your place to apologize for me." The lady's tone was a warning. "Nor do you need to be present when guests arrive."

Looking toward her at last, the priest said, "Your pardon, my lady. I didn't mean to upset you." He spoke to Roark and Alain again. "She's been fragile since her poor father's death."

"Father Eudo." With a look that was anything but fragile, Lady Alyss moved to the table. "These knights are tired and hungry and carry news of my brother. I will tell you what it is when I learn of it."

The priest finally had the good sense to shut his mouth, but his lowered brow spoke loudly. Rather than returning to the chapel, however, he trailed them to the table. The lady gestured to a bench, then sat in the smaller of two carved chairs at the center of the board. Sir Baldwin stood at her back. He had not spoken since their arrival, but he had not taken his gaze from them, either.

As they sat, Roark and Alain exchanged glances. Roark could read his friend's thoughts as clearly as if he'd spoken. Lord Ulrich was dead. Sir Henry was dead. Lady Alyss was unmarried and alone in a castle that was undermanned and in need of repair.

They were home.

Chapter Seven

The maid glanced at Roark with a shy smile of welcome when she set the food before him.

"Thank you, Annie." Lady Alyss's militant attitude startled Roark. God's bones, was this Sir Godfrey's meek, compliant lady?

He sighed. Might as well get it over with. He sipped the ale. Cool, delicious. He let it trickle down his parched throat, then looked up. He would try to be gentle, to spare her feelings as much as he could.

"I gather from your priest's words that Lord Ulrich is no longer with you," he began. "I am sorry to hear it, my lady. I hope his passing was—"

"My father died defending his castle from attack," she interrupted. "As you can see from looking around, he was successful. My brother is now the lord. If you have word of him, tell me with no more delay."

Well, then. If the lady wanted blunt words, he would oblige her. "Sir Henry died protecting the king the day your messenger caught up to the army."

Her eyes glazed, and her face paled.

He stood but Sir Baldwin leapt to her side. He grabbed a cup of ale and held it to her lips. "Drink, milady."

She jerked her head away and gasped, her breath held. Then she exhaled slowly. She rose, her gaze unfocused. "Thank you." Her voice tightened. "We will

Barbara Bettis

discuss this after you have eaten."

Roark had never seen anyone cling to control more desperately as she moved in measured steps toward the stairway. Sir Baldwin followed, calling for Rose to see to her mistress.

"If anyone touched her, she would shatter," Alain observed.

Roark motioned to the priest who sat looking not at Alyss, but at the two of them. "Father, shouldn't you be with her? She could use some words of comfort."

Father Eudo shook his head and left his bench, ale cup in hand. "I believe the child would prefer solitude right now, to say her prayers in private. In my three years here, I've found she likes to go her own way." He stopped beside Roark and Alain, managing to insinuate himself between them as he sat.

"A pity she's so headstrong," he added. "Later, when she has had a chance to compose herself, I will talk with her." He gestured to the places on either side of him. "Now, eat and rest."

Roark *was* hungry and knew Alain must be also. They'd broken camp well before dawn and had only a bit of dry bread as they rode. Both sat now and reached for food.

Father Eudo picked up a hunk of cheese, bit into it, and spoke as he chewed. "Sir Roark? What took you from the king's side and brought you here? Is your home this way?"

The little priest was inquisitive. Choosing the words he and Alain had rehearsed, Roark replied, "My friend Sir Henry spoke with affection of his home and family. When Sir Godfrey found me recovering from a slight wound, I offered to ride ahead with the message while he gathered Chauvere's men. The lord I served fell in the same attack as Sir Henry, and the king gave me leave to return. Stopping here was the least I could do for a friend."

That's all the priest needed to know.

The holy man studied the chunk of cheese he held. "Who did you serve, Sir Roark?"

Roark's answer was abrupt. "A lord from the south."

"Will you return there, now that you've delivered your message?"

Very inquisitive. "I'm needed elsewhere."

The priest looked as if he wanted to ask more, but Roark rose from the bench and tossed his uneaten bread to the hounds. A soft gasp from the side of the dais had him turning.

The young maid, Annie, stood with her hand over her mouth. She rushed forward, retrieved the bread, and carried it toward the kitchen.

"This is an unusual household," the priest explained. "The lady allows few dogs in the hall. And she insists we not feed them from the table." He sucked the crumbs from his fingers. "I believe I missed the name of your late lord, Sir Roark."

If the name of someone a country priest could not possibly know would satisfy him, why not. "I served Lord Martin of Cantleigh. Now, Father, I must check on my horses."

An odd expression of speculation came over Father Eudo's narrow face, accompanied by a slight smile. "You are well come, Sir Knight."

****

Roark wanted to make certain Cin had settled in.

His war horse tended to be as temperamental as a maiden if he didn't like his surroundings. Sure enough, the large mount proved restless in the spacious stall, bumping the sides and stomping hay into the floor. Roark recognized the behavior as simple boredom. Cin was in the process of making the stables his home. Grabbing a brush, Roark stroked the horse's dark red sides in long, calming motions.

"It's a nice place. We'll like it here," he reassured Cin in a murmur. "Time to rest. We've earned it, certainly. No more fighting."

A whinny punctuated a toss of the mane and a hoof to the floor.

"Think you might miss that life, do you? No one to stomp? Bloodthirsty beast."

Roark's ears picked up a slight rustle at the back of the enclosure. From the corner of his eye he saw, easing over the top of the stall, a cap of black curls topping a high forehead, brown eyes, and an upturned nose liberally sprinkled with freckles.

"But there are plenty of boys in this place," Roark continued, louder. "I saw enough when we arrived to give you many days of entertainment. Surely the lady won't miss one or two if you feel you must crunch someone." A nod of Cin's head and a whicker seemed to signal agreement.

The rest of the young face popped into view. Chin resting on the top board, the boy who greeted James earlier watched in wonder.

"Your horse answered," he said in awe. "I saw him. Does he understand what you say?"

Roark looked from Cin to the youngster and back. "Here's one now," he told the horse confidentially. To the boy he said, "Certainly he understands me. Just as important—I understand him. Have you come to provide fodder for the great Cin?"

"Oh, no. I'm Will." The youth's earnest gaze remained on Cin. "I work 'n the stables, but there's not many horses t' do for now. Most of the good 'uns Sir Henry took. Our knights got the leftovers, 'cause we never go anywheres to fight. They all come t' us."

"Well," Roark allowed, "in spite of his bad temper today, Cin can tolerate a young voice or two. Would you like to meet him?"

Before the words were out, Will had rounded the end of the stalls and raced toward them.

"Slowly," Roark cautioned, holding up a hand. "He's nervous enough right now. Dashing about won't calm him. Haven't you learned that, working in the stables?"

Will pulled up in a blink. "I know, but I forget sometimes when I really want t' be somewheres. Lady Alyss says I'll run out of my shoes someday if I can't slow down. I won't really." He lifted his foot for Roark's inspection, showing a sturdy boot. "They're good and tight."

"You're fortunate. Many boys I know are barefoot."

"Aye." Will looked unconcerned. "My lady sees to it. She says it helps us keep healthy. A healthy body is a happy body and a happy body is a working body, she says."

"And is it?"

"Mostly. But sometimes my healthy body is not happy t' work."

Roark's mouth quirked up at the ingeniousness of

the boy's answer. He stepped aside and gestured at the mount, which was standing still, eyeing the youth.

"Will, this is Cin. Cin, this is Will." He leaned in toward the horse. "He's young and tender," he whispered loudly. "Do not stomp him."

The huge animal continued to watch the youngster until Will stuck his hand inside his tunic and produced a withered apple. He held it out. Taking a suspicious step forward, Cin tossed his cream-colored mane and swished his cream-colored tail. Will placed the apple on the ground and moved back.

Roark was impressed with the youth's respect for a horse that, as yet, did not know him. "Smart lad. I wager Cin warms up to you quickly. In a few days, he may let you brush him.'

The boy took a last look at the horse, now munching contentedly, and dashed toward the back of the stables. "Gotta find James," he called.

Roark walked to the open double doors and gazed out at the activity. One youth dressed in a simple dark tunic headed toward a side entrance of the keep. At the wall to his left, two men checked the condition of a stone. To his right, a cauldron of water heated over a fire, and a robust woman, flushed face apparent even at that distance, carried buckets-full into what must be a small laundry hut against the wall.

From around the corner, a girl herded three geese whose minds seemed set on investigating the fire. Waving her arms and shouting to divert their attention, she was joined by the washer woman to shoo them back the way they came.

All normal busy-ness of everyday life in a castle. Roark liked what he saw. He had dreamed of the moment he took charge of his own land. It had been nothing but a dream until this morning, when he saw Chauvere in the distance. Limned by the sun, it gleamed gold.

He'd felt a tightening in his chest then. Against all odds, this place would be his.

Even the unwelcoming Alyss would not deter him. With her father and brother dead, she'd end up wed to someone. Better him who would value her as well as the land, than another who wouldn't.

He would deal fairly with his wife. He would not beat her. Out of respect for her, he would not keep a leman within the castle walls. Perhaps, if she were not as cold as she appeared, he would not need one. He might wish for a marriage as loving as his parents had shared, but like most knights bent on bettering themselves, he could not afford to marry for love.

At the sound of footsteps, he turned.

Alain joined him in the doorway. "Looks peaceful."

"I was thinking the same. And quiet."

Alain raised his eyebrows as the honking geese, which had made a circle, flapped toward the washhouse again. The washer woman bellowed and waved what looked suspiciously like a wet pair of men's hose. The goose girl shouted and a yapping dog joined the chase, alarming the birds even more.

"We may have goose for tomorrow's meal," Alain quipped.

Ignoring the tableau, Roark asked, "What do you not hear? Or see?"

Alain listened. "No sound of training. Of course, they may not have started for the day."

"Should have." Roark nodded toward the wall. "Only two men-at-arms at the gate. One lookout in the tower. No sign of others when we arrived."

"Could be they're repairing the wall."

Roark didn't reply. Both knew the men should be training.

"What do you plan to do now?" Alain at last prompted.

"Talk with Sir Baldwin to discover the threats we face. Establish a training schedule. Increase the number of look-outs. Find the seneschal, learn what stores we have, and if we have coin. You talk to the men, see what you can discover."

Alain interrupted him. "Did you forget a small detail?"

"No." Roark looked grim. "Find Father Eudo. After I meet with Sir Baldwin, I'll take myself a wife."

Chapter Eight

Alyss sat in her bedchamber, back lance-straight, heart as clenched as her hands. Henry, dead. The brother she'd followed around as a youth, gone forever. What would she do without him?

He'd often led her into mischief. Once he teased her into climbing a tree in the orchard, and she'd gotten stuck on a high limb. When he had laughed and offered to help, she said no. She would do it herself.

And so she did. Ripped clothing and all. As young as she'd been, her pride and independence burned strong. Stubbornness, her father called it. Henry merely hugged her and dubbed her his intrepid sprite.

A lump lodged in her throat. She forced it down. Tears welled but didn't fall. Alyss never cried, not anymore. She'd order Father Eudo to say a special mass, and she'd declare the next Lord's Day a village holiday, in memory of Henry. She brushed a hand across her face, tucked a strand of hair behind one ear. A plan of action always made her feel better.

She stood and clasped her hands. Now she must see to the strangers. In the corridor, she found Rose sitting against the wall.

"Do ye need aught milady?" The girl sounded anxious as she climbed to her feet. "There were a messenger come, but Sir Baldwin took care o' him. We thought ye might want a bit o' privacy."

Alyss inclined her head. "Thank you, Rose. You did just right. Please ask Martha Cook to hurry the meal so our guests can be on their way."

The maid trotted down the stairway. Alyss longed to race after, to dash outside, through the gates, and into the freedom of open countryside. To lose herself in the woods for a moment of solitude. She didn't. Instead, she followed at a more sedate pace. Her people needed to see that their lady stood firm. They must be reassured that life at Chauvere continued unchanged.

If only it were true.

At the bottom of the stairs, she paused to look out over the hall. Sir Baldwin stood there, Father Eudo, and the guest with light hair, whose name she hadn't learned. Sir Roark stood to the side, confidence in the set of his broad shoulders and the tilt of his square jaw. Her stomach gave a little lurch. When he turned to hold out a large, strong hand, her pulse raced and her heart pounded.

For a moment she dared not move, uncertain her suddenly weak knees would support her.

"Come." His deep voice sent shivers down her spine, but his commanding tone aggravated her. He had no right to give orders in her home. Yet her mind refused to supply a proper sharp retort.

She needed more time to adjust to the shock of Henry's death. That must be the reason the knight's presence affected her so. A traitorous part of her responded to the promised comfort in his strong body. She fought the urge to reach out, take hold of all he offered. But before she made a fool of herself, he spoke again.

"Come along," he repeated. "We must honor your

brother's dying wish."

He had been with Henry at the end? Alyss clasped her hands at her waist. "And that was?"

"Your safety through our marriage. Father Eudo has agreed to oversee the vows. Let us say them now, then I can set to the wall's repair after the meal."

"Pardon?" Alyss's voice came in a whisper, but he seemed to hear well enough.

"I said your brother wished us to wed."

The sound of a million crickets chirruped in her ears. His lips continued to move, but she heard nothing as her bottom hit stone, and she collapsed onto a step. Her eyes saw only him.

He loomed over her, fists propped on hips, dark hair brushing those broad shoulders. She raised her brows in a level gaze—and inhaled sharply. Hazel eyes, sprinkled with green and gold chips, gleamed back. Luring. With effort, she recalled his recent words, and her thoughts focused.

She shot to her feet. "You must be mad. I have no intention of wedding a stranger who appears at my gate with some imaginary story of my brother's last commands. I remind you, sir, you are a guest. In fact, I must ask you to leave. Your behavior is intolerable."

His big hands closed around her shoulders. They were warm. Firm but gentle. She shook them off.

"I'm afraid I can't do that, my lady," he murmured for her ears only. The tickling sensation of his breath on her face warred with the alarm in her mind. "This demesne is in danger, and you know it. I can keep it and you safe. Be the sensible lady Sir Godfrey described. Do not create a greater scene. It only serves to upset your people."

Anger drove her to answer without thought. "No one can force me to marry."

He stepped back. "Sir Baldwin, tell Lady Alyss of the messenger who just left."

Baldwin shot her a pained look of apology. "From Windom he came, milady. The new master there commands an interview tomorrow, under order of Prince John. I sent him on his way, but it don't look good. This new master'll be here early in the morn, I'm bettin'."

Alyss stood, chin high, arms crossed beneath her breasts. "Let him come."

Sir Roark chuckled. "By God, my lady, we'll deal well together." He grabbed her shoulders and pulled her against his broad chest.

Before she could protest, Sir Roark's mouth was on hers, and she was forced to clutch his sleeves. Only to keep from tumbling over, of course, because her traitorous legs threatened to collapse. Then the tip of his tongue brushed the seam of her lips, and she lost all thought but his taste and the strangely comforting arms holding her up.

****

The kiss had been a damned mistake. Roark had meant it as a statement of possession. But her softness hit him like a mace. When he inhaled the rich fragrance of spice and roses and woman, his intent changed. He hauled her closer, slanted his mouth, stroked his tongue along the seam of her lips. At her whimper, a flicker of guilt undercut Roark's stirring of desire. He ought not do this to the lady. He ought to gather his belongings and be on his way.

But the memory of the recent messenger lingered.

That one portended nothing good. If Roark gave in to his inconveniently awakening conscience, by tomorrow night Chauvere, its people, and its lady would be the property of the neighboring lord. Of that, Roark was certain. So the way he saw it, either Lady Alyss married him or she'd be forced to accept someone else. And if Windom's representative was any indication of his master, she'd not like that alternative.

What would it take to persuade her? A sudden pain burst between his legs, and he gasped, eyes blurry. The little hell-cat kneed him in the balls. Even though chain mail deflected some of the impact, he used every bit of his willpower to remain standing.

Apparently, persuasion took more than a kiss.

He drew a steadying breath. "You don't understand, my lady. You will be my wife before the sun sets. It was your brother's dying wish. It was my pledge to a comrade."

By God, he'd begun to believe it himself.

Alyss met him toe to toe. "This morning I had never seen you, and by tonight, you think, I will marry you?"

Her head tilted back and she glared into his eyes. "Were you, perhaps, wounded in the head during a fight? Have you lost your senses as well as your hearing? How do you propose to force me to the altar? With your army?"

With an exaggerated look around, she nodded toward Alain. "Ah, yes. There it is. Impressive to be sure."

Turning from Roark, she said, "Sir Baldwin, see that these two knights are outside the gates by sundown. Call every man in the garrison to help, if need be. I want them gone."

Head high as if confident her word would be enforced immediately, she strode to the stairway.

Frowning, Sir Baldwin started forward. Roark lifted a hand to halt him. He glanced at Alain, then back to Alyss. "One moment, my lady. Hear me out."

She continued to walk, but everyone in the hall had no trouble hearing her. "Unless you intend to apologize, you can say nothing that will interest me."

Roark had known this would not be easy, but he had expected the female to at least listen to reason. An obedient, well-behaved lady is how Sir Godfrey described her. An excellent housekeeper, but helpless to defend herself if her menfolk were all dead. Obedient, well-behaved. Helpless.

That Lady Alyss wasn't this Lady Alyss.

"You are at the mercy of your neighbors," he said, "all of whom want your home. You need someone who can protect you and organize a defense."

Alyss whirled and stalked toward him. "*I* will defend it as I always have. Who defended it before my father was killed? Who defended it after he died? Who defended me but a few days ago when I refused yet another offer of marriage? Where were you? I believe I can take care of my people and myself."

If eyes could shoot sparks, hers would flame. Her skin was flushed, and that wayward wisp of honey-brown hair danced with energy. No longer narrowed in sorrow or displeasure, her lips were full and red. For a moment Roark stared at the glowing beauty before him.

Then he shook his head. "Do you not recall the messenger from Windom and the lord who's calling tomorrow? Don't think he's coming to offer sympathy on the loss of your father and brother. The messenger said he has an order from Prince John, and that means one thing. You *will* be wed by tomorrow. Your only choice now is the husband. One who is the prince's lackey, or one who fought alongside your brother and called him friend?"

****

"Whether or not he comes is none of your concern." Alyss's voice quivered, and she hated that sign of nerves. She wasn't stupid. She knew very well whoever now ruled at Windom wouldn't give up. But how could Sir Roark know it, the rogue? She didn't need this arrogant stranger invading her home, her life. She could take care of everything. As she had for the last years.

Extra guards had been posted each night, scouts sent toward Windom the last three days. Morning and night, she prayed Henry would return with the rest of Chauvere's force before Windom's army arrived. And when he did…

Henry isn't coming. Our men aren't here.

The realization slapped her like an icy blast. Before she could continue, Roark lifted his hand for her silence.

"Lady, I think you must realize that your new neighbor will not give up. It's a matter of time. And if he's defeated, what then? King Richard will be in England soon, and you'll be married to someone he chooses. You don't have enough coin to compete with the men who will pay for your hand."

"Ha. For my land, you mean," Alyss snapped. Warmth washed her cheeks. "I won't be bartered like a sack of wool, and I won't be carried off by some barbarian."

****

Roark felt stirrings of admiration and, surprisingly, desire. He squelched them. He didn't like spirited women. They were more trouble than they were worth. Just ask poor, dead King Henry, who spent his life trying to harness Queen Eleanor.

Still, he had to give a grudging respect to this woman who wanted to stand independent.

Trouble was, she didn't have a moonbeam's chance at midday of remaining unwed. In time she would see it.

Time was something Roark didn't have.

"You won't be given a choice. And you can lay odds whoever threatens you knows it.

"His days grow fewer and fewer. He must make his move before Richard arrives, because the king won't stand for one of his lords attacking another."

"But," he added, "if the king is presented with the accomplished deed and a big enough purse in reparation—well, you understand?"

Judging by Alyss's expression, she did. From her tilted chin, he could see it didn't matter. He sighed. This challenge he'd set for himself was proving more complicated than he'd imagined. He'd won entire tournaments with less trouble.

"Is that what you intend?"

Roark frowned. "My lady?"

"Do you intend to offer the king a huge purse to excuse our forced marriage?"

Tension reverberated along every nerve, and his damaged eyebrow twitched. Jaw clenched, arms held out to his sides, he said softly, "Force? As you point out, my army is elsewhere."

Alyss took an involuntary step backward. He softened his gaze and began again. "My lady, I am here because your brother loved you. Because I vowed to a comrade to defend his land, his people, and his sisters. His last thoughts were of your safety. Give him credit for protecting you with his dying breath."

God's bones, he sounded sincere. A muffled cough from Alain made Roark realize how far into his deception he'd sunk.

"I..." For an instant Alyss seemed to waver. Then without another word, she turned and walked with stiff composure toward the stairs.

Chapter Nine

The moment Alyss disappeared from sight, Roark turned to Sir Baldwin.

Frowning and with mouth pursed, the captain ran a finger along the side of this chin. "Best give our lady some time to consider what you've said. Been a tough morning for her, I'm thinkin'."

A plump older woman harried the servants to their duties. They dashed quick glances at Roark, whispering to each other. Sir Baldwin nodded toward the lady who changed directions toward them.

"My wife, Lady Isobel," he said, holding out his hand. "I've been blessed with her for more than two score years. One of Lady Gwen's attendants, she was, Lady Gwen bein' Lady Alyss's mother."

Lady Isobel stopped in front of the pair. Her husband made the introductions while she looked Roark over, then pinned him with a glare. "We hear you're on a mission from our boy, Sir Henry. If that's true, it *could* be you have our support. Time will tell. Our lady needs a good man. If she marries you, see that you are. You may think Lady Alyss is unprotected, but you're wrong."

Having delivered her opinion, Lady Isobel nodded her head sharply and trotted off toward the kitchen where, from the smell of it, the noon meal was being burned. She stopped and turned.

"We have a bathhouse not far from the kitchen. Sir Baldwin will show you the way. You'll want a wash before you talk with our lady again."

Maybe she had a point. Roark couldn't recall the last time he'd done more than slapped cool water on his face. He supposed it might help his case if Lady Alyss needn't hold her breath around him. He followed Sir Baldwin through the doorway. Nowhere did he see the second sister. Sir Godfrey mentioned two, and James had filled their journey with stories of Lady Evie. "Is your lady's younger sister about?"

After a silence, Sir Baldwin answered, "Best ask Lady Alyss."

A slight odor of the stables drifted up as they neared the bathhouse, which also served as the laundry house he'd seen earlier. Roark looked down to find James at his elbow.

"Hello, Sir Roark. She's making you take a bath, is she?" The youngster nodded wisely, then skipped to match his step to Roark's. "I remember how she is. Pages have to wash our hands and face every day and sit down in a tub after Sunday Mass. She says no one wants to be served at table by a man with dirty hands and a smelly body."

Sir Baldwin chuckled. "Aye, it's a trial for you, isn't it? My Lady Isobel insists I have a wash right often too. And look what it's done for me." He pointed to his face. "Wore out my skin, it has. Look at these wrinkles."

James giggled, then said to Roark, "Ralf found you a corner in the knights' chamber. He's unloading your belongings."

They went inside the wooden shed to find two

caldrons of water warming. Despite the chill breeze outside, the temperature in the small structure was comfortable. A cauldron of cool water, with a dipper hanging on the side, sat near a large flat-bottomed, waist-high wooden tub. No doubt it served as the laundry tub as well.

The young page took a deep breath and launched into his spiel. "I could help with your mail, Sir Roark. I helped Sir Henry sometimes when his squire was busy."

Roark considered the youth Sir Godfrey had insisted they bring home. To make their passage easier to Chauvere, he had told James, but Roark understood the old knight's desire to send the youngster ahead.

"I would appreciate your help, lad," Roark said. "Once we have removed my hauberk, find Sir Alain and ask him to join me."

Sir Baldwin stood by for a moment, studying Roark. He looked like he wanted to say more. Finally he grumbled, "You can find your way back, I'm thinkin'. I'll just leave you to your bathin'."

The shed had no windows but contained a small hole in the thatched roof to permit steam to escape. The door offered the only other ventilation, but that arrangement ensured relative warmth during cold days. The smooth planks underfoot indicated another bit of unexpected luxury. No dirt floor to become mud. Slight gaps between the pieces of wood allowed water splashed out to drain onto the ground below. Of course, it also could send up gusts of frigid air.

After filling the tub, Roark settled in, his mind teeming with plans he'd been framing for weeks. But the warm water curled around his body, soothing the ache of the sword wound in his thigh. His head dropped back against the tub's edge.

A soft moan sent a slight ripple across the surface of the water. His mind eased, and he thought how good it would be to have this homely comfort always waiting for him after a hard day's labor or a hard campaign.

It would be. He would not allow this chance to slip away. He sat and reached for a dish of soap. He had to prepare for one campaign right now. He had to capture Lady Alyss in a swift attack.

The room brightened as the door opened, bringing a slash of midday light and a gush of cool air, then dimmed again as Alain closed the door. His friend hooked a foot around the edge of the bench between the fire and the tub, pulled it around, and dropped onto it.

"Looks like there's room for two in there." Alain nodded to the tub.

"Not if I'm one of them." Roark's mouth quirked up. "Patience. You're first after me."

"You've tried to teach me patience for years."

"Right now, I am teaching by example." Water sluiced down Roark's muscular body as he stood. It parted around the new scar and channeled down other, healed, slashes. "Hand me the drying cloth and tell me what you've discovered."

Alain obliged. "The guards are mighty loyal. They didn't have much to say, except they hoped the new lord at Windom didn't take it in his head to attack until the walls are repaired. Damage was the work of Windom's former lord. He attacked after his offer was turned down. Marriage in exchange for protection or the like. She didn't like."

"That must have been Jasper, the one Sir Godfrey

worried over."

Alain rose and added a stick to the dying fire. "There's a mystery here. It seems the previous master of Windom was killed in combat with Lord Ulrich, in the lord's bedchamber. The lord was recovering from an affliction that had left him unable to speak or move."

"And where," Roark added thoughtfully, "he rallied miraculously to defeat his foe."

"Perhaps not so miraculously," Alain put in. "It had happened before. He'd suffered a seizure months ago. He was unconscious for a day, then suddenly opened his eyes and asked for the priest. They said his left hand was weak after that, and his speech slurred, but his right hand was good as ever."

Roark applied the drying cloth vigorously to his hair, then wrapped it around his waist.

"If Jasper of Windom was inside the lord's chamber," he mused, "where were his soldiers? There's no evidence of damage inside the castle."

"A mystery, as you say."

"See what else you can find out." Roark contemplated his friend. "You managed to get a lot of information out of reluctant guards."

Alain smiled and winked. "The milk maids were not reluctant."

Maids or matrons, women were never reluctant around Alain. He had a twinkle in his eyes that could coax the habit off a nun.

"I hesitate to ask—why are you out here and not inside trying to persuade your bride?"

"Have to get rid of the scent of the road before my wedding, don't I?" Roark finger-combed his hair, then motioned to the tub. "Your turn."

"Don't forget to scrape your face and trim your hair," Alain reminded him. "You'll look less like a wild beastie."

Leaving Alain to bathe, Roark walked to the keep. No more postponing the next confrontation with Lady Alyss. His fists clenched and unclenched at his sides. He should not have waited.

Pity she had experienced so many losses the past months, but she had no more time for grieving. She obviously needed help. She was a lady, after all, and couldn't be expected to handle all the responsibilities of running the castle and the village.

The holding had been without supervision too long. Sir Baldwin had done his best, but the old knight could not do it all. The business of the unrepaired wall showed one of the problems from a lack of authority. He would take care of that. And he would take care of Lady Alyss. Marriage to her would not be so dreadful, once she learned who was in command.

He found her spark and her strength appealing, true. Here was a woman who knew how to manage a household, he did not doubt. He could take care of the rest. And her ready tongue? Roark's body tingled. He adjusted himself and redirected his randy thoughts away from the uses he could find for her ready tongue. Once she was safe, her temper would settle down. She just needed reassuring.

Chapter Ten

Lower lip caught between her teeth, Alyss leaned against the closed door of the solar. It had taken all the self-discipline she possessed not to toss aside her dignity and race up the stairs. But he would *not* overset her.

She didn't know who he was, and it didn't matter. He would *not* have control of Chauvere; he would *not*. Even if an army threatened at the gate.

An army could be dispersed; she'd done it before. The disturbing man in her hall required a different tactic. He wanted to marry her. *Sweet Jesu.* What was he about? Did he really think she would stand for such a thing? She would marry no one. Certainly not some nameless knight who claimed friendship with Henry.

For all she knew, it was a lie. For all she knew...but James would know. James had been with her brother. He could tell her about Sir Roark. Opening the door, she discovered Rose just outside. After bidding the maidservant to find the young page, Alyss sat to wait. Scarcely had she touched the seat then she was on her feet again, striding around the chamber.

He was one more thing to handle. Evie, Father, Jasper, Henry. And now this Sir Roark. She halted and flattened her hand beneath her breasts. No use to go over the list of trials again; the process would only lead to more upset.

Alyss found herself at the wide window her father had lovingly created for her mother. She slipped the latch and opened the shutter. A stirring of air cooled her burning cheeks as memories of earlier, happier, years filled her mind. Her parents had shared a deep and lasting love. Once she'd longed for that kind of marriage, knowing how unique it was. Life's reality discouraged such romantic notions. Marriage was for business; love was for pleasure.

Certainly Alyss's first betrothal had been business. Two old friends—her father and his—had agreed their lands should be joined; their son and daughter were the means of doing it.

But the arrangement hadn't been business at all. She'd learned four years ago, painfully, the betrothal had never been formalized. Alyss felt no pain now when she thought of Gareth and his wife. Time healed that wound.

True he'd been handsome, with his blond hair and mustache, his fine manners, and entertaining stories. So unlike the rogue glowering in her hall right now.

Sir Roark. She didn't trust his threatening look, the days-thick growth of beard, the long and ragged hair. His eyebrows were much too straight, except for the scar that slashed through one. She didn't recall the color of his—scheming hazel eyes with green and gold flecks. And his nose. Like the beak of a hawk. It would have overpowered his face if his jaw had been less square, his mouth less mobile. Altogether, he appeared entirely too commanding, and she wasn't about to be commanded.

A quick scratch on the door brought Alyss around. She clenched her mouth against a disappointed sigh when Father Eudo stepped in and stood poised in that way of his that invariably irritated her. What a sinner she must be, to react that way to a man of the church.

"Such a sad day for you, my child, left all alone," Father Eudo said, his tone morose. "I am sure your brother died bravely defending the king. I regret I didn't know Sir Henry better, but in the brief time he was here, he showed himself an honorable knight and a loving son and brother. I will arrange a memorial service for him this Lord's Day."

The priest's words were meant to be comforting and, indeed, Alyss was grateful for his efforts. At least, she should be. Right now, she just wanted solitude. She wasn't to get it.

"With your father and your brother gone now, you are alone," he repeated. "Chauvere is unprotected."

"I am not alone, nor am I a child," Alyss pointed out. "I have my sister and the people here."

A soft "tsk" floated in the air followed by a murmur Alyss couldn't catch.

When he continued, his voice had lost its conciliatory tone. "I didn't say it earlier because you'd just suffered a shock, my lady. But the time has come to face a difficult truth. Without a strong man to take charge, you are at the mercy of any army that attacks."

Alyss rounded to face him. "Haven't I managed to withstand all challenges before now, Father Eudo?"

A bitter look flashed across his face, but it was gone in an instant, replaced by his unctuous smile.

"You and your faithful Sir Baldwin. Yes, my lady, I know. Your people know it too, and love you for it. And you are right. The defense has been well done since your father—left us, and I know Sir Baldwin has benefited from your suggestions. Yet consider. A lady alone, commanding a rich but severely undermanned holding, is temptation itself. When word of Sir Henry's death becomes public, the trials you've experienced in the past will seem nothing, indeed."

Alyss clenched her lips. She didn't want to admit it, yet he was right.

An expression of benevolent concern creased his cheeks. "I fear for you, my lady, and for your people. The truth is, Chauvere will not be left in peace while you are unwed. It is the way of the world."

"Are you trying to say I should marry this stranger?" Anyone who truly knew Alyss would be wary at her soft tone. "A man we know nothing of, who appeared at our gates practically alone? Would you have me give over to an unknown knight all those things we fought to keep from someone exactly like him?"

Kicking at the confining robe that wound about his left leg, the priest eased toward the brazier. "He is a stranger," he agreed. "Yet he comes in peace, not with an army behind him. He has served an estimable lord. He is courageous."

"Or desperate," Alyss murmured. To put distance between the two of them, she strode to the table that served as her desk. "I don't care whom he served. I will not marry him or anyone."

Father Eudo paused at the brazier and held his hands out to the warmth. "It is not an easy choice, I know. Remember the words of our Lord, who said a woman's duty is to marry and a husband's to defend. To refuse to obey the church is a sin. The knight waiting below offers protection at a time when your need is greatest."

He had an inexhaustible store of platitudes he blamed on the Lord. She wanted to roll her eyes, but manners prevented insulting a priest.

Running footsteps sounded in the corridor, and he turned to the door. "Consider his presence an answer to your prayers."

The Lord sent Sir Roark? Not likely. She braced both hands on the table. *I can do this. I did it before Father died. Henry wasn't here then. I can do it now.*

Can't I?

Her thoughts sounded like defeat, even to herself.

James nearly barreled into Father Eudo as the two passed in the doorway.

The boy's shoulders hunched. "Rose sent me, my lady," he began, "but I swear, I wasn't poking around in Sir Roark's gear. He said for me to straighten it up."

Alyss motioned the boy to the padded bench next to her. "I don't want to talk to you about that, James." A look of relief flicked over his face. "I want to ask you about Sir Henry. You were with him before the king was set free, weren't you?"

She didn't wait for him to nod, but continued. "When did he and Sir Roark meet? Was it on the ship, or after they arrived?"

James's brow crinkled. "I don't know, my lady. I know Sir Henry had lots of friends, but I didn't see them all."

"Well, then, did you see Sir Roark and your lord together?"

"No, my lady." James fidgeted on the bench.

Alyss struggled to keep her tone gentle despite her pounding heart. "Did Sir Henry ever mention him by name?"

"I never heard Sir Henry mention none of his friends by name." Then he cocked his head. "Oh, sometimes he talked about the king, and sometimes he talked about Sir Geoffrey and Sir Amos—they was squires together."

Sitting back, Alyss clasped her hands. "One last thing, James. How did you know Sir Roark and my brother were friends?"

"Sir Godfrey told me when he came to camp. He said Sir Roark was going home, and he had volunteered to tell you the bad news, and that I should go along to help him." The boy was looking worried again. "Did I do wrong, my lady? Should I have stayed with Sir Godfrey? I were sick a lot after the fight."

Alyss patted his hand. "No, James, you did right to obey Sir Godfrey. You may return to your duties." The youngster had made it to the door when she thought of something else. "James, did Sir Roark talk about Sir Henry on the trip here?"

"Yes, my lady." James pushed the hair out of his face. "He said he knew how hard it was to lose someone you love and that it was all right to cry. He said Sir Henry would want me to grieve for him some, but he would want me to go on and live a good life and remember him."

Either Roark had known Henry or he was a shrewd, conniving liar who covered his tracks. She smiled at the youth. "That's very good advice. Thank you."

After James left, Alyss walked to the window again, trying out explanations in her mind.

Roark is a fraud, an opportunist who never met my

brother. He heard Henry had died and snatched at the chance for a wealthy holding.

But he knew so much about them all, so much about the castle, the people, Henry himself.

Roark knew Henry and agreed to provide his protection for the family.

But what about his own home—surely he belonged somewhere? Had he, his friend Alain, and the two pages traveled all that way alone? Very dangerous. He obviously commanded men, an air about him made Alyss certain of that. If he commanded men, where were they? Why had they not accompanied the tiny contingent the long distance north? Oh, she should have asked James.

Alyss paced across the room and back. Something about the knight made her uneasy. She couldn't identify it, yet she felt unsettled around him. At times during the hours since he arrived, he appeared confident as well as competent. But at others he'd appeared surprised, even uncertain.

Mary's tears, her head throbbed with indecision. Voices floated up from the courtyard, and her back stiffened. She would not let a momentary weakness affect her. This was her home; no one would usurp her place.

And so she would tell Sir Roark.

Chapter Eleven

Alyss halted in the shadows of the stairway to watch the scene before her. Trestle tables were being readied for the midday meal. Sir Roark stood on the dais, his back to her. Father Eudo spoke quietly at his side.

Near the kitchen entrance, Lady Isobel beckoned. She turned a shoulder from the crowd when Alyss approached. "Alfred sent word from Windom," she murmured. "His new master's coming here. Got some kind of paper from Prince John that he's been bragging over. Says he'll be wed soon."

Alyss closed her eyes. What Sir Roark had told her earlier was true, then. Not that she'd doubted, but perhaps she'd held out a small hope. She glanced at him fully then—and blinked at his changed appearance.

With his scraggly beard gone and his hair trimmed, he was even more striking. Strong, compelling. Unexpected. Her face flooded with warmth that swept into her chest, and she looked away. The last thing on earth she wanted was to feel anything for this usurper. Isobel caught her eye and smiled. Obviously she'd had a hand in his transformation. Alyss flicked another look his way.

He intercepted her gaze and prowled toward her. Like the kitchen tomcat cornering a mouse. Her breath caught. Her throat felt dry as week-old bread. She swallowed and took a step toward the stairs.

Roark's hand on her arm stopped her. Looking the image of a solicitous suitor, he whispered, "Are you ready? We will say the vows now and celebrate with the midday meal."

"No," she gasped. "I'm not...prepared. I must..." she gestured to the work gown she wore, "...change."

He frowned, then gave a quick shake of his head. "Make haste then. And bring your sister. I've yet to meet her."

****

Roark paced for what seemed like hours. How long could it take to change one blasted gown? The noise level in the hall rose as more and more people gathered for the meal, which Lady Isobel held back. Looked like he had one ally at least.

It seemed his bride would not make a voluntary appearance. What did a man do in these circumstances? Didn't the woman understand plain facts? He'd tried to deal reasonably with her. Couldn't she make simple decisions? He was obviously the best choice of those facing her; must he take drastic measures?

Finally, he gestured to Father Eudo. "Make ready."

"But Sir Roark, weddings should be celebrated before midday. It's long past now. The church..."

Roark leveled a gaze at him.

The priest cleared his throat. "Under the circumstances—"

"Then get on with it."

"If only your bride obeyed half so well," Alain murmured. "Don't narrow your eyes at me, it's the truth. Unless I missed something earlier, the lady never agreed to wed you. You simply told her it would be so."

"This isn't a time for your blasted humor," Roark grumbled. Usually his friend's remarks made him smile, but not now. "Find Sir Baldwin and assemble the fighting men outside. In truth, I'd rather confront them than the lady. They will understand the threat to the castle and the village."

As for the Lady Alyss, Roark had no words certain to sway her. He had used his words, and they hadn't worked. That left other persuasion. He leaned his left hip against a table, crossed his arms, and considered his alternatives.

He could force the lady's compliance. She loved her people. She'd preserve their safety at any cost to herself. But would he really threaten her in that manner? Did he want the holding at such cost?

He and Alain could simply leave and avoid the almost-certain fight ahead with the neighbor. This wasn't his nor Alain's battle. If necessary, the two of them could hire out as free lances, mercenaries.

There were bound to be other places to claim, other women to wed. Yet in his heart, he knew there wouldn't be. This was his time, his place. He felt it the first night he met Sir Godfrey at that inn. He had to persuade the stubborn woman above stairs to agree. By God, agree or no, she would be his wife.

Father Eudo seemed to read Roark's thoughts and stopped at his side. "What if she won't agree?"

Roark shook his head. "It doesn't matter. It will happen."

"You can't force her. The church requires consent."

Soldiers had been leaving the hall and finally, Alain gestured. Roark pushed away from the table. "I'll get her consent."

He paused, flashed an intent look that sent the priest back an involuntary step, and lowered his voice. "Or I'll get yours."

If only he were as confident as he sounded.

Outside, the knights and men-at-arms stood at the base of the stairway. Their conversations quieted when Roark appeared. He paused. For years, he had stood where they stood now. But no longer. He squared his already straight shoulders.

"Men, no doubt you have heard that Sir Henry won't be back. Before he died, I vowed to him to take his responsibility as my own, to protect Chauvere and its people. I intend to do that, beginning now." He kept talking through the mutterings.

"I've heard of the recent trouble with your neighbors who wanted this holding. They failed before. But you're all fighting men—you know they'll be back." Roark saw many of the soldiers nod, expressions grim.

"You're concerned for the safety of your families and friends, I know, and for your lady." The men glanced at each other and at Sir Baldwin as Roark continued. "So am I. Nonetheless, if you can't swear loyalty to me, you can pack your belongings and leave tonight. If you stay, you'll be required to fight. Tomorrow we begin training. You will take your orders from Sir Alain. Sir Baldwin will assist him."

Several coughs and a few curses followed that pronouncement. Sir Baldwin nodded at the men. Amidst the angry talk, one voice called out, "We owe allegiance to Lady Alyss. I say you have no right to take command."

Roark pointed to the man, a knight from the look of his clothes and his carefully nurtured black mustache. One of the young ones who had not followed Sir Henry.

"Step forward," Roark ordered. "Who are you?"

The knight sauntered to the front, his wavy black hair gleaming in the sun. "Sir Roland, son of Lord Fredrick of Barksdale." He smirked. "Who are you?"

The insolence silenced the men, a few of whom nervously inched away from him. No knight would stand for his insulting tone. Roark didn't intend to. Still, he knew the others hoped for an answer to that question.

He looked out at them once more and said simply, "I am your new lord."

He glanced toward his new captain. "Sir Alain, see that Sir Roland collects all of his *own* gear before he leaves for Barksdale. Now."

The cocky knight straightened, the smug look arrested. "You can't send me away. Lord Ulrich gave his word to my father..."

The door closed on the protest as Roark stepped back into the hall.

Some of the tables had been pushed up against the wall and set with pitchers of ale and platters of meat pasties. The talk quieted as he walked to the center of the room and looked around. Roark spied the female who had attended Lady Alyss earlier.

He motioned to her. "What are you called, girl?"

"Rose," she answered, eyes lowered.

"Well, Rose, go and tell your lady that I await her." He turned to Father Eudo. "Are you ready?"

The priest looked at Roark for a long moment before he nodded once.

They did not talk while they waited. Muffled sounds drifted down from the solar, then a heavy door slammed. The maid reappeared, a sly look on her face.

"Milady said you could wait until doomsday. Sir Roark." The courtesy title was added begrudgingly. From somewhere among the servants came muffled laughter. Roark set his jaw and headed for the stairway. When he reached the solar, he lifted a foot and kicked open the door.

Alyss stood by the window, mouth tight, face flushed, eyes wide. "There was no need to bully your way in. The door wasn't barred."

Roark clenched his teeth, and the cords in his neck tightened. He deserved the reprimand, but he couldn't allow the lady to keep the upper hand. He took one step, then another, toward her. "I sent word for you to join me in the hall. You ignored me. Never again ignore my summons."

He almost winced. He never spoke so harshly to any woman. His mother would have boxed his ears.

And he didn't want to be angry. He wanted to scoop her into his arms, to promise he meant no harm. Only good. Only protection.

Only she refused to cooperate. How did a man handle a woman so independent? If only he'd been more observant when his father spoke to his mother. If only he hadn't been so young. Before the tragedy.

Alyss stood her ground and lifted her chin. "You didn't summon me, you said you awaited me. Perhaps your knightly training did not include language. 'I await you,' is a statement. 'Come to the hall,' is a summons."

Again, the lady had found a weakness in his armor. He had no language training at all, no reading, no writing but for his name. Most knights did not, but his inability rankled him.

"If my speech doesn't move you, then I won't bother with it." He leaned down, grabbed her around the knees, and upended her onto his shoulder. A thought raced through his mind: This wasn't, perhaps, the ideal way to scoop her into his arms.

The unexpectedness of the action brought a squeal from Alyss and the sound of running feet from the hall below.

"Put me down." She smacked him on the back and squirmed, kicking out at any part of his body she could connect with. He clenched her legs with his right arm before she managed to unman him with a lucky blow.

"Hold still." A smack to her bottom punctuated his words. "And that was a command." *God's elbow.* Another act guaranteed to increase her ire. Would he ever learn?

He strode out the door, Alyss anchored to his shoulder. Half way down the steps, he paused. He didn't want to embarrass her before her people. He set her on her feet and patted her back.

His anger had been replaced by bewilderment. Nothing had gone according to plan today, from the moment he and Alain rode through the gates. Least of all the reaction of Lady Alyss.

He had to persuade her one way or another. The more he learned about past attempts on the castle, he more he realized time was, indeed, short. Although he hated what he was about to do, he murmured, "Make no mistake. You will marry me now. If you value your home and your people, there will be no more foolishness."

Alyss swung her hand. He caught her wrist before she could connect with his face. She glared at him, her eyes filled with anger. "Do you think you can force me into marriage with threats? Better men than you have tried and failed."

Sliding his hand down to cover hers, Roark said,

"Understand lady, I do this for your protection." His low voice was fierce. "Luck has been with you. For whatever reason, no one has used the kind of force needed to capture this place. Once word about your brother is out, they will come.

"It won't take much, believe me. I've overrun castles manned by more fighters than you muster, and I have done it with fewer soldiers. I'm here now, and I will defend you and your people. Consider their safety, if not your own."

Her lips tightened into a line, and Roark mentally cursed his rough words. Even when he tried to be reasonable, still he sounded like a warrior, not a courtier. Well, she needed plain speaking, if only she'd recognize the rightness of what he said.

****

Roark's words had Alyss rebelling at any attempted coercion, but he was likely right. Her displays of independence, her boasts of driving away the Windom army and its lord had been that, boasts. If Chauvere just had more fighters, she *could* manage. None were coming.

As a child, she once saw a juggler who twirled a staff burning at both ends. She felt like that juggler. For months now she'd kept the staff balanced, but she couldn't forever, and no matter which way she moved, she would get burned.

Did she have a choice? He hadn't exactly threatened her people, but he had implied—what? What had he said? He had talked of protection, not conquest. Could she trust him?

Closing her eyes, she pictured her people, her sister, her loyal friends here. Their welfare was her responsibility. They deserved the best protection she could provide. As much as she protested, as much as she resisted the idea, Alyss knew in her heart Sir Roark was right. With Henry gone and Sir Godfrey and the other men God only knew how far away, Chauvere's garrison could not hold out indefinitely.

At last she could admit: The only freedom she really had lay in her choice of a husband—the new lord of Windom or Sir Roark. Although Sir Roark had a talent for irritating her, and no matter how she'd insulted him earlier, for some inexplicable reason she trusted him. Her trust had nothing to do with the unwelcome warmth his touch sparked, nor the unexpected breathlessness that squeezed her lungs at the sight of his strong face. Certainly not.

Alyss looked Sir Roark squarely in his eyes. They held confidence, determination—and something more. An intensity, a drive. Beneath his grim stare, she vowed, lay sincerity.

She prayed she wasn't mistaken.

As if from a distance, she heard herself say, "Very well."

****

The ceremony was brief, cloaked in unreality. Alyss repeated what was needed, but her mind refused to focus. And when the final vows were over, she felt no different. Yet everything had changed. She was married. She had staked her life and that of everyone here on a man she knew nothing about. She prayed the decision hadn't been a mistake.

A shout of laughter made her start. Servants and men from the garrison were celebrating the wedding with ale and meat pasties. No formal midday meal this day.

The villagers should be told, although word undoubtedly had spread. She needn't trouble announcing anything. No, that wasn't her way. She did her best to keep her people informed of any change that affected their lives.

"We will go out to the village now." She raised her voice to reach Roark, who looked up from a conversation with Sir Alain. "I will introduce you."

"I don't need you..." He stopped, grasping her intent, then inclined his head. "My thanks."

She walked past him on the way to the door. "I'm not doing this for you."

****

All in all, Roark decided, the trek through the village went well. Folks seemed friendly, but cautious, reserving judgment on their new lord.

Most of the talk had been for their lady, to whom they offered condolences on the death of her brother. However, Sir Henry's long years away meant that few people knew him. It was to Lady Alyss they went if they needed something. It was Lady Alyss who was familiar to them, who had grown up in their midst.

It was to Lady Alyss they owed their allegiance and, just as important, their affection.

As they returned to the castle, Roark realized the sister—Evie—hadn't appeared at the wedding. Her existence had fled his mind in the turmoil of the proceedings. Was his new wife keeping her hidden? Did she fear him that much?

"Where is your sister?" he asked. "Why have I not seen her around the hall today? At the wedding?"

Alyss picked up her stride but he kept pace. At last she slowed, then stopped as if reaching a decision. She faced him, defiance in the set of her mouth. "Evie is with friends. I sent her away when the castle came under attack, before our father died. She's safe."

"Where?" he repeated, his tone gentle but firm. "She can return now. I will see to her safety."

Turning, Alyss resumed walking. Again, in silence. He was about to insist on an answer when she said, "Evie is at St. Ursula Convent. And I want her to remain there until…that is, for now. Until the trouble with Windom Castle is settled."

Roark considered the request. A convent. The girl might well be better off there for now.

"Very well."

The afternoon light had weakened and temperatures had dropped by the time they made it back to the castle.

"I'll see to a room for you," Alyss announced as they approached the door.

"No need," he said. "Sir Alain unpacked my gear while we were gone."

"Then I will bid you good night."

"No need," Roark repeated. "We will retire together. We have unfinished business."

Barbara Bettis

Chapter Twelve

Alyss strode toward the stairs. Sir Roark was a...she couldn't think of a low-enough name for him. She knew perfectly well to what unfinished business he referred.

The bedding. Her stomach plummeted. Her palms itched with nervousness. Well, he was in for a surprise. His 'business' would remain unfinished.

An unexpected touch on her back made her jerk, but the firm pressure remained. Alyss hadn't realized he walked so close.

Entirely too close. She felt the warmth of his hand through her clothing. And she smelled him. Faint perspiration from the walk to the village mingled with a slight fragrance of soap from his earlier bath. And something else she couldn't identify, not an herb but an earthier scent. His own.

It wasn't offensive.

Untrue. Everything about him was offensive. His shoulders were too broad, his chin too stubborn, his nose too hawkish, his attitude too inflexible. And his hands, too callused, too strong, too...warm. Alyss arched away from the hand that lay just above her waist.

When they reached the solar, she paused. Sir Roark urged her on. "To the lord's chamber."

She glared over her shoulder. She refused to argue in the corridor.

She stepped into her father's old room and stopped short. She couldn't speak; she didn't trust her voice. All her father's things were gone. Fresh rushes covered the floor. Along the wall opposite the window ranged Sir Roark's belongings. Only three bags? She raised her brows.

He seemed to read her thoughts, because he shrugged. "That's all I've ever needed."

"Then you've done well for yourself today."

****

"I believe I have." Roark let her think what she chose. He'd send to Cantleigh for the rest of his hard-earned possessions once he'd settled in.

He walked to the center of the room, looking at the left wall, the one she hadn't noticed. Alyss's gaze followed his, and she gasped.

"No." Anger gave her voice a sharp edge. There, arranged neatly, sat chests from her chamber.

Her reaction was immediate. "How dare you confiscate my personal belongings as your own. Have you no shame? Have I no privacy?"

"We're married." Roark kept his voice calm. "We'll share a room. I thought you'd want your things close."

Alyss glared at him, then turned toward the door.

He got there first, arm blocking the latch. "I can't let you leave right now. We must finish this."

He expected her to argue further. She didn't. She merely walked to the wall near the bed and showed him her back.

He'd hoped her anger over the room arrangements

might divert her from the bigger issues of the quick marriage and the story of Henry and Roark's friendship. That story was proving shakier than he'd imagined.

Hundreds of miles from England, the plan had seemed simple. A grieving sister was bound to welcome her dead brother's friend to fulfill the brother's dying wish that they marry. In so doing, the friend would take control of the sorely under-defended keep she struggled to hold. The epitome of knightly duty to a meek and mild lady who needed protection. A woman whose youthful betrothed once rejected her.

Could he have been more wrong? This woman wasn't so grateful for his appearance that she never questioned it. God's blood. This woman would question a messenger from heaven. She'd probably insist the Lord didn't know His own mind.

Roark was as far from being God as Lady Alyss was from being…an unappealing woman who couldn't hold a man. Her hair was as sleek and golden brown as meadow honey. And that damned strand that kept falling in her face. He wanted to twist it around his fist and drag her to him. He wanted to shake her, just before he kissed her witless. One way to silence her.

Her lips would be soft and mobile, provided he could work them open from the compressed line she wore now.

That thought surprised a growl from him, and she turned her head. At this distance, he couldn't see her eyes, but he remembered the smoky blue-gray as they lit in anger. His body recalled their fire too.

Damn. At least he could achieve the bedding tonight. It had been many long weeks since he'd known a woman.

The left side of his mouth curved up. "One last step to take, my lady." He looked at the bed.

The end of her long braid swung back and forth across her bottom as she shook her head.

"I will not." Her voice came low and steady. "We are wed, in God's sight and in the world's. You have what you came for. If Henry did, indeed, send you, then the vow is satisfied. You have command of the garrison, the servants, and the village." She turned, her back pressed against the wall. "You will not have control of me."

Roark raised his brows. "Not according to the church."

Alyss's short laugh sounded bitter. "The church. The church is run by men, for men. Don't knights swear to kind and gentle manners in the name of the church, and then go out to rape and kill?"

"I will not kill you, lady," Roark murmured, "and I will not rape you." He took a deep breath. "But we will go through with this. Consummation binds a marriage, and I won't take the chance this wedding can be challenged."

Alyss stepped away from the wall, her chin raised in her own challenge. "I refuse."

Roark hadn't actually planned what would happen after the ceremony. If he'd thought of the wedding night at all, it was as an accomplished fact. He never imagined he'd have to drag his wife to bed.

"I have never forced a woman in my life," he told her. "I don't want to start now. I can make the joining easy for you, if you will allow it. But if not...well, that's your choice, again."

"What *choice*?" She ground out between clenched

teeth. "My *choice* is for you to be gone from our lives. My *choice* is for the last six months never to have happened."

Her frustration filled the air. "I told you my *choice* and you *chose* to ignore it."

She faced him, then, her eyes brimming with anger. And beneath the anger, Roark judged, lay fear. Natural for a woman to feel fear. He understood that.

He tried to reassure her. "Lady, why should I harm you? You are my wife now. I have just vowed to protect you. You will bear my sons and daughters, and I will treat you with the respect you deserve. You have nothing to fear."

What more could the woman want? He offered her security, protection. She would continue managing the household. And he, Roark, would be far kinder than another knight in this situation. He reached out for her, but she backed away, shaking her head.

****

Sons and daughters. Breath locked in Alyss's lungs. This knight expected her to have his children? Of course he did. They were married, what else? But she wouldn't. She flung out her hand to keep him back.

"Wait." Alyss gave a deep, shuddering sigh. She didn't know which emotion took precedence—anger, reluctance, or embarrassment that she might be forced to concede another obstacle to their joining this night. "Give me time. A little more time. That's my choice."

He studied her with eyes that seemed brown in the dim light filtering into the chamber. Assessing. "How long?"

Forever. "A few days. Let us grow to know each other." A few days could be stretched into weeks. And then…she would think of something. The answer would come, if she just had time to consider.

He took a step forward, then another, slowly extending his right hand, as if she were an animal needing reassurance. Her gaze never wavered from him. His fingers slid behind her shoulder to urge her closer. No longer able to keep her eyes on his, she focused on his left ear. As he drew nearer the ear blurred, and her neck tilted back to keep it in view.

The tilting stopped with her head cradled in his hand. Blessed Mother, he was going to kiss her again. She tried to twist her face to the side, but his grip was firm. His hand moved to the strand of hair at the side of her face, and he wrapped his fingers in it. She struggled for breath.

Then his big, warm body was close to hers, and his lips were there, gentler than the first time, softer than she could ever have believed. He tasted of ale and seduction. She breathed in the aroma of wood smoke, the castle's herb soap, and a spiciness…heady, comforting…him. The hard muscles of his chest tightened beneath her fingers.

She stiffened. Her hands pressed flat against his chest. Roark moved back slightly, and Alyss saw the gold flecks glimmering in his eyes. She felt as if her body had pulled into itself, poised on the brink of bursting, yet she could not move. Her mind fogged, and she didn't know whose arms held her captive. A sudden wave of revulsion swept through her. She panicked and shoved.

****

She fit fine in his arms. But Roark detected the trembling of tensed muscles beneath his fingers. Her body felt brittle, stiff but fragile, ready to crumble at the wrong touch like a skim of ice on a winter's morn. For an instant, Alyss's lips relaxed, along with the rest of her body. The near-softening was over in a flash, and she tried to pull away, her hands pushing at his shoulders.

He obliged her by leaning back, and the contact sent a surge of energy through him. This rapid turn in her life must surely be a shock. How could it not? But once she adjusted to his presence, once she realized she no longer had to bear sole responsibility for every duty, she'd be persuaded.

She'd resume directing the household, sewing, and holding court with her attendants. All ladies liked that. In his experience, their thoughts never strayed long from parties, new gowns, flirtation.

There would be no flirtations involving Lady Alyss. No new gowns, either, for a while. And no parties. Roark knew the challenges he faced in building his position at Chauvere. He could not afford to welcome people he didn't know. Not yet. Too much to do. Rebuild and strengthen the walls, train the few soldiers and knights remaining, perhaps try to hire more. He'd see how deep the coffers ran.

A shame his men from Cantleigh weren't here. Yet, they weren't his men. He had trained them, lived with them, led them into battle, but they were pledged to Cantleigh.

Alyss's breathing had returned almost to normal, and her muscles began to unclench in his grasp. She turned away, her chin lifting again in what Roark was beginning to realize was not defiance, but uncertainty.

"I will have Rose move my belongings back to my

bedchamber," she said in her calm voice. "Until we have come to know each other."

She started for the door again and again Roark stopped her.

"That won't be necessary, my lady," he said. "I think I am coming to know you quite well. We won't need more time."

"*I* need more time."

"I can't give it to you." Roark stepped to the table to light more candles. The waning evening had left the room in near darkness, and he wanted to see her. "You are wed," he said, voice hard. "You must accept it."

He sounded like a bastard, talking to the lady that way. But he couldn't afford to give ground. He was too close to success. Nothing, not even his new wife's feelings, could get in his way. If he were challenged, there must be no doubt of his right to hold Chauvere, no grounds for annulment.

Roark watched Alyss for some reaction to his declaration. He thought he detected a look of panic in her eyes, but it disappeared so quickly he couldn't be certain. Then he saw nothing, save for a flaring of her nostrils and an even firmer compression of her mouth.

"Very well, if you must humiliate me, I confess." Her face blazed, but she maintained eye contact. "We cannot consummate the marriage tonight. I have...that is, I'm..."

What was she trying to say—that she wasn't a virgin? He didn't like the thought, but her condition wouldn't stop consummation. Then he realized what she meant, and for the first time in his memory, Roark stood speechless. From the way his neck burned, he likely appeared as embarrassed as she did.

She must have mistaken his reaction, because she crossed her arms beneath those tempting breasts and glared. "Surely you understand what I'm referring to. In order for females to reproduce—"

"Stop." He raised a hand, palm out. "No need to explain. I know your meaning."

"I thought you likely did." Her voice carried a trace of smugness, and he'd be damned, if her eyes weren't sparking with humor.

He'd never come across such a lady in his eight and twenty years. Still at a loss for words, he turned and stalked across the chamber. In one brief moment, she'd regained the upper hand in their confrontation.

"Let me consider," he said.

The church discouraged intimacy between man and wife during times like she endured tonight. He respected that. The fact remained, however, with no proof of consummation... He faced her. "Understand that if this marriage is challenged within the next sennight, you must submit to an examination. Once proof is found that we have not been together, my claim is weakened. I can't have that."

For a moment, the significance of his words didn't hit the mark, because Lady Alyss stared at him, her forehead pleated in uncertainty.

Then she must have realized his meaning, because she looked away, her lower lip clenched between her teeth.

At last she shook her head and murmured, "It won't come to that."

It was his turn to be perplexed. When he grasped the import of her implication, he wanted to roar, to throw something. Instead, he asked, "Who was he? Tell me his name."

She shook her head, her eyes wide. "What?"

"Is he here? Will I see your lover in the hall every day?"

"I don't understand what you mean." Her words were little more than a whisper.

He struggled to keep his voice calm. "If you're lying to me and I find him, he will be."

"You need not worry. No such man is here."

Roark didn't answer. As in battle, he didn't allow feelings to interfere when he plotted action. "Tell me this. How many know? Were you discreet? Or does every villager whisper stories of your meetings?"

Lady Alyss drew in a breath, then another, before she answered. "There is no one."

Something in her tone skidded across his mind. She met his eyes and lifted her chin. He didn't believe her.

Roark paced the length of the chamber, then went to the bed. He motioned to Alyss. "We'll have some kind of proof tonight. I'll step outside while you see to a spot of blood on the sheet."

****

Alyss's hands shook when she pressed them against the door. He'd misunderstood. He thought she implied she wasn't... She'd only meant that she would submit later, when necessary. But if he thought otherwise, perhaps he'd leave her be.

A flutter passed through her stomach. She wasn't good at deception.

Working quickly, she made sure the required evidence stained the white bedding. It was a blessing her time had come when it did. She wasn't about to inform Sir Roark that personal maids and washer women knew when women of the keep bled. But perhaps with all the excitement of the past days, they'd not notice this slip.

When Roark opened the door, Rose trailed him in.

"See that your lady's belongings are moved back to her quarters," Roark directed the maid. He pulled the sheet off the bed and threw it in her direction. "And show this in the hall. Tell Lady Isobel to store it. I may have need of it one day."

Without speaking, Alyss made her way to her bedchamber where she sank onto a bench. If only this day had been a nightmare, if she could wake to find everything as it was yesterday.

Her mind struggled to take in the events of the past few hours. Wed to a stranger, a man who came as a guest, but who remained to wrest control of everything Alyss held dear. How had it happened?

When he stood before the gates that morning, he seemed like a simple knight, weary from the long journey. There'd been nothing to alert her to the devastating message he carried, nor of the absolute coup he'd achieve.

Yet with no threats, no superior forces—no forces at all—he conquered. Speaking of honor and duty, he played upon their grief. He hadn't needed a battle. With just those sympathetic eyes and a few stories of her beloved brother, he wormed his way into a position that others had not gained after prolonged fighting.

She should have listened to her head and sent him away. Instead she allowed emotions to rule. Alyss shook her bowed head then forced her eyes closed. She had to sleep.

Hours later, she stared at the ceiling. She had not

For This Knight Only

slept, but she had not wept. Who was he, really? His trickery replayed in her mind, but a nagging notion intruded. In spite of his inflexible insistence on marriage, afterward he'd shown some consideration. The way he tried to ease her fears, his attempt to explain the benefits she held as his wife. He might be a lying schemer, but he had shown thoughtfulness.

Until he thought she wasn't a maiden. Then he behaved as she'd expected of any man she wed and gave no chance for an explanation. Nor even asked for one. For which she ought to be pleased.

The pain in her chest made breathing difficult. She rolled over, flung an arm over her eyes, and groaned. The cycle of pain, anger, regret, and fascination had to end. Time for another day.

Work didn't halt for the recriminations of foolish virgins. She was scrubbing cold water on her face when a sound alerted her. She cracked open the door to hear clamor from the hall and saw Roark dash from his chamber, followed by Sir Alain.

An emergency? No one had alerted her.

Chapter Thirteen

Roark's eyes had flown open at the quiet knock. He was on his feet, sword in hand, before a shadowy figure stepped into the doorway, carrying a candle. Alain. He relaxed his stance.

"Come in."

"Sorry to…" Alain looked at the empty bed, at the wall where Alyss's belongings sat earlier, then at Roark.

Roark shook his head.

Alain set the candle on the table near the brazier. "Scouts report a sizeable group coming from the west."

Roark tossed his sword onto the mattress and reached for his clothing. "If they move at night, they must be familiar with the land."

"Think they'll attack?"

"Could be." Roark pulled on his tunic. "Or set a siege. Whatever they plan, with part of that wall still down, we're not ready." He reached for a boot. "How long till sunrise?"

"Maybe two hours." Alain handed him the other boot. "I've sent for Sir Baldwin."

"Good. Rouse the garrison and gather the weapons we have." He continued to talk as Alain followed him out the door. "Find where the grain is stored and where to keep the extra livestock."

In the great hall, servants chattered in confusion.

Sir Baldwin had arrived from his cottage already, along with Lady Isobel, who was directing the maids.

Alain pointed out the two who had espied the oncoming troop. Beckoning to Sir Baldwin, Roark headed toward them. Neither scout could estimate numbers, but they agreed on where the troops came from.

"Windom," insisted one, "no doubt. Nothin' that direction but Windom."

"Last time Windom came," Sir Baldwin said, "the troops camped outside the gates, there, while Sir Jasper gave Lady Alyss time to make up her mind. Not that she didn't tell him right away she wouldn't have him. She did, that. He waited two days. At dawn on the third, he attacked."

"What happened?"

"Somehow the devil got into the castle alone and struck down Lord Ulrich in his bedchamber." Sir Baldwin didn't quite meet Roark's eyes. "Before our lord died, he killed the man. We sent Windom's body home with his soldiers. They had no reason to fight after that, don't you see."

"We'll have no surprises this time," Roark said. "Come with me."

He gave Baldwin the duty of moving in as many people and supplies as possible from the village, then motioned Alain aside.

"Position the men on the parapets at each tower and at the corners of the wall." He frowned at the activity buzzing around them. "This test has come a bit sooner than I'd hoped."

"You're up to it." For once, Alain spoke without his perpetual half-smile. He nodded toward the stairs as he left. "Good luck with that."

Before Roark could turn, he heard Alyss.

"What's happening?" Her voice lifted only slightly, yet the noise level in the room diminished.

He met her as she came down the last few steps. Her eyes were puffy, but not red. Her braid was loosened and soft hair streamed around her face.

"It seems your new suitor from Windom has arrived," he said. "The scouts spotted troops marching from that direction."

She ignored his words and looked out over the activity. Swiping hair from her eyes, she demanded, "Where is Sir Baldwin? We must notify the village and get the garrison up."

"Don't worry." Roark followed her across the room. "Those are my duties now. I'm taking care of them. You organize the household. Show the men where to store the grain when they return."

Alyss stopped so quickly, Roark bumped into her. He grasped her shoulders to steady them both.

"You surely didn't order grain brought in from the village?" She shook his hands loose. "There's no time for that. And no place to put it."

"Find a place," Roark ordered. "We may need all we can get if this turns to a siege."

Lady Isobel had spotted Alyss and trotted toward her. Alyss looked at Roark, finally meeting his eyes. In that moment, he saw anger, defensiveness and, he could have sworn, hurt hidden beneath the antagonism. Then she was off across the floor to consult with Isobel.

****

Paxton, newly named Lord of Windom, observed as his troops established themselves before the gates of

Chauvere. The sun had just cleared the horizon. They'd made good time.

He was pleased.

His troops objected to traveling in the dark. They liked even less his insistence on quiet as they drew closer to their object.

He didn't care. Their surly attitudes and not-so-quiet predictions of bad luck had failed to sway his determination. Fools. So long as they obeyed without question, he wouldn't be forced to make any more examples of them. Stupid peasants.

Right now, little could penetrate his good humor. His lips curved as he imagined the guards' surprise when they awoke to find a small army spread out before them.

And the lady. What was her name? Ah, yes, Alyss. She was in for a greater surprise. Paxton inhaled and felt the leather-wrapped parchment press against his chest. She'd present no trouble. The keep was what he concentrated on, and it didn't disappoint, looming in the dawn like an immovable block.

He approved of the reward Prince John had presented him, while the royal brother still had means to do so. The last lord of Windom hadn't been up to the charge given him, but the prince had at last found the man to do the job properly. Himself.

A head popped above the wall outside the guard tower. Paxton's lips pulled tight against his teeth. Nearly time. The troops spread out in such a way to alarm the people inside, help them make a quick decision. He'd warned the soldiers to leave the villagers alone—for now. A rapid response to his demands by the lady inside would save a great deal of time and trouble.

With the wedding ceremony out of the way quickly, he'd continue to secure this part of the midlands for John. The prince considered Chauvere an essential piece in his chess game with his brother, King Richard. With its location, its two manors and a village, Chauvere had strategic significance. It needed to be brought into the prince's fold with a minimum of damage.

And here it lay, unprotected, like a shorn lamb in a winter fold. He, Paxton, was the wolf to devour it.

Actually, he preferred to think of himself as a fox. And the female inside, a trembling rabbit. The first thing he'd do—get rid of the old man who'd been handling the defenses so adroitly. Sir Baldwin. That piece of news had been delivered to Windom three days ago, courtesy of a friend at Chauvere. Paxton didn't know the friend's identity, but he would.

One helmeted figure appeared on the battlement, followed by another, then a third. At last.

The first stood between two merlons and called down. "Who are you and what do you want?"

Paxton kneed his horse forward. "Open this gate immediately. I am your new lord. Notify Lady Alyss that her husband has arrived. Now."

If the trio on the wall made any response, it was drowned out by the murmurs from his own men. He ignored them. They had not, of course, been told why they were here.

The soldier who had spoken disappeared, but the two others remained. One carried a lance, the other a bow.

Waiting was not something Paxton excelled at. He

allowed what he considered enough time for the gate to open by picturing in his mind someone climbing down from the wall, walking to the gate, and...

When nothing happened in the period he allotted, he nodded to his second in command who pointed to an archer. The archer whipped up a readied crossbow and fired so quickly, the pair on the wall scarcely had time to duck. The arrow sailed through the opening between merlons and dropped out of sight.

A faint cry drifted up. Lord Paxton smiled.

****

Roark heard a shiver in the air. A lone arrow swacked down to quiver in the bare dirt of the bailey, not far from a two-year-old village girl who had toddled away from her mother. Turning at the sound, seeing the near miss, the woman screamed and swept up the child, who caught her mother's fear and began to wail. A stray pup trotting behind the girl yapped in response, prompting an answer from a dog in the kennels. In seconds, the other dogs had joined in.

Alain dashed up the steps while Roark gave a last look at the men crouched around the walls. Some of the villagers looked grim, others frightened. All looked determined as they awkwardly clutched their borrowed bows, lances, and swords, weapons usually reserved only for knights and nobles.

"Remain still until you see the signal," he told the soldier nearest him, an older man-at-arms who had helped position the village men. "Pass the word."

Roark was waiting when his captain hit the bottom stair near the gate.

"Could you hear?" Alain asked.

Roark nodded. So Alyss had a husband. Perhaps

that's why she agreed to wed Roark, knowing the vows to be illegal. Or perhaps the man's words were a bluff.

****

In the midst of the din, Alyss raced down the steps. After making sure the child and the mother were unharmed, she sent them to the hall. Lady Isobel followed to herd the remaining women and children inside.

Alyss spied a familiar freckled face in a group of boys gawking at the hubbub. Will. "Quiet the dogs, please," she bade him, then paused beside Roark. "Who is it?"

He spared her a brief glance. "Wait inside."

Alyss ignored the command. "Is it Windom?"

"It is your first husband, Lady Wife," Roark answered. "Has his name escaped you? He calls himself the new lord here."

"Foolish, foolish," Alyss grumbled, shaking her head. "You know I have no—"

His eyes met hers, and the noise seemed to fade as she recalled the night before. She looked away quickly.

"I will see about this." Alyss ran for the stairs near the gate, but Roark caught up with her in a few strides.

"Stop." The authority in his low voice halted her. "Sir Baldwin will take care of it."

The former captain of the guard was already at the top of the steps. He stood, partially shielded on the battlements, and called, "By what right do you demand entrance as lord of Chauvere? You are not Lord Ulrich's son. You are not wed to Lady Alyss."

A showy bay pranced forward from the advance line below. The rider's voice lifted. "By order of Prince John, the land and the lady are mine. Open the gate."

"Until Lady Alyss can see proof of these claims, only you may enter."

The knight didn't like that stipulation and a short period of negotiation followed. Agreement finally was reached for him and four of his men to be admitted. He didn't look happy with the concession.

****

As the portcullis was raised, Roark looked around the littered bailey. Rays of early morning sun oozed over the stone walls, nudging sleepy shadows into retreat. They huddled in cold corners and clotted around piles of belongings the villagers couldn't bear to leave behind to possible pillage. All in all, not an impressive sight.

The few Chauvere soldiers gathered inside the gate were joined by Baldwin. Standing beside Alyss, Roark nodded, and one of the gates began to open. Alain took up his place at Roark's other side. The barking dogs and crying children had finally quieted. The men were silent. Sounds of groaning wood and creaking chains swelled, then the five men rode in.

The gate lumbered shut. Alain gave the signal, and the men on the wall straightened into view. Half faced the force gathered outside, half faced the group inside. The four accompanying soldiers registered surprise, but the knight's attention was fixed on Alyss. He pushed his coif back and urged his mount forward.

****

Alyss stood motionless as the bay walked toward her, coming closer. Instead of stopping the horse, the rider held the reins steady. His gaze challenged her, but she refused to budge. She'd raised her hand to whack the horse on the nose when Roark stepped up and grabbed the reins near the bit. The knight chose to ignore the interference and looked down at Alyss.

"My lady, I am Paxton, Lord of Windom. Prince John sends his greetings and other messages." He dismounted and threw the reins toward Roark. "I trust you have food and drink."

Alyss eyed him. He must think his cockiness passed for confidence.

"Let us not pretend this is a neighborly call," she said. "You brought your army to my home in the middle of the night. You have fired on my people. What do you want?"

Lord Paxton smiled ingratiatingly. "We will be much more comfortable inside."

Alyss caught Roark's eye, and he nodded. He beckoned to James, handed him the reins, and fell in beside her. His mouth thinned, and his eyes narrowed. Did he recognize the visitor? How would he know the man?

The intruder looked around as he walked. When the group stepped inside, he stopped and considered the large hall crowded with women and children from the village. "You have a sizeable household."

Alyss disliked his caustic tone. Her own was mild when she replied, "Only until your men leave. Then my people can return to their homes without fear."

She moved to her carved chair at the high table. Before Lord Paxton could act, Roark slipped into the matched chair next to her. His gaze didn't waver from Paxton, who in turn stared at Roark with a puzzled expression. It suddenly turned to recognition.

"Sir Roark of Stoddard? Cantleigh's man?" His voice shook with fury. "I thought you were dead."

"Your information is wrong."

Expression grim, Lord Paxton sat on the bench at Alyss's other side. For a moment he glared, then a smug smile took over as he unlooped a cord from around his neck and pulled a flat leather packet from beneath his tunic. He took out a parchment and opened it.

"A message from Prince John to Lady Alyss of Chauvere," he announced. "I will read it to you."

Alyss's brow arched. She plucked the parchment from his hand. "Thank you. I will read it for myself."

The man narrowed his eyes. Then he seemed to remember himself and nodded genially. "A lady of many parts," he acknowledged. "How convenient." He sat back, a satisfied look on his face, as one of the young pages poured a cup of ale.

Alyss scanned the note. She heard Roark clear his throat and glanced up. He likely wanted to know what it said. After the terrible night that had passed, he had no right to expect anything from her. Yet if the stranger sitting at her side was correct, Roark would certainly be involved.

"Prince John sends his greetings and his condolences," she said. "He has heard of the unfortunate death of my father and the sad, untimely death of my brother in service of the king."

A murmur moved through the hall at what appeared to be very proper condolences. She paused for a moment, then returned her attention to the message.

"The prince says he is sympathetic to my difficult position here alone. Because Chauvere lies within Nottinghamshire, and because Nottingham Castle is his to command, he feels responsible for my well-being and for my future. He recommends that I marry the bearer of this message, Lord Paxton of Windom, a loyal man and one strong enough to protect me."

She lifted her gaze to Lord Paxton. "And, of course, my home."

"John has no power here now." The sound of Roark's voice cut through the mutters swarming around them. He rose, looming over Paxton. "Even so, there can be no marriage. Lady Alyss is my wife. We were wed yesterday."

Chapter Fourteen

"No." Lord Paxton's fist hit the table as he leaped to his feet. "That's impossible."

Alyss jumped at the unexpected outburst and found herself looking at Roark's solid back.

In a blink, he'd placed himself between her and the other man. How could anyone that big move so quickly and silently?

Mary's tears. She refused to have a fight in the middle of the hall. She slipped around Roark, pushing between the two warriors. Roark's hands gripped her shoulders in what may have looked like a protective embrace to others, but the force of his fingers digging into her skin left no doubt of his intentions. He wanted her still and quiet.

He had a lot to learn about his new wife.

Hands clenched at her waist, she looked at Lord Paxton and spoke in what she hoped was a calm voice. "Let us all sit and discuss the message from the prince. Nothing can be settled with anger."

Alyss turned to Roark. He glared back at Paxon, the two apparently willing to settle the issue with a great deal of anger.

Alyss turned to Roark. "Husband?" She managed the word without choking. "Will you sit?"

She placed her hands on his, feeling the tension in his fists.

Alyss glanced back at the intruding knight. The wild look that accompanied his outburst had been replaced with narrowed eyes and lips pursed to a knot between narrow moustache and pointed beard.

Roark's strong hands remained tense beneath her own. Realizing she still held him, she lifted her fingers and again clasped them at her waist.

A movement in the room caught her eye. From the direction of the kitchen, Father Eudo threaded their way, gaze fixed on Lord Paxton.

"My lords, my lords," the priest called, his face intent, "let us not be hasty. Neither God nor Prince John would want blood shed here."

He trotted up the two steps to the table and bobbed his head in Lord Paxton's direction.

"My lord, it is true that the lady is wed. I blessed the ceremony between them."

Father Eudo's gaze pinned Lord Paxton. "Sir Roark arrived only yesterday with news. Our own Sir Henry charged him with protecting Lady Alyss and the people here. You must agree, that changes everything."

For once, Alyss was perfectly willing to let the little priest talk. Although he behaved strangely, even for Father Eudo.

Lord Paxton lowered himself into a seat. Roark did the same, his gaze never leaving the other man.

Taking advantage of the momentary lull, Alyss motioned for ale. Everyone needed a drink, but she didn't intend for wine to rile emotions even more.

****

Paxton's gaze landed on Sir Roark. Without a beard, the knight looked different, so he couldn't blame himself for failing to recognize him. Not dead after all.

How in Hell's hinterland had the lowly knight made the acquaintance of one of the king's inner circle like Henry of Chauvere? In any case, Sir Henry would never give his own sister to a landless knight. There was only one reason Cantleigh's man would show up here.

John sent him.

Anger simmered in Paxton's gut. What game did the prince play? He shifted on the bench and absently picked up his ale cup. He'd thought it almost too good to be true when John granted him Windom, along with the authority to take Chauvere and organize support for the prince in the area.

He deserved every prize he got, and with what he knew about the insidious plans of the king's brother, he'd counted on a bright future. But if John sent Sir Roark here, if he promised both knights the same prize, what did John hope to gain?

Paxton would wait. At least until he knew what John was up to. Carefully setting the cup on the table, he said, "So. I'm too late."

He bared his teeth in the best approximation of smile he could muster. "The king may yet have something to say about it. Orphaned heiresses don't marry without royal approval. Do you have that?"

****

Roark clenched his jaw and made an effort to choose his words. He would like to challenge this *poseur* now, but that could be disastrous. He'd be damned if he let his temper burn away this chance.

"I gave my word as a knight to protect my friend's sister. Surely no permission other than God's is necessary. Vows were freely made, and the bedding

115

complete. She's well and truly mine."

Paxton was silent for another moment, his eyes cold, his face still. Then he said, "I saw you in a tournament once. The other knight was bigger and his blade was better, but you moved from side to side, advancing and retreating, confusing him until he dropped his guard and you scored the winning hit. You bluffed him."

Roark lifted his hands to the sides. "Don't mistake me. Today I'm standing still."

An unctuous tenor slid like oil across the roiling conversation. "My lords, why don't we move to a more private place to continue this discussion?" Father Eudo gestured toward the stairway.

Paxton stood and pushed away from the table. "Not necessary. I'll return to camp." He inclined his head. "My lady."

In a glaring insult, he ignored Roark and Father Eudo as he strode toward the large doors.

"My men will accompany you." Roark's voice followed Paxton across the still-silent hall. "I wouldn't want you to think we're inhospitable."

As Paxton passed, his four knights joined him. Alain nodded and a half-dozen Chauvere men fell in.

When the doors closed behind them, Roark exhaled and worked the tightness from his clenched jaws. He sure as hell wasn't giving in to Prince John's puppet.

Something didn't feel right about this. How had John known about Sir Henry? Why did this Paxton think he, Roark, was dead? Questions for which he had no answers. At the moment.

Nor did he know what the man planned next. He'd consult with Alyss about stores, then order the guards doubled. This was his first challenge as the new lord of Chauvere. He dare not fail it.

****

Alyss conferred with Martha in the kitchen, then made the rounds of the villagers who were settling in. They had brought all their food and as many personal belongings as possible to keep from marauders.

When she'd done all she could, she escaped to the solar where she sat at the worktable and rested her forehead against folded arms. Her mind was as jumbled as the threads in her sewing basket.

Why did Prince John care about her and Chauvere? If he gave the holding to Lord Paxton, he must have known Sir Jasper was dead. If John had appointed Jasper as well, her old enemy's behavior fell into perspective. Alyss had always attributed his behavior to greed. She was not so vain as to think the neighbor sought her charms.

No matter what her father had said, when the betrothal to Gareth was set aside, Alyss blamed herself. Lord Ulrich, as a good father, assured Alyss it had nothing to do with her. Alyss, as a good daughter, pretended to believe him. In her heart, she was certain she lacked what it took to be an acceptable wife.

But today she'd stepped into the role. How odd it had been to keep peace between her *husband* and a stranger. Come to think of it, both knights were strangers. Yet when an opportunity to escape from an unwanted marriage came in the form of Lord Paxton, she instinctively aligned with Sir Roark.

All this furor over land.

The bottom dropped from her stomach. Had Roark really wed her for Henry's sake—or had he done so only to gain control of Chauvere? Last night, when the two of them were alone, what had he said? *I won't take the chance this wedding can be challenged.* Why would he be so concerned their union be questioned?

Had he lied? Had the clever Lady Alyss spurned offers from obviously land-hungry lords only to be trapped by a simple knight? The insight sent an icy shaft through her. *Stop this*! Alyss curled her hands into fists. It wasn't like her to overreact so.

She leaped to her feet and ran to the window. In the bailey below, he spoke with Sir Baldwin. His manner reflected steady determination. Despite his overbearing manner when he arrived the day before, today he'd sought her opinion. What was she to think? She pressed her fingers to her temple in confusion.

Below, villagers mingled with the castle's servants, going about their duties, reminding her—as if she needed it—of the new threat beyond the walls.

Ironic that, if it had not done so yesterday, the castle would be preparing for a wedding.

Sir Roark had arrived first. Alyss didn't know whether to thank God or curse Satan.

****

Furious, Paxton rode back to the encampment. He didn't know at whom to direct his anger, Sir Roark for beating him to the prize, or Prince John for perhaps arranging Paxton's failure.

Claude, his second in command, rode to meet him. "Is it true, my lord? Is the wench married?"

Paxton ignored him.

"Do we attack, then?"

"Shut up."

Claude swung his horse around, and they rode in

silence to the tent erected for Paxton's use. Paxton knocked the flap aside and flung his gloves at the opposite wall, ignoring a twinge the movement caused to the poorly healed sword wound on his arm. "How, by the fires of hell, does Sir Roark still live? I was told he died of his injuries."

"Never mind," he said before Claude could answer. "He's merely a dullard who moves swiftly and swings a heavy weapon. His kind is never smart enough to use their strength for themselves. They always serve a master."

Except Paxton knew full well Sir Roark was no dullard. He was damned dangerous.

Stopped at the doorway, he lifted the flap and gazed out at the castle. What master did Sir Roark serve now? Paxton had best discover that before he took the next step.

"Settle the men here," he said over his shoulder. "Post guards and see that no one goes in or out. I've got—"

"My lord, I've toured the village. There's not enough food there. And most all the animals have been moved inside the castle walls."

"You can hunt, damn you." A muscle at his neck throbbed. He jerked a dagger from his waist and slashed the tent flap he still held in his other hand.

"We didn't come prepared for a siege," Claude reminded him.

"I know what we came for," Paxton roared. He clutched the dagger and turned on his friend. Claude stepped back, balanced on both feet. Paxton froze. Sucking in a breath, he struggled to control his fury. A moment later, he released a tight and measured sigh.

"Captain," he said formally, "return the men to Windom and begin gathering material for a longer visit to our new neighbor. Leave three soldiers here to keep watch."

Paxton intended to send a message to Prince John. And if that didn't answer, he'd appeal to Richard. He had waited a long time for this reward. He had no intention of losing it.

Chapter Fifteen

From the platform at the top of the guard tower, Roark and Alain watched the partially assembled camp break up and the soldiers retreat along the west road.

"He took failure well." Alain's tone implied exactly the opposite.

"You're right. We've not seen the last of him. And it appears he left a few watchdogs. I'll have some of the men keep an eye on them."

He set out to locate Sir Baldwin. He also wanted two shifts working on the wall. Those fallen rocks had to be replaced by the time Lord Paxton returned. Roark had no doubt the man would be back.

In a corner of the great hall, Alyss consulted with Baldwin about supplies. They glanced up as he approached.

"With what was brought up from the village, it looks as if there will be enough to last for several days," Alyss told him, then turned to Baldwin. "You've done well this past month, but we simply haven't had time to replenish the stores. If Lord Paxton remains long—"

"He's gone," Roark interrupted.

"Send out hunters—" she said.

"Order the men to—"

Alyss glared at him as they both stopped speaking. "We must put in some meat," she said. "Now, while we have the chance."

"The wall must be finished," he countered, "before anything."

"You won't say that when you eat pottage for every meal."

She knew what the keep needed, of course, but he also spoke true. The holes should have been filled days ago. Without a strong wall, Chauvere would have no need for food.

"Very well," she said. "We can do both. Sir Baldwin, see to the men who are working with the stone. I will pick others to find game."

Roark should have known she'd challenge his first commands. But today they had no time for such bickering. His voice lowered and hardened. "I will lead a hunting party of men *I* choose, after I give Sir Baldwin orders for the repairs. *You* see to the household."

"Don't narrow your eyes at me," Alyss murmured, her jaw set. "This is *my* home, and I will give the orders to *my* people."

"This is *our* home and *our* people." Suddenly aware of the unusual quiet of curious servants, he lowered his voice. "You'd not get that concession from John's man. Remember, if I weren't here beside you right now, he would be. And *my* orders will be much more to your liking." He turned toward the doors. "Sir Baldwin, with me."

****

Alyss pressed her fingers to her forehead. *Be calm.* Why couldn't she have had time to adjust before facing such a trial?

"Sorry, my lady." Her old friend didn't quite meet her eyes. "I'd best see to his orders, I'm thinkin'."

"It's all right," Alyss assured him. "Do what you must." She watched his progress across the hall. His hitched gait seemed worse lately. Perhaps sharing duties with Sir Alain would benefit her father's old comrade. Perhaps Roark's plan had merit after all.

She stretched her neck forward to relieve the tension, then frowned at the shabby work gown she'd grabbed when the commotion began this morning. It wouldn't do to appear haphazard before her people. Perhaps she'd don a wimple, although the head coverings were annoying.

How would *he* react? Would he think she'd bowed to his authority? She ought to resent his domineering attitude of ownership when they'd been wed less than a full day, but something in his manner made her tolerant.

It was his eyes. Sad eyes that looked longingly at his surroundings. A cruel man was not sad—bitter, perhaps; hateful or mean. Without understanding a thing about Roark, Alyss knew no matter how he had behaved the night before, he would never physically harm her.

Still, he did have the tendency to overrule her, and she must not allow that to continue.

As she ran up the stairs, Alyss didn't call for Rose. *Surely I can dress myself for once.*

The rest of the day passed in a stream of activity. Sir Alain sent several men-at-arms to assess damage in the village, while Alyss consulted with the women who packed for the return to their homes.

Most of the castle's men were helping repair the walls, on watch, or were part of Roark's well-guarded hunting party. Ignored among carts being loaded under the noisy direction of chattering females, children shouting as they ran back and forth, and mounted hunters milling around in the bailey, three men drifted toward the woods.

Alyss had insisted Baldwin send scouts. When she discovered Sir Alain planned something similar, she swallowed a sharp retort, then calmly recommended the best tracker, and stood by while Alain and Baldwin chose two others.

The hunters returned late with enough game to last several days. Having retired earlier, Alyss watched from her window as the band rode into the bailey. Martha had kept stew warming, and the hungry men piled into the hall. In the dark from that distance, she couldn't identify any of them, until two veered away and made toward the guard tower.

The one on the right was Roark. Perhaps she hadn't known him long, but she could distinguish the set of his wide shoulders, the length of his unwavering stride. Determined. That described the new lord of Chauvere. Her husband.

She leaned her forehead against the cool stone at the side of the window. She couldn't seem to think straight. Sir Roark turned her world on end. Was he their protector, or was he the conqueror?

The fiasco of the wedding night didn't help clarify her thoughts. Before revulsion overtook her, Alyss enjoyed his embrace, swept up in the unexpected emotions. Then memory intruded, and she had been repulsed. Praise heaven he'd been the one to reject *her*, for she couldn't bear to have him touch her again.

But if that were so, why did she keep recalling the feel of his warm muscles against her, the clean, musky scent of his body? For an instant their embrace had seemed—right.

Her eyes burned with unshed tears. Sighing, she pushed away from the wall. Perhaps a good night's sleep would help. As she turned, Alyss saw the knight pause as he entered the guard tower. He raised his gaze to her window then went inside.

****

That night set the routine for those that followed. Roark found a pallet in the garrison or the guard tower, and Alyss saw him only at meals. Even then he usually was deep in discussion with Sir Alain or Sir Baldwin. He avoided her when he could and said little when he couldn't. Two periods, however, stood out in her mind.

On the second day, Sir Baldwin came to her for the accounts, saying Sir Roark wanted to go over them. Without a word, Alyss handed him the carefully scribed parchments she had tied between smooth, thin squares of wood. That evening at the meal, she asked her husband if he had any questions about what he read.

"Not yet," Roark replied. "I'll ask Sir Baldwin if I do."

Alyss had nodded and sipped her wine, hiding a smile. Sir Baldwin couldn't answer any questions because Sir Baldwin couldn't read. She'd maintained the records since her mother died, and no one at Chauvere thought anything about it. They knew the lady of the keep recorded tithes and counted the harvest, whether the lady was mother or daughter. Not only that, but villagers and servants had grown used to seeing Lady Alyss at her father's side when grievances were heard. It was a small step to bring their complaints to her when Sir Ulrich became ill.

If Sir Roark questioned any of the accounts, he

must come to her. Would he wonder about the periodic contributions to St. Ursula Convent begun two months ago?

Father Eudo took a small amount with him each time he visited her sister. In fact, he had left for the convent soon after Lord Paxton had gone. He carried Alyss's letter to Evie, telling her of their brother's death. Ironically, in all the confusion Alyss had neglected to add a note about the wedding. Father Eudo undoubtedly broke the news to her sister. He, at least, seemed content with the marriage. Perhaps soon she'd tell her husband more about Evie.

On the third day, when she visited the wall repairs, Alyss discovered the lord of the castle hefting rocks with the workers. The day was warm for mid-March, the kind of weather that presaged a storm. The sour odor of sweating males hung in the air as the men wrestled with the boulders.

Roark had tossed his tunic and shirt to one side. He strained with three others to maneuver a large stone into place. Moisture dotted his back. She watched one drop slide from his shoulder over bulging muscle and down his dirt-streaked side.

The sight of that rivulet trickling its way across dusty skin should not have mesmerized her the way it had. She couldn't take her eyes off the clean trail left as it meandered down his body.

Alyss tore her gaze away. And met Roark's stare. His head jerked in a short nod before he turned back to the stone.

Spying Sir Baldwin near the stables, Alyss hurried toward him. He saw her coming and stepped into the doorway's cool darkness.

"How are the repairs coming?" she asked, ducking inside.

"Better. No accidents since *he* came. That's a good thing, I'm thinkin'." In a few words, Baldwin filled Alyss in on Roark's activities. "He's fittin' in. Acts like he knows what the folk need. They're takin' to him."

"So he knows how a village operates. How is he with the men?"

"Works as hard as they do, he does. Gives orders like he's used to it. But that's as should be, I'm thinkin', if he's been with another lord these past years."

"Is there nothing he's failed at?" Alyss asked dryly. She was a bit surprised when Baldwin pursed his mouth.

"Don't seem like he knows a lord's business in the keep," Baldwin said thoughtfully. "He wanted the accounts, but he's not looked at them. Hasn't asked me about them, neither."

"Is that all? Perhaps he hasn't had time."

"True. Early days yet, Lady Lissey," Baldwin had agreed, forgetting for a moment she was no longer a pesky eight-year-old. "We'll see."

****

Roark lowered himself into the wash shed's tub-for-two, groaning in pleasure at the warm water lapping around his shoulders. Mornings on the practice field, afternoons lugging rock, evenings visiting with the people—his people, now. Nights sleeping among the men or in the guard house.

God's mercy, he was tired. Tonight, he would seek his bed in the keep. The knights and men-at-arms had been exposed to him for the last few nights. He'd shown he knew their world, was once a part of it.

But no longer. Whatever he had been trying to prove, it was enough. Resting his head against the rough wooden side, Roark closed his eyes and pictured Lady Alyss. His wife. He had lost himself in work since the wedding night, avoiding her and trying to avoid thinking about their problem. Time he faced it.

The door opened. Roark lifted an eyelid enough to identify his friend, then closed it, grunting. Dropping onto a bench, Alain sighed. He lounged in silence for a while, neither man speaking.

"We need rain," Alain said at last.

"That's not all we need." Roark sat up in the cooling water and reached for the soap. "A few more men would be right handy."

"A storm's not likely to blow them up."

"The old knight from here—Sir Godfrey." Roark ducked under the water, then flipped his head back, smoothing his hair with both hands. "Said he was going to look for Chauvere's force and bring them home. They may be on their way now. If we have those soldiers back, we can make a stand."

He stood and wrapped a large linen drying cloth around his hips. "How about the men's training? I'm with them in the mornings, but that's not enough to tell."

"They grumble," Alain said. "Seem to think they're in as good a shape as they need to be. Sir Baldwin's been trying, I'll say that for him. But next week they'll be better, whether they like it or not."

Roark nodded. "None of them have much to say at night."

"Speaking of sleeping arrangements," Alain

ventured, "I overheard one of the maids say that her bed was available if the lord didn't find Lady Alyss's soft enough."

Roark's head jerked up. "Who said that? I won't have servants gossiping about their lady."

"Are you going to order them to stop? How exactly do you think that will work? You've not slept in the same room with your wife. You've not slept in the same building."

"Where I sleep is nobody's business, not even yours." Roark's voice was a growl as he slung a clean tunic over his head.

Alain said nothing until Roark buckled his sword belt then, "Actually it may be everyone's business." His tone was uncharacteristically serious. "Look at it as they do. You sweep in, convince Lady Alyss to marry you, then desert her. They see it as an insult to their lady, and they're beginning to talk. If word gets back to the king that your marriage isn't real, he may decide to take a hand."

Roark ignored him and opened the door.

"One more thing." Alain's voice halted him. "There's some wild tale being whispered around that you threw Lady Alyss out of your bedchamber on the wedding night."

Roark sighed. He hadn't counted on servants' gossip. The fault was his for avoiding the inevitable. Past time he dealt with the situation. Then the talk would die.

In the great hall, men and servants took their places at the lower tables. Roark made for the dais where Alyss, already seated, talked with Lady Isobel. He passed Father Eudo sitting at a lower table. He didn't recall seeing the priest since the wedding, but then, Roark never attended Mass.

Leaning toward Alyss, he murmured, "I want to speak with you later." She turned her head and parted her lips as if to answer, but her gaze caught his, and she said nothing. Shadows circled her red-rimmed eyes. A slight gauntness of cheeks seemed to emphasize a strain around her mouth—she did have a beautiful mouth. Alyss was exhausted. Yet she'd die on the rack before admitting it.

Tired as she looked, Roark still found her appealing, and he remembered the way she watched him fitting rocks on the wall. He never thought the lady of the castle would show up in the work yard, or he would not have removed his tunic. She certainly seemed to enjoy looking. Any servant maid who lingered like that signaled her availability. His wife obviously didn't know those signals.

Glancing at her profile, with its straight nose, curved lips, and firm chin, he was struck by her vulnerability, her innocence. No, whatever her story, she didn't know those signals.

Chapter Sixteen

Roark followed Alyss into the solar. "I've ordered your belongings moved back to my bedchamber. We will share the room beginning tonight."

"You have ordered my...?" Alyss closed her mouth with a snap of teeth. "I will *not* sleep with you. You banned me from the bedchamber, if you recall."

"I've reconsidered."

"Why?" Of all the reasons she'd imagined he wanted to see her, this was not one.

He paced to the hearth and stood with legs apart, arms crossed over his chest. Alyss slid onto on the bench behind the table that served as her desk. She placed her clasped hands on the surface, although she really wanted to throw something at him.

Candles were not yet lighted; the room's dimness, coupled with an occasional crack and pop of the small fire, had a calming effect. Until she inhaled. Beneath the faint but familiar odor of smoke, rode a tangy mix of musk and of air and earth—like a hot, mid-summer twilight. Roark's unique scent. He had bathed, but even the herb soap soldiers used in the bathhouse didn't erase it.

The damaged side of his face was turned toward her. The blow must have been serious to leave such a ridge of scar across his brow. Alyss had seen head injuries before. The bleeding could be the devil to staunch. Without proper stitching, the wounds healed roughly.

A slight hump on the bridge of Roark's nose showed at least one break. A commanding nose, it balanced his square jaw and strong chin.

Strong—Sir Roark personified the word. Alyss's face grew warm as she remembered the day at the wall, the way his muscles moved beneath his skin. She shivered and suddenly found her folded hands of great interest. She jumped when his voice cut through the silence.

"You know this Lord Paxton will return. Whether the king declares the marriage illegal or whether he accepts it, whether Prince John lets the matter drop or whether he pursues it, there will be trouble."

The direction of Roark's voice told Alyss he had turned toward her. She glanced up, lest he think her timid.

"We must be ready for whatever that decision is." He paced in front of the fireplace. "Men like Paxton will go to any lengths to get what they want. He will not be satisfied if the king allows the marriage to stand. He will find a way around the order."

Alyss studied her hands again. "And if our marriage is declared invalid?"

Roark crossed the space in two strides to brace his hands on the table in front of her. "*I* will not be satisfied. *I* will fight."

Alyss nodded, looking into his eyes. "You gave your word to my brother. Your word as a knight." She spoke slowly, gauging his reaction. "Yet you would find a more willing bride elsewhere."

"I promised to protect you all." His jaw hardened

and his expression was fierce. "Make no mistake. Chauvere is mine now. I will not give it up."

He ignored her other remark. This wasn't the time to settle that difference, she admitted.

"You say we will fight, and my men are up to any battle." Alyss rose from her bench. "But the army Lord Paxton brought is larger than the previous one from Windom. Now would be a good time for your men to arrive. You did say they were coming with your belongings, did you not?"

Roark turned away, avoiding her eye. Had he told her so? "Did I? Well, I gave them several duties to discharge before they left Cantleigh. Those may take some time."

A tingle skittered down Alyss's spine; he didn't want to answer. "Exactly how many men do you have?"

Her voice was deceptively calm. She was proud of her control.

"Several died protecting the king." Did he sound defensive? "And some have families at Cantleigh."

She pivoted in front of him and caught his arm. "How many?"

He glanced over her head at the fireplace. "I have never seen a structure like that in a solar," he said. "How did it come to be here?"

She didn't turn. "My father wanted my mother to be warm in her new home. He brought a castle-builder from Normandy to design it."

"A waste of money. He should have spent the coin on stronger defenses."

What nerve he had to denigrate her family and her home. Alyss's control slipped and her voice rose. "Our defenses have never been a problem until now."

She jerked her hand from his arm. Her fingers throbbed from the contact. She turned away—there wasn't enough room in the solar.

It was him. He was too big, too overpowering. He needed to leave.

In the distance, she heard a dull rumble and glanced at the window. A quick light illuminated the clouds on the horizon.

"The rain finally comes."

She jumped at the deep voice beside her. How had he done that again, move so softly and quickly? Big hands settled on her shoulders. Their warmth was comforting, even in the closeness of the room.

Light flashed in the sky. The thunder cracked, closer. Alyss shivered again, and Roark turned her toward him. A rough, callused palm slid up her neck. She grabbed his hand and drew it away.

Roark's hazel eyes darkened to brown. He lifted a brow. "Have you always been so contrary? Is that why your betrothed broke the contract?"

The unexpected blow of that question left Alyss speechless. How did he know of that? She couldn't draw breath around the knot in her chest. Somehow she gained the door, then her own chamber where she made for the bed. She turned onto her side, pressed her palms to the fiery knot in her stomach, pulled up her knees, and stared at the wall.

Roark's cruel words brought back the humiliation, the shame the young girl of seventeen felt when she heard her childhood friend had married another. The support of Prince John had enabled Gareth's family to break their understanding easily. Her parents took the news with surprising calm. The betrothal had never been committed to formal contract, between friends as it was. Her father had accepted a manor on the border of their adjoining lands as recompense. The manor now formed part of her marriage portion. She didn't care.

"It's truly a blessing, my dear," her mother had insisted. "You're better out of the messy politics."

In the years since, Alyss had stopped fretting over her inadequacies. She had healed. Yet a few words from Roark stripped away her own ridge of scar and left the old wound burning in her stomach. *After all this time, I should not care.* She did.

Sir Roark should not have the power to wound me. He did.

****

Satan's arse. Roark stared at the closed door. Alyss was crushed.

It wasn't like him to speak without thinking, but the words about her betrothal popped from his mouth without passing through his brain. He'd intended to tell her why they must pretend to the marriage, but her arguments had distracted him. She seemed to have that effect on him.

He shook his head. If he fought the same way he dealt with her, he'd never have made it to manhood. Still, he hadn't meant to offend her. And why must he worry over his words to his wife? Marriage wasn't as simple as he'd imagined.

Lightning skipped across the near-dark sky. Thunder boomed. Soon the rain would arrive. Roark should check outside, make sure everything was settled for the storm. Halfway down the stairs, something occurred to him. Surely Alyss hadn't thought he meant to bed her. Had he implied so? No. Did he want to? Not yet. Too many questions and no time for answers. He likely wouldn't want to hear them, anyway.

****

A rumble then a loud rush nudged Alyss from her doze. Eyes closed, she identified the sounds as thunder and rain. Thank God. With spring planting near, a wetting would help the earth. Not too much, however, or the field work would be delayed.

She pushed herself to the edge of the bed and sat for a moment. The memories were gone and with them the pain. Perhaps weariness had made her overreact. What happened with Garrett lay in the past. She must make sense of the present.

For some reason she couldn't fathom, Sir Roark had changed his mind about sleeping arrangements. Alyss couldn't bear to lie with him. The thought of doing so brought back images best forgotten.

Yet when she was near him, she felt an awareness, an expectation. Less than a sennight ago, she hadn't known Sir Roark of Stoddard existed. Today, irritating and stubborn though he appeared, she felt as if she knew him somehow, as if something in her recognized something in him.

Levering off the bed, she straightened her clothing and looked around. Yes, the chests were gone. Very well. She would accede to his demands without argument, at least where anyone could overhear. Presenting a united front to the people was more important than her pride. She sighed. The night was going to be a long one.

Alyss didn't see Roark again before she retired. Shutting the bedchamber door behind her, she stood considering the bed, then the chair, then the floor.

I'm not sleeping in the cold. Let Sir Tyrant rest there. She placed the night candle on a nearby chest, kicked off her slippers, and climbed onto her mother's prized goose-down mattress. She'd scarcely lain back when she realized she hadn't washed her face, and slid off. She had just dried her hands on a soft linen square when the door swung open and Roark entered, his clothes rain-drenched.

She looked away awkwardly, not meeting his eyes, then covertly glanced up as she replaced the toweling beside the mazer and pitcher, another luxury her mother brought from Normandy. "Is anything amiss out there?"

"Not that I can find." He placed his candle on the small table near the wall and unbuckled his sword. After tossing the belt on the floor, he picked up the drying cloth and began to wipe off the blade. "Your stable lads know their jobs. My war horse sometimes takes exception to lightning. They've got him settled right well."

A safe topic of conversation. "My father loved his horses, and he made certain anyone who worked around them felt the same. Mistreating a mount brought as much punishment as any trespass. Martha's Will is especially good with them, although I suspect he spoils them with too many treats. Have you met Will?"

Roark nodded, a side of his mouth lifting slightly. "He and James are friends."

He examined the blade, made another swipe with the cloth, then laid it aside. "James is my new page," he announced.

Alyss considered for a moment before answering, "All right."

"What, no arguments?"

137

She thought she heard a smile in his voice, but the flickering candle flames didn't illuminate his face.

"James was Henry's page. It's only right you continue his training."

Roark didn't answer as he placed the sword beside the bed. Then he stripped off his wet tunic and draped it over the end of the table.

Alyss watched, horrified. He was undressing, and she didn't know what to do. Outside, the storm had relaxed into the steady, comforting rustle of rain. Inside, silence roared and the air crackled. Roark plopped onto a bench to remove his boots. Alyss had yet to move.

Finally he said, "I plan to sleep in that bed. You can stand there watching, or you can join me. It's your choice."

Alyss's stomach plummeted. He expected her to submit to him, it was obvious. Her voice snapped, "I will take the bed, you will take the floor."

He looked at her, the boot dangling from his hand. "No, wife. We won't play that game. I will not be on the floor. If you have any sense, you won't be on the floor, either."

"I won't sleep with you."

"Then lie there awake, but lie where it's warm and soft." Concentrating on his other boot, he said, "I may not have made myself clear today. I won't touch you. That hasn't changed. But no one must doubt our marriage is real."

He was so matter-of-fact, Alyss nearly believed him. Though God knew she didn't want to lie next to him. She felt skittish when he was near, as if her skin itched all over.

She considered the bed. It was large—big enough for both to keep their distance from each other. Perhaps she could arrange something. Occupying that bed had become a matter of principle. This was her home, and she refused to be pushed out of any part of it. Anyone who tried would come up against an immovable barrier.

A barrier. Alyss started for the door.

"Where are you going?" Roark's voice was deadly calm.

"I must fetch something from the solar. It won't take long." Not a waver in her tone. Good. She mustn't allow him to guess her unease. He might think she feared him. She did not. Mother Mary, she didn't.

Alyss reached the corridor and paused, gulping the cool, damp air like a parched traveler. No torches burned, but she knew her way in the dark. The solar sat near the top of the stairway. Her bare feet made no sound as she approached the door, so the soft scrape of boots alerted her. She stopped.

"Don't follow me here again," came the wisp of a whisper. "I've told you that before." A softer reply escaped Alyss's hearing, until "...see me."

"No one will see you if you're careful, foolish girl. Go." A rustle of movement, stillness, then a grumble. Another swish, then nothing.

She thought she could make out two darker shadows against the black before they disappeared.

The whispered exchange had been too soft to identify the speakers. Alyss couldn't tell if they were men or women, except for that last, scornful comment. A man and a woman, then.

Who in the entire castle would sneak away like that? Alyss knew every person in her home, and not one would need be involved in a secret meeting in the family's quarters above stairs. Unless one of the soldiers bothered a serving maid? Alyss did not permit any of the women to be forced into a relationship, so any liaisons should be in the open. Tomorrow she would ask Rose if any of the girls had been importuned against their wills.

Grabbing a long cushion from the solar window seat, Alyss hurried back to the bedchamber. Hand on the door, she paused and bit her lips. *Let him be in bed.*

Gently, she pushed it open. The night candle flickered on the chest. In its shadows, she saw Roark's bulk stretched out. She couldn't climb over him, so she made her way to the bottom of the bed and clambered up on her hands and knees. Pausing with her feet in the air, she brushed the soles together to remove any dirt, then crawled forward. She arranged the long cushion like a wall down the center of the bed and lay on her back, hands folded beneath her breasts.

After a few moments, a low voice came from beside her. "Breathe."

Air puffed from her lungs.

Alyss could have vowed Roark chuckled, but when he spoke his voice was serious. "I said I wouldn't demand anything of you, lady wife. So sleep. If you don't rid yourself of your exhausted look, the people will think I torture you in private."

If he only knew how close he came to the truth.

"Look you," he murmured, elbowing the cushion between them, "this is one wall even I will not storm." With a rustle of mattress and tug of cover, he turned away.

Alyss watched the deep shadows above the bed

sway with the slight, flickering candle flame. Space around her seemed to tighten. Extending her elbows, she verified she had plenty of room.

Then why couldn't she relax? Her eyes would close, only to jump with repressed blinks, then fly open. She heard Roark's slight snore, slow and steady. He was asleep. So soon.

Inhaling deeply, she concentrated on counting slowly as Sir Baldwin had taught her. Deep breaths helped focus a fighter's attention, relaxing tense muscles. Control.

At last, Alyss felt her neck, then shoulders, ease. Turning slightly for comfort, she caught Roark's scent. Nostrils flared as she drew it in. Through the bolster, his heat radiated. Tingles moved across her skin and bumps popped up, as if nudged by a cool breeze. She shifted restlessly.

Even if he seemed familiar at times, still this strange man disturbed her. She didn't recognize the sensations he caused; she pressed her hand to her chest. *I don't like it.*

But in a small, private corner of her mind, she wondered if she lied to herself.

Chapter Seventeen

Roark's waking mind registered a soft bulk beneath his arm, moving it gently up and down. His eyes opened and in the diffused light of early morning were confronted with embroidered, saffron-colored linen—a cushion.

Beyond that, he glimpsed a strand of golden brown hair lying over a firm, straight nose. His right arm raised and lowered again. Looking down he identified the motion—the arm was draped over the cushion and the clad waist of Alyss.

Easing up, Roark verified the suspicion. His wife had slept fully clothed. *God's toenails.* He didn't need this complication. Why in the name of St. Jude was she so stubborn? The sight of this headstrong, troublesome woman relaxed in sleep was a revelation. Lines of care were wiped from her forehead. Her beautifully molded lips curved slightly, as if with pleasant dreams.

He brushed the back of his forefinger to her cheek. Soft, warm. Not so prickly as her attitude. His mouth quirked at the sprinkling of freckles, and he blew a gentle breath. A honey-colored curl lifted, then settled again. Alyss moaned slightly and burrowed her face into the mattress, moving the fabric of her neckline further to the side.

She must have been uncomfortable, all bound up in that gown. The hem was bunched around her knees and the bodice had twisted, pressing against her breasts. Full breasts. A good handful. A better mouthful.

He fought the urge to gather her into his arms and hold her curves against his body. To ease his knee beneath the hem and raise it farther up her soft thighs. To cup the roundness of her bottom. To pull her musky, moist heat to his hardness. Roark shifted his hips away from the cushion in an effort to ease his already firm morning arousal, and his freed cock sprung up.

Better think of something else, or I won't be keeping my word not to touch her. What would she say if I did?

His lady might blister his ears with her caustic wit, or she might freeze him with detachment. He'd been subjected to both since his arrival. She was determined, he'd say that for her.

Throughout the turmoil of the past days, her image had lurked at the back of his mind ready to pop in.

Alyss had coordinated the villagers, when they were confined to the castle, with the ease of an experienced lady of the manor. Now the people were home, she visited them each day. She ran the household effortlessly with the help of Sir Baldwin's wife. She no longer countermanded Roark's orders—in public. She no longer argued with him—in front of her people.

Everything was as it should be.

Except Roark couldn't shake the feeling that something was not. He couldn't put his finger on it, but he often caught a look in Alyss's eyes, a twist of her smile, a firming of her chin.

As if she waited.

When he had hit on this plan to gain land, he hadn't given much consideration to the woman he must wed to get it. The times he had thought of a wife, he imagined a shadowy figure who gratefully fell upon him as her rescuer and didn't bother him again. He'd envisioned his children, clustered at his side as he strode through the keep. But their mother was never a part of that picture.

The reality was a striking woman whose presence affected him physically. The reality was…staring him in the face. Alyss looked startled. She didn't shriek, she simply lay there, looked at him. Then she slowly rose up on an elbow, taking in the long cushion crushed between them. Her gaze hopped from the cushion to Roark's legs to his hips. She gasped, and pink washed her cheeks.

"You're naked."

"You're not. Obviously you didn't believe me last night when I said you had no worry."

He rolled over and stood, his now-softening arousal arcing heavily from his body, swaying as he moved. He grabbed his braies, walked to the window, then pulled them on.

****

Alyss sat cross-legged in the middle of the bed, clutching the long bolster to her chest and eyeing her husband's form. As lady of the castle who saw to villagers and servants, she had seen naked men before. No, she had seen unclothed men before. She had been unaffected by men without clothing. The word naked carried feeling with it. This man was naked.

Her mouth opened and closed, but no words came. The sight of his large manhood transfixed her.

As he turned away with his clothing, she marveled at the alternate flex and relax of muscles, the slight indentations on the sides of his buttocks. She found herself longing to trace the hills and valleys of smooth skin that were fast disappearing beneath sturdy cloth. The long scar curving along his side.

A strange, tingly feeling enveloped her again, skating across her chest and tickling her stomach. Chills popped up on her shoulders, and she shivered. She'd shivered a good deal lately. She hoped she wasn't sickening. No time for illness.

Roark glanced at her as he opened the door. "You look rested. That's good. The villagers will approve." Then he was gone. With an indignant gasp, Alyss hurled the cushion at the door, but its length slowed it to undulate half on, half off the bed.

Scrambling to the floor, she headed for the basin where she splashed water on her face then took up Roark's recent place at the window. The rain had stopped, but early morning mist bathed low-lying spots; wisps curled upward like smoke tendrils.

She looked closer. Perhaps one of those gray spouts just inside the woods was smoke. No fire danger, but still it seemed strange. Until she recalled the lookouts that were posted there. Voices floated up from the bailey. On tiptoe she craned her neck to see below. She could make out only dark figures in the dim, damp light.

Returning to the water, she took up a cloth and quickly washed. Selecting a gown from one of her chests, she changed, rebraided her hair, and collected yesterday's clothes.

It wasn't until she left the bedchamber that Alyss realized Roark's nakedness had not panicked her, as she might have expected. Rather, it intrigued her. Odd.

As she rushed down the hall, Alyss met Rose at the top of the stairs.

"Oh, milady." Rose gasped as she nearly collided with her mistress. "I was on my way to see if ye needed me." She opened her arms, and Alyss handed her the bundle.

"Would you see these get to the laundry house?" Alyss looked at girl. "Rose, did the storm keep you awake? You look pale."

Rose glanced up quickly, then lowered her eyes. "Yes, milady, the lightning were fierce. Since I was a babe, storms has scared me. They make me jumpy, although I'm too old for such foolishness now."

Alyss patted the maid's shoulder in understanding. "Age doesn't seem to matter to our fears, does it? Has Lady Isobel arrived?"

When Rose nodded, Alyss said, "Send her to the solar, would you? And Rose, ask Martha for some of her healing salve for your poor hands. They're red. You must have touched ivy again."

By the time Alyss had retrieved the cushion from the bedchamber and returned to the solar, Isobel waited with news.

"Our thief has hit again," she said. "The rope from the wall. Gone. The men are outside now, but Baldwin says there's no trail, what with such heavy rain last night."

Not again. Why would anyone want to hamper repairs on their home? Delays threatened everyone's safety. It angered her that one of her people would endanger others by his action.

When the person was found, Alyss would deal with him.

****

"The man who did this will be sorry," Roark said, after he examined the ground.

"What if the thief is a child in a harmless prank?" Father Eudo asked.

"Theft of the rope is not a prank," Roark said. "It prevents final repair of our defenses. I can think of only one reason for it."

Alain looked at the three other men gathered around the stone that had been destined for the top of the wall, one of the last to place before the work was done. His blond hair appeared to have been plastered back quickly when he awoke, but some dry strands fanned across his forehead, giving him the look of a mischievous boy. The quick smile that usually played around his mouth was gone, and his lips were narrowed.

"I didn't notice any men missing from the garrison, but I wasn't awake all night," he said. "I'll question the guards." He glanced at Roark, eyebrows raised.

Roark stood back, surveying the ground. "We can't learn more here. The rain washed away any footprints. Sir Baldwin, you question the servants. Perhaps one of them saw something unusual. Father, you know the people here. Do any have reasons to keep the castle weakened?"

"My lord." The priest seemed shocked. "They have lived here all their lives. Who would want to see harm come to their home?"

Roark brought his sharp gaze to the holy man. "That's what we're trying to discover, Father. Unless you believe this was the job of angry spirits, at least one of the men in the castle is to blame."

Roark checked the stables, but lads there assured him they had heard nothing but the storm during the night. Will slid to a halt in the mud as Roark was leaving.

"Do you need help, lord?" he gasped, out of breath. His dark curls bobbed around his short, freckled nose, and he swiped them aside. "I can maybe scout ahead. I'm a good scouter. Lady Alyss says I come up with all kinds of things she never saw."

On the verge of dismissing him, Roark paused. The boy could use a mission.

"All right, Will. Keep watch for anything that doesn't look right, or anyone who is not where he should be." The lad bounced with eagerness. "But you must do it quietly."

Big brown eyes gaze up at Roark earnestly. "I can be quiet, my lord. You'll see."

By the time Roark returned to the hall, word of the rope's theft had spread. Servants and soldiers, breaking their fast with bread and ale, talked of little else. Some chuckled over what they considered another small indiscretion. Others weren't so glib, having heard that the new lord wasn't amused.

When Roark strode into the hall, mud falling from his boots and a look of thunder on his face, no one had any doubts how he felt. He went directly to the dais and held up his hand for silence. When it didn't come fast enough, he lifted his voice.

"You've all heard that a length of rope was taken from the work site during the night."

When the din quieted, his voice lowered. "The rope doesn't matter. We've rope aplenty.

"What matters is that someone is trying to prevent

the wall from being finished. The wall represents security during attack. Attempts to undermine safety is the act of a traitor.

"I've learned that similar efforts took place in the past. This is the first to occur since I arrived.

"It will be the last."

His glance passed over the crowded tables in front on him. "Anyone who attempts to weaken the castle's defenses will be punished accordingly."

A few gasps sounded in the quiet hall as he sat down and motioned for food.

Talk resumed cautiously. He knew they considered his words harsh. One stone wouldn't topple the wall, true. It was the blatant defiance the theft represented. That, he could not tolerate. Not and maintain his new position.

He would not show weakness. His people had to understand the seriousness of what happened. They had to accept who commanded the castle now. If Roark had learned one thing at Cantleigh, it was that firmness early prevented weakness later. Of course he didn't expect to mete out harsh punishment. He expected the disruptions to stop.

****

The ground had been so dry, one night of rain absorbed quickly enough to cause little interruption in work. By midday another rope had been secured around the rock, which then was hoisted into place. Alain stood beside Roark while the last of the mortar was smoothed away.

"Did you consider," Alain said, "if somebody truly wanted to wreck the repairs, he would have chosen something harder to replace, like the pulley?"

"I've thought that. Sir Baldwin said no real harm was done over the weeks. Just enough pilfered to create delay and aggravate everyone. As if the culprit stalled for time. But no matter how slight the damage, morale was undermined. Suspicion was sown."

Alain nodded. "Garrisons can't be strong if every man thinks his neighbor might be plotting. Households probably operate the same. God's teeth. Plots under every pillow. Suspicion around every corner. That sounds like the royal court."

Roark's head came up sharply, and he stared at Alain. "It does at that."

For some reason, Alain's remark stuck with Roark. Could it be possible? If so, then why did Prince John take such an interest in a small holding so far away, and at this time, when the king was en route home and John's own plotting was sure to be discovered? Why chance another problem for himself?

Yet the king's brother was obviously involved in Paxton's arrival at Chauvere. That fact had not been far from Roark's mind during the past few days. He understood a knight's desire for land—none better than he. If John wanted to reward a follower with Windom, which was in John's territory of Nottingham Castle, who would question it?

With marriage to his neighbor Alyss, Lord Paxton would have received a second sizeable gift. Many at court might wonder at that. Exactly what service had the knight performed for Prince John that qualified him for such honors?

Roark recalled the fateful day when the attack on the king went awry. Could Paxton have been there? Roark saw the event, frozen in place behind his closed eyes. He checked off those who fought for the king. No. He knew them all. Even Sir Henry, who had dispatched Roark's future when he dispatched Lord Martin.

And who's to blame for that? I made the choice when I shouted the warning. He'd relived that moment over and over in the past weeks. He'd made the right decision, duty to king and country before all.

Other images flashed in Roark's mind. Things he had done to repay Lord Martin over the years. At first Roark had been glad to do any task. His willingness had quickly gained him a place of honor in Cantleigh's garrison. He was not proud of some jobs he performed.

As years passed, the orders grew increasingly objectionable to the sense of right and wrong his parents had instilled. After one last job, he made his opinions known to Lord Martin.

From that night on, Roark's role in Cantleigh's service changed. On the heels of "proving loyalty," Roark had been named captain, but he'd never again been asked to take part in his lord's underhanded business.

He knew Martin tapped others to fill the role he previously played. He often lay awake on his pallet, listening for the return of a surreptitious night ride, speculating what had occurred. Yet the lord still praised Roark for his leadership, for his battle prowess. And promises of his own place were reaffirmed often enough to ensure loyalty.

How could he have been so foolish to have remained, to have believed after all he'd known of the man? Yet he had. And what had it gotten him? Roark smiled grimly. All he'd been promised, actually, and much more, although Lord Martin hadn't planned it thus. God surely had a sense of humor.

Roark would never allow anyone to usurp his new position. In spite of the lack of knights and men-at-arms, he would fight. It was time to increase training for the garrison he did have.

At the evening meal, Roark and Alain outlined which exercises would be emphasized, and Baldwin soon joined in to discuss which fighters excelled at what skills, and how best to employ the villagers.

Later the three adjourned to storerooms where they took stock of armor and other supplies until the blue-gray evening became gray-black night.

Sir Baldwin and Lady Isobel had retired to their cottage set against the wall of the inner bailey, and guards were securing the gates when a shout went up from the lookout tower.

"Riders approaching."

Chapter Eighteen

Torchlight dotted the walls at the front gate, unusual for this time of night. "Visitors outside," a guard called down. "Some knights, from the look of 'em."

A deep, rough voice floated through the air from beyond the walls. "We're friends, seeking Sir Roark of Stoddard."

Roark broke into a run. It couldn't be. God be praised. "Raise the portcullis."

When the gates opened, a half-score strangers stood in a cluster, their tired mounts and several packhorses drooping nearby. The sharp zing of metal sounded as he and Alain drew swords.

Two of the strangers stepped forward, hands raised.

"What?" called one, a tall, burly red-beard. "You'll strike us down for being late?"

Roark lowered his sword. "Bernard. By God's legs, I hoped I recognized your rocky voice. Where did you spring from? Is that Nicholas? By all that's holy, man."

He shook his head in disbelief. Alain strode forward to greet them.

When a third knight came forward, Roark roared. "Rance. God's mercy, we thought you were killed."

"Wait," he said, finally, "Why are you here? How did you find Chauvere?"

Bernard answered in his rough voice. "As to how,

we asked the way. As to why, Lady Elinor released us from service at Cantleigh. We're mercenary knights, now, selling our blades to the highest bidder. Who would we come to but our captain? What can you offer?"

Roark shook his head. "All I can promise at present is bed and board, a likely feud with John, and a battle from our neighbor."

"More than enough." Bernard's laughter boomed. He pounded Roark on the back. "Did you think you could get rid of your men so easily?"

A touch on his hand told Roark Alyss stood at his side. "You know these knights?"

He suddenly was glad she had come to welcome his friends. He slipped his arm around her waist, realizing what he'd done only when her muscles tightened.

"These miscreants, my lady, are from my former garrison. Men, let me make you all known to my wife, Lady Alyss."

Before she could utter a word, Sir Bernard grinned and said, "Wife? Wife? There's a word we never thought our captain would utter, eh, lads, eh? Will you welcome us here, then, my lady?"

****

Good humor seemed to pour off the large knight. Alyss liked him instantly.

"With pleasure, Sir Knight," she said, smiling in return. "You are most welcome. You all look well able to defend anything in sight."

After the gathering trooped noisily into the hall, she met each new man, ensured food was plentiful, then climbed the stairs to her bedchamber.

So these were some of Roark's company, who'd chanced the trek north on a search for their captain. A half-dozen knights, accompanied by a few squires. Quite the sign of respect for her husband, because she didn't for a moment believe they'd come only in search of hire for coin. And from the evidence of the loaded horses accompanying the men, they'd brought along Roark's possessions. His expression when he recognized the newcomers had been stunned and then happy.

Warmth welled through her. She'd been happy for him. Glad some remnant of his former life had found him. A different side of her husband had been revealed.

She liked it. She liked him—the him that laughed and jested with his men. The him that surprised her with a kiss before she retired, just as her father used to salute her mother. Perhaps, just perhaps, there was hope for her marriage.

Alyss lay back on the soft mattress and sighed. Deep voices and laughter from below blended into a reassuring low murmur.

Comfort. She rolled to her side and slept.

A bang against the rock wall awakened her, and a stab of fear scattered her thoughts. But time and place coalesced immediately, and alarm gave way to calm. Her husband staggered into the room, the night candle's flame giving his shadow an exaggerated wobble. With attempted stealth, he closed the door and slid the bar into its cradle.

"Has the welcome ended?"

"Ah, wife, sorry to wake you." His voice sounded remarkably steady, given the unsteadiness of his walk. "Yes, the men have bedded down in the barracks."

"I was glad to meet them. They appear to be competent knights."

"I'd match those six against a score of ordinary fighters." He sat on the edge of the bed. The mattress tilted and she clung to the side to keep from rolling toward him.

In the dim light, she made out his pursed mouth and a frown.

"Have they decided not to stay?"

"What? Of course they'll stay. They're my men. Where else would they go?"

"Then what is wrong?"

"Wife—" He paused.

Oh, dear. She feared she wouldn't like what he had to say, with that tone of voice.

He ducked his head. "Events are moving quickly. We don't know how long until Windom returns, and with our new reinforcements, I need to spend time with the men in training."

What was he trying to say? She reached over and placed a hand on his arm.

He sucked in a breath, then cleared his throat. "We must consummate the marriage."

A chill raced down her back and she shivered. She hadn't expected *that*. "I can't... I'm not ready."

"We have no more time. It must be tonight."

Alyss knew he was right, but could she? He wasn't as overbearing as she'd first thought. She'd become rather used to him—and that change of mind had nothing to do with her growing awareness of his physical presence. Certainly not.

Alone, what chance did she have at continued independence? Blessed little. To be truthful, she'd prefer the husband fate sent her to an unknown replacement.

"Would it just be once?" Blast her quivering tone!

At first she thought he wouldn't answer, then, "For now. But eventually we *will* have children."

"Of course. Just give me time. After tonight, more time."

He sighed and nodded sharply.

"All right." She could do this. Once. She scooted to the center of the bed, closed her eyes, and spread her legs. A buzzing in her ears quieted somewhat. She tried to breathe slowly and deeply. There was nothing to fear. It would be over quickly. At a touch on the arm, she jumped and gasped.

"There's nothing to fear." His gentle words echoed her thoughts.

He brushed the hair off her face, the roughness of his fingers rasping against her skin. Alyss did not move, but she opened her eyes.

He stood and turned away to pull off his tunic and shirt. She could see his naked back. In the flickering candlelight, she made out a scar low on the right, running across his side. And the dimness could not obscure the width of his unpadded shoulders. She shivered. The room seemed warmer when he pulled the strings of his braies.

Holy Mother.

Alyss trembled and squeezed shut her eyes again. In a tiny corner of her mind, she heard her mother's voice from long ago. "Control. You must learn to control yourself if you are to control your household."

How many times had Alyss heard that as she grew? She drew on the memory now, opened her eyes, and lifted her chin.

He came down on the bed beside her, his mouth on hers, firm and insistent and tasting of wine. For a moment Alyss forgot her fears and allowed herself to feel the intent movement of his lips working gently, urging hers to relax. If she didn't know otherwise, she would swear he wanted her to open her mouth. But how could people kiss with open mouths?

Alyss's hand made contact with Roark's skin, and she pulled away as if burned. It was warm and a bit damp, still, from his clothing. He caught her hand and pressed it back to his side. She touched skin soft yet textured and gasped at the tingling that ran up her arm into her chest.

Roark took advantage of the gasp and fit his lips more fully to hers. The tingling spread, and Alyss pulled her mouth away to gulp air. The smell of him was all around her, musk and spice, headier than before. She liked it. She slid her hand farther around his side, up his back.

He pulled her closer, and she felt a hard ridge press into her hip. A chill washed over her. She dropped her hand.

****

Alyss's muscles stiffened beneath Roark's hands, and he lifted his head. What now? She'd been responding. Even through her smock, he felt her breasts firm and her nipples harden. What happened to take that away? Was her analytic little mind working again?

"My lady," he murmured, "if you will let yourself relax, you will not feel pain. Not much. The first time will bring some discomfort, but I will try to go carefully." Roark rubbed his hand up and down her thigh, but she rolled away, onto her back.

"Just get it over with," she interrupted in a low voice. "Do it and be done."

"I can't just—"

"You won't be forcing me. I'm willing. But please hurry."

God's blood, but she was stubborn. Perhaps if he took his time, persuaded her. But she might as well be on her deathbed, still and resigned. What had happened to cause such a response?

How in the name of all the saints was he expected to perform this duty without forcing her if she refused to cooperate?

"Open your legs farther." Alyss moved them a few more inches. At last he was able to settle himself between her thighs. But her reticence began to have an effect. His cock halted at her entrance and began to retreat.

Roark lay propped on his elbows, head in hands, his hair brushing Alyss's cheek and neck. He could howl his frustration to the whole castle, or he could laugh.

His body shook.

"You're laughing? Why?" she hissed. "What are you doing?"

"Nothing, it seems." His glance met hers.

He slid up to kiss her and her muscles tensed. Again.

He slid his hand down her hip. Beneath the soft linen of her smock, he felt her flinch.

Her on and off reactions drove him mad. Roark had to concentrate, or he'd never accomplish this deed.

"Will you allow me to touch you? I can make your

body ready for mine; you'll be more comfortable."

The silence dragged so long, he feared she wouldn't answer. At last she said, "All right."

But when he reached beneath her hem to brush her leg, she grasped his hand in place and jerked away. "Sorry. Give me a moment to adjust."

After two deep breaths, she whispered, "Ready."

He stroked her inner thigh then stopped.

"Go on. I'm willing. Perhaps if you kissed me again."

Slowly, gently, Roark worked to relax her rigid muscles. Nothing helped. He refused to force her. Her body wasn't ready and the discomfort would likely make her even more reluctant to try again. Given time, perhaps he could ease her fears. Time. He'd give it to her and find a way to deflect any challenges to the marriage. None might come after all. But his compulsion to secure possession of this land could drive Alyss away for good, and he wasn't willing to chance that.

Damnation. He'd grown accustomed to the woman. He leaned back. "We will wait until you're ready."

She grabbed his arm. "No. I'm ready now. Please."

"Your body is too dry. I'll hurt you."

"Can nothing else be done?" Her voice wobbled.

What would help? He leveraged off the bed and rummaged through one of his packs on the floor. He returned almost immediately, a tiny cloth-wrapped pot in his hand.

He held it up. "This ointment may ease the way. It won't hurt you."

He scooped out a bit and set the pot on the floor by the bed. Then he climbed back between her thighs and took his cock in his hand. It responded to the warmth of the ointment and the rhythmic movement, lengthening and thickening as he rubbed on the cream. His breath quickened. He rose above her, positioned himself.

And eased forward. The tightness of her passage was a problem. To thrust through, he had to use firm pressure and repeated tries until at last he had advanced as far as he could go.

No mistaking the barrier he breached. She'd been a virgin. An unexpected surge of satisfaction made him smile. She was his completely.

****

Alyss held her husband as he lay above her. Except for a pinch at first, she felt no discomfort, only a sensation of fullness. And, oddly, no sense of panic. She expelled a long, slow breath. He held still, as if waiting for her to react.

"It's all right," she murmured. "Not painful."

"Good." The word sounded strangled. "If you're sure."

She moved her hips, and he groaned. Perhaps he was uncomfortable. But before she could think how to ask him, he began to move.

Alyss forgot all her previous fears and sighed.

Chapter Nineteen

Roark awoke in the dimness of breaking day to find his arm again draped around a bundle. But this morning Alyss, not the cushion, pillowed him. He was content to study the woman at his side in the faint strains of early dawn until she began to thrash around. Her dream must be troublesome. He tightened his arm.

She snuggled into him, the press of her curves reminding his body of their real wedding night. He ran his hand lightly over her back, caressing her bottom, before he stopped himself. No need to awaken her yet. She was bound to be sore from her first time. He'd been the first, after all. The knowledge made him feel smug.

Alyss had charmed his men at their meal the night before. She had even laughed when Alain related some of his milder stories of Roark's time at Cantleigh. When she left the gathering, Roark had pressed his mouth to the side of her neck in a brief farewell. She'd been startled, but he vowed she'd leaned into the kiss before turning away. His hand had even brushed the side of her breast, causing her face to redden.

And then, later. Surely the strangest wedding night in Christendom. How would she react this morning?

The brush of eyelashes against Roark's chest signaled his prickly wife was awake.

Her muscles tensed. Then her clenched breath broke free in a soft but controlled exhale that slid across the right side of his chest. His body hardened, and he fought the impulse to bring her lips to his nipple. The bud swelled tighter when he thought of her warm, wet tongue on it, and his cock jumped.

Rearing back, Roark looked into her now-wide eyes alert in the dimness. "Good morning, wife."

"Good..." Her voice broke. She cleared her throat and tried again. "Good morning."

He lifted his left arm, almost numb from her lying on it, and drew her nearer. His right hand slid to her throat, then around to the back of her neck. Lowering his head, he brushed her lips with his. Neither of them closed their eyes. Hers were startled, wary. Ah, she'd remembered.

"How do you feel?" he whispered.

"I'm fine." She placed a hand on his chest to push away, but the movement brought their lower bodies closer. Roark's hips jerked forward in a reflexive action. He drew his partially open mouth along her clenched jaw, to her neck, where she seemed to enjoy his attention the night before.

Tension eased from her as he nuzzled, the tip of his tongue dotting its way to her ear then to the sensitive flesh behind. She shivered. He pulled her closer.

He exhaled and against his chest, one firmed nipple grew taller. Kissing his way up the side of the breast, he captured the tip in his mouth, pulling, sucking until his mouth was full of soft, tasty woman.

Arching, Alyss gasped. Using his forehead to nudge her shoulder back, he released that breast and trailed the tip of his tongue to the other. Her fingers stroked into his hair, a tentative touch. He slid his hand down her side, down the back of her thigh, to her knee.

Barbara Bettis

Hooking it, he pulled her leg over his hip.

The shock of her heat against his erection took his breath away. Hips jerked forward again, and the underside of his hard sex pressed against her soft curls. Roark's brain turned smoky, his body, afire. This was his wife. He wanted her.

Alyss came alive, twisting away in what appeared to be fright. He let her go. But rather than leap from the bed, she lay with her arms crossed over her breasts, her cheeks reddened. His prickly, independent wife was embarrassed.

"Why did you not tell me you were a virgin? That first night, you let me assume differently."

Her eyes widened. "I…"

Roark turned to her and propped himself on an elbow. "You didn't know? How is that possible?"

"Of course, I knew. It just brings back…unhappy memories." Alyss covered her eyes with her forearm.

He pushed himself to a sitting position, the answer hitting him like a club to the head. "You were attacked. Who was it? Who should I kill for you?"

She jerked her arm from her face. "No one. He's dead now. Sir Baldwin…"

Roark wrapped his arm around her waist and dragged her against him. "Shhh, it's all right. Won't speak of it now. But I owe Sir Baldwin a special thanks for finding you in time and killing that bastard."

"Of course," she murmured. "Sir Baldwin arrived to help me."

"I'm your husband, not your attacker." That was an inopportune remark, but he wasn't good at speaking of feelings.

"No," she said, her voice low again, shaky. "But

164

the sense of being surrounded brings back the memories."

She hadn't condemned him for his stupid remark. That was a good. Perhaps she could forget now. When he tentatively eased an arm beneath her shoulders, she turned toward him.

They lay quietly for a few moments, wrapped in the heat of each other's body. Suddenly, she gasped.

"Oh my. I told Isobel I'd meet with her this morning. I must go." She climbed over him and off the bed, the mattress dipping. Roark listened to the rustle as she donned her gown. She turned at the door and caught her lower lip between her teeth. Did he detect an almost-smile? Ducking her head, she left.

He clasped his hands behind his head and sucked in a deep breath, an unfamiliar lightness filling his chest. He wanted to smile, to call her back, to wrap his arms around her soft body. With a sudden grunt, he sat. He hadn't expected such a flood of feelings, didn't understand these emotions. He understood reason. Action. The thrill of combat, exuberance of victory, pain of injury. Even the compulsion of lust, which satisfied a natural urge that brought relief. Perhaps those *were* emotions, but he understood them.

His feelings for Alyss were more than physical desire. She affected him as no other woman had. A prickling sensation along his shoulders or at the back of his neck always told him when she was nearby. He swore he could hear her chuckle, soft and low, across the din of a practice field. The wayward strand of hair that always danced free beckoned him to tuck it away. And her spirit...

His wife was a contradiction. Calm and agreeable

one day, stubborn and contrary the next. At first, he believed she would willingly give him the reins once she realized he was a strong master. He had ignored her occasional outbursts, given her time to adjust to the changes in her life. But in a few short days, she had taught him the error of his previous encounters.

What had changed? Nothing and everything.

He snorted. He'd been distracted too long. Time to get on with the day. He had stomped his feet into his boots, dressed, and was halfway down the corridor when Alain intercepted him.

"We have a visitor. You'll want to hear this."

"Has Windom sent a messenger again?"

"He's not from our neighbor."

Roark loped down the stairs and found Alyss standing next to a youth. Father Eudo was on the other side. She looked up. "My lord, we have word of our men. This is Wilbur, one of the squires. King Richard has kindly allowed him to bring us a message."

Wilbur rose, lingering over a bite of cold venison and swiping his greasy hands down the sides of his dirty tunic.

He bowed quickly and looked grateful as Roark motioned him back to the bench. Throwing a narrowed glance at Father Eudo, Roark sat in the spot the priest vacated just in time. After a sip of ale, Wilbur cleared his throat and delivered his obviously memorized speech once again.

"Sir Conrad said to tell you Chauvere's knights and men-at-arms are with the king, and they will be home soon. They will accompany the king north."

Roark frowned. "Sir Conrad?"

"One of our knights," Alyss said. "Henry's second

in command."

The messenger sent a perplexed look toward Roark, then turned to Alyss. "The king permitted me to leave when he stopped in Rochester. He also sends his condolences on the loss of Sir Henry."

"But Wilbur says Sir Godfrey is not with the men. He remained near Cologne to search for..." Alyss cleared her throat. "Henry's body was not found at the battle site, and Godfrey couldn't bear to leave without locating and burying him properly."

"I'll go now, my lady," the squire said, then looked to Roark. "My lord?

"You'll rest before you return," Roark ordered.

Alyss agreed. "Sir Baldwin will prepare a pallet for you."

Drooping as if he could fall asleep on the table, Wilbur shook his head. "Thank you, my lady, but I must get back at once. It may yet come to a battle, and I should be there. I am one of the squires, you know."

"Well, Squire Wilbur, you won't be of use to anyone if you can't stand." Roark's tone of command left no room for argument. "We expect our squires to be wise as well as ready. A few hours won't make a difference."

Her tone quiet and level, her eyes wary, Alyss asked, "What battle?"

"It's the king, my lady. Some of Prince John's castles didn't surrender when ordered, and they've fought. King Richard is visiting them to make sure they surrender and know he's in charge now."

When James appeared to lead Wilbur away, Father Eudo accompanied them, deep in conversation with the squire. Roark, Alyss, and Alain sat at the table. She

167

spoke into the silence as they waited for food.

"Wilbur said there had been resistance from the prince's castles, but I don't understand why anyone would fight their king."

"John has been consolidating power since Richard went off to Jerusalem," Roark said. "When the king was captured returning from crusade, it seemed as if the one-hundred-fifty-thousand-mark ransom couldn't be raised, and he would never be released. John intended to have the throne, whether or not he was named heir."

"Well," Alyss said, "all his manipulation was for nothing. The king is free."

"John won't give up," Alain said thoughtfully.

Roark caught his eye and nodded. The pouch. They both rose.

With a vague excuse to Alyss, Roark strode beside Alain out the doors, toward the garrison and Alain's gear. They were silent as they went.

Across from the knights' sleeping quarters was another room used as storage where Alain's small chest was hidden. As Alain reached for the latch to the chamber, Father Eudo swung out of the garrison door. He stumbled when he saw the pair. For an instant, Roark thought he saw surprise, and something else, flick through the priest's eyes before the man's normal, placid expression slid into place.

"Father Eudo. Is one of the knights unwell?"

"No, no, my lord. I simply offered prayers for Squire Wilbur. He's resting now."

Roark followed Alain into the storage room. They had pulled the chest out when Roark felt someone watching. Looking up, he saw Father Eudo in the open door.

"I have been meaning to ask, my lord, why I have not seen you in mass these past days?" With a quick glance toward the wooden box at Alain's feet, he was off.

Alain pursed his lips. "Oddest priest I have ever seen. What do you think he really wanted?"

Hands on hips, Roark watched the holy man walk away. "I think he has his nose in too many places."

"His way of feeling important?"

Roark shrugged.

Liberating the hidden compartment at one corner of the case, Alain removed the leather pouch Lord Martin had worn on the day of the attack and held it out.

Roark slipped the cord over his head and dropped the packet beneath his shirt. "With time, I will work this out."

He only wished he felt as confident as he sounded.

After the midday meal, he took refuge in the solar where he spread out the parchment on Alyss's—now his—worktable, near the accounts he'd ordered Baldwin deliver. He'd never learned to read, but he could write his name, something Lord Martin had insisted upon for all his knights. R-O-A-R-K.

With knowledge of those four letters, Roark hoped he might be able to decipher the words. The sun was high when he at last rolled his neck to ease the tightness. He could make out a few shapes of the letters here and there among the black lines on the parchment, but none made sense. Why had he thought differently? He had to find another way. His instinct cried that the message was important, that it was from Lackland.

Sighing, Roark began to fold the note when he heard, "Is that from the king?" As Alyss walked in, he quickly stuffed it into the pouch which he slipped over his head.

"No. It's not from the king."

****

Roark was hiding something. The way he shoved the parchment into that tiny bag, the guilty look on his face, both gave him away. But Alyss wasn't about to let this opportunity pass.

"Sir Baldwin tells me he gave you the accounts. Do you have any questions? Some of the entries may be unfamiliar."

He shoved back the bench and rose. "No questions, yet. I'll tell you if there are."

"But I want your opinion on whether we could afford to buy new oxen for the harvest. Do you think we have the coin? My estimates on the cost are in the third set."

Alyss picked up one of the stacks. From the corner of her eye, she saw him round the table.

"We'll discuss it later." Roark was gone before the words left his mouth.

He was hiding information. If it affected Chauvere, she had a right to know about it. As she straightened the account books, her thoughts wouldn't stay on the mysterious parchment; they strayed to the maddening man who carried it. The episode in bed earlier had shaken her. At the memory of Roark's callused fingers on her body, his soft lips along her neck, she shivered. It had been rather wonderful, and the shimmery waves that coursed through her body had nothing to do with fear.

Astonished, Alyss was considering the revelation when a wide-eyed, breathless Rose found her.

"There's another messenger, my lady, but this one's not a friend by the looks of 'im."

What now? "Our day for visitors, it seems." Alyss straightened. "Let's hope this one brings us good news as well." Rose looked dubious as she stepped aside. All thought of the packet around her husband's neck vanished when Alyss heard loud voices from below.

****

Dark curls bouncing, Will caught up with Roark headed for the stables.

"We got a man here says he's from the sheriff, my lord," the boy announced. "He's eatin'. Lady Alyss says you're to come right now." Roark turned and Will followed.

Meeting Alain outside the great hall, Roark nodded to the doors. "That was quick. If Lord Paxton rode to Nottingham, he must not have stopped to piss."

Alain grinned and stood away from the door. "From the way this one's shoveling in two-day-old mutton from the kitchen, he didn't stop to eat, either."

"Mutton? Who gave him that?" Roark remembered the fine meal of venison Martha had prepared last night.

"Your charming wife." Laughing outright, Alain followed Roark to the stairs.

****

Alyss directed Annie to refill the offensive visitor's cup as she battled for self-control. The man had crudely demanded entry to the keep, then threatened the servants with the sheriff's anger if he wasn't served food immediately, a threat Alyss heard as she walked into the hall. Grimly listening to Lady Isobel's report, she'd personally ordered food for their "guest."

Shoving his mouthful of food to one side with his

tongue, he mumbled, "Wans t'see Sir Roark of Stoddard." A gulp of watered ale washed down the mass. "Need to deliver this message, now," he added, "'n see'im back."

Alyss felt Roark's arrival in the tingle that skittered across her skin. Wordlessly, he reached around her, plucked the dirty, folded sheet of parchment from the man, and checked the seal. He didn't recognize it.

The messenger mumbled, "The sheriff says as how if you cain't read, I should jest tell you he wants to see you in two days." The man's tone was an insult as well.

Roark crumpled the sheet in his fist and stalked toward the man, who at last seemed to realize his danger. His eyes widened at the advancing bulk of muscled knight, and sound roiled in his throat.

Although in this instance Alyss sympathized with Roark's natural urge for violence, she didn't want murder in her hall. Quick as lightning, she was in front of Roark, facing the messenger.

"You have insulted my husband, my home, and me." Her voice rose in indignation. "You will leave. Now. And you can be sure the sheriff will know how you have shamed your office by your actions. Sir Alain, escort this person to the gate. He can find shelter in the village."

Eyeing Alain, the messenger recovered some of his courage, stretched to his inconsiderable height. "Well, now, milady, I don't see's how you kin toss out the sheriff's messenger."

Alyss clenched her fists. "Then you'd best look sharp, so you won't miss a thing."

At Alain's signal, three other knights surrounded the man and herded him toward the door.

Roark's fingers dug into Alyss's shoulders. His low voice roared in her ear. "You should have let me handle him. Don't interfere again."

"Murder would have been difficult to explain to the king," she said, dryly.

"I wasn't going to kill him, just make him think so." From his tone of voice, his anger still simmered. "That messenger is nothing better than a stable hand or a rough from the streets. His presence was meant as an insult."

Alyss frowned and reached for the wrinkled letter still crumpled in Roark's hand. He allowed her to pry it from his fingers. She unfolded the sheet and sucked in a breath. "This is a summons 'to answer in the matter of forced marriage to Lady Alyss of Chauvere.'"

The sound in the hall rose as servants talked among themselves. Some stared openly at their lord and lady.

"Do you have nothing to do but stand about?" Lady Isobel's voice sailed across the room and snapped the gaping cluster into action.

Alyss smoothed out the parchment on the table, then folded it into a careful square. "When do you plan to leave, my lord?"

Roark had started for the doors but looked up, startled, as if he had forgotten she was there.

"As soon as I've given orders to the men and met with the miller in the village. Tomorrow morning, then."

"I will prepare food for the trip."

A look passed over his strong face, one that Alyss could almost think was surprise—perhaps gratitude. "Thank you, my lady."

Watching as he disappeared out the door, she

smiled.

"You look mighty smug." Isobel regarded her warily. "What's in your mind?"

Alyss turned, her smile broadening. "Not a thing, old friend. Will you help me get my clothing together? I've not visited Nottingham in years."

Chapter Twenty

Shortly before dawn the next day, Roark rose from a pallet in the barracks where he had caught a few hours rest. He'd explained the problem to the new men, and asked Bernard to act in his stead at the castle. Roark expected no problems, but he chose not to take chances. He would have liked more time at Chauvere before facing outside challenges. Looks like he'd have to make the best of what he had.

Alain, Ralf, James, and two men-at-arms were accompanying him. Alain met him in the stables. "The lady wasn't a ward of the court, you know. Her brother promised her to you before he died."

Roark cut him a glance. "You sound as if you believe it."

"You'd best start *acting* like you believe it, if you expect anyone else to."

Roark sighed. Alain was right. No one could prove his story false. The only other one to know the truth, the lady's brother, was dead.

Now he must bid Alyss goodbye and vow to be home quickly. Home. Chauvere. It was his. Bedamned if he would relinquish it.

Roark needed to don his mail for the trip; Ralf had been cleaning it. Again. Heading for the hall, he saw Ralf and James had brought the packed horses around. Good. There was a cart, as well. Whose idea had that been? All their supplies could be loaded on the horses. He could buy an extra cart to carry supplies he'd obtain in town.

At the top of the steps, he nearly collided with Alyss. She was dressed in a sturdy but stylish gown he had never before seen. Her hair was covered by a proper wimple, and she was directing two men carrying a chest.

"Good morning, my lord. We're ready." She motioned to Rose, who was likewise dressed for traveling.

His wife smiled at him. "It's been years since I visited anywhere. Let's be on our way."

As she brushed past him, she leaned in and said in a determined voice only the two of them could hear: "There's no use arguing. I'm coming along. This involves me as much as it does you, and I'm not going to be left behind." She smiled again and patted him on the chest.

The expanded party didn't leave until mid-morning. With the addition of Lady Alyss and her maid, more men had to be drafted to accompany them and changes made to the defenses at home. Finally, they rolled out: a cart for the maid and for baggage, two extra horses, two extra knights who shared a squire and page, four men-at-arms, Ralf, James, Alain, Roark, Alyss, and Rose.

Ignoring Roark's order that she share the cart with Rose, Alyss rode her favorite mare, Berry, a black-maned bay with a flirtatious arch to her neck.

The cart's wooden wheels rattled and creaked as they lumbered through the gate, sending James's horse sidestepping at the unfamiliar noise. Once the skittish mare settled, the entourage found its pace, stopping to pick up the sheriff's messenger in the village, where someone had taken pity and given him a place to sleep.

Roark was surprised to see Father Eudo with the man. He'd been meaning to ask Alyss who said mass when the holy man was gone, as he seemed to be frequently. Not that it mattered to him, but a castle's people needed a reliable churchman. As lord, he was responsible for seeing one was present.

The messenger was pale and clutched his stomach.

"This poor man is too sick to travel. He was up most of the night purging himself." Father Eudo frowned, his tone indignant. "Surely you can postpone the trip for a day."

Roark shook his head. "The sheriff has demanded my presence. And he"—nodding toward the messenger—"must go with us." The man lifted bloodshot eyes in a wordless plea but was motioned to the supply cart.

Privately, Roark was glad the disrespectful little rat was suffering. Served him right for the display of insolence he had shown the day before. And for the gluttony he had indulged in at the table.

The cavalcade hadn't gone far when the messenger leapt from the small wagon and dashed toward the side of the road.

"Hope whatever he's got's not catching," called one of the knights, watching the man disappear behind a bush.

Lady Alyss flicked Berry's reins. "I wouldn't worry." Her voice lifted as the mare moved ahead. "Likely, it was something he ate."

For a man on horseback, Nottingham was a long, hard day's ride from Chauvere. Traveling with loaded cart and two women, the party could take up to three days to make the trip. But despite Roark's misgivings, the group made good time. Nearing sundown, Roark pulled his horse alongside Alyss's. "We'll look for a place to rest for the night soon."

His statement was met by a rumble from her stomach. She smiled. He started to remark on it when Alain called out and pointed to a horseman coming up fast behind them. The cart was moving toward what cover could be found before Alyss recognized the rider as one of the guards from home.

Roark and Alain rode back to meet him. Alyss, determined not to be left out, followed.

"My lord," the man gasped, pulling to a halt. He nodded to Alyss, "My lady. Sir Baldwin sends a message. He has word that Windom plans to move on Chauvere while you're gone."

"How did he get this information?"

"He didn't say, my lord."

"We should return immediately," Alyss said, certain of the message's origin at Windom. Allowing a servant from one holding to wed a servant in another often had unexpected benefits.

"Damnation." Roark wheeled his horse toward Alain. "The sheriff's message was a fake. Lord Paxton's trying to draw us away so he can attack." He jerked his head toward the messenger. "Get some food and change horses."

They returned to the small group in silence. He wished they were not hindered by the cart and the women. On horseback, Chauvere was a few short leagues.

"We could make faster time if we rode ahead," Alyss said, mirroring his thoughts. "What if we left the others to come at their own pace?"

Once again, his wife surprised him. No complaints, just an assessment of the problem and a solution.

"I'd like to," he said. "Alain and I will leave now. The others will stay to protect you and your maid."

He could have sworn he heard a snort. "Perhaps you didn't hear me," Alyss said. "*We* will ride ahead. I can keep any pace you set. And I don't need a maid."

"No," Roark's voice rose. "It's too dangerous, I said. You're my wife, and I'll protect you the way I think best."

Lifting her chin, Alyss looked him in the eye. "You might as well know, I'm not staying behind. Chauvere is my home, and I will not allow anyone to threaten it. Either I go with you, or I follow right behind, alone. Your choice."

No doubt she would do just that. He could order his men to guard her closely, but she'd find a way. Roark had enough to worry about; he didn't need a wife galloping around the countryside unattended.

He ordered one knight and two men-at-arms to accompany Rose and the luggage wagon. The rest were to travel with him. The fake messenger was nowhere to be found.

They rode hard while the light lasted, then slowed. Alyss kept pace, although her body strained forward and worry marked her mouth and eyes. She uttered not one word of complaint.

His new wife was quite a woman.

Chapter Twenty-One

Alyss breathed a sigh of relief when Chauvere loomed up in the light of the waxing moon. No attackers occupied the space in front of the castle. She swung down from her mount and approached Roark. Bernard appeared out of the shadows.

"Glad you're back," the knight said. "The army's still hours away. He's taking his right old time, thinking you're off to Nottingham."

"Windom likely won't bother with talk," Roark answered. "We'll prepare for an attack."

Alyss started to ask Sir Baldwin's location so she could rally the soldiers... She stopped before speaking. Roark had that duty now. But would he... She stopped herself again. She had to trust him.

She should check on food supplies. "Merciful Mother," she cried. "The villagers. They must be brought inside the walls again."

She dashed toward the keep. In the great hall, Lady Isobel already had the servants in action. Picking a half-dozen, Alyss sent them to the villagers with orders to bring what they could, but to come quickly. No doubt word had already reached them and packing had begun.

"Milady, where do you want the extra water stored?" Martha called.

Bless the woman for remembering. Alyss turned to show the cook where to place the tubs and barrels. The water-filled containers would be scattered around the hall and bailey for use in the event of fire.

The last of the villagers had nearly made it into the gates when Lord Paxton's men came into view. Three of his over-eager soldiers galloped ahead, attempting to harry the stragglers.

Alyss raced to the gates to see the trio retreat when Sir Alain and Sir Bernard appeared, mounted and in full mail and accompanied by a pair of men-at-arms. They were just in time to meet Rose and the guards driving the supply cart at harrowing speed along the opposite trail.

Lady Isobel caught Alyss's attention as she returned with Rose.

"My lady." Isobel hauled the miller's wife up beside her. "Betts has offered to organize some of the women to help."

Alyss nodded at the two. "That's perfect. Send those with knowledge of healing to the hall. And find a safe place for the children when the fighting starts."

Her usually jolly face serious, Betts bent a knee and trotted away.

Roark caught up with Alyss sometime later. "You must rest. Windom won't take action immediately. Don't know what he thought he'd accomplish, arriving in the dark."

"Perhaps he intended to give the people a surprise when they awoke with an army outside and no lord inside for protection," Alyss said.

"He knows better now."

After making sure as much as possible had been done to prepare the castle, she urged everyone to rest. She hardly recalled closing her eyes before light streaming through the window awoke her. Alone in bed.

****

Roark rested briefly in the barracks before rising to arm all men who could handle a weapon. Never mind the foolish rule that prohibited peasants from having knightly weapons. They deserved to fight for their homes. Alain commanded the soldiers, while Sir Baldwin directed the few castle archers. They waited.

The first volley of arrows from camp came with the dawn. Most missiles fell to ground, or landed harmlessly among the villagers' possessions stacked around the outer bailey.

Chauvere's archers took their turn. That set the day's pattern. Minutes became hours and still only arrows were exchanged periodically. Such a method of fighting didn't make sense to Roark. Windom's lord must be preparing some kind of attack. The nature of that attack became apparent during a routine patrol of the walls about mid-morning.

In the distance near the tree line, well out of range of Chauvere's bowmen, workers were building something. Roark signaled Alain, who was reassuring some soldiers along the battlements. When Alain reached his side, he nodded toward the activity. "What do you see out there?"

"Looks like—Satan's snowballs, it's a damned catapult."

"What I thought. Today is a delaying tactic. Keeping us busy until that thing's ready. We'll have to take care of it tonight."

Roark called for Bernard, Alain, Rance, and Sir Baldwin to join him in the barracks. It never occurred to him to include Alyss until Sir Baldwin asked.

"Lady Alyss is busy with castle duties," Roark said. "No need to disturb her for our battle plans."

Sir Baldwin raised his bushy white brows and narrowed his mouth, but didn't reply. Roark could imagine what the old knight thought, but no matter how brave Alyss might be, no woman belonged around fighting.

He outlined his idea, and the others agreed. The plan was dangerous, but under cover of darkness it might succeed. After the army settled down for the night, a handful of volunteers would leave through the postern gate, work their way to the catapult, and destroy it. He doubted Lord Paxton would expect such a bold attack.

If they couldn't get to the catapult, they'd destroy whatever was in their way.

The meeting broke up, and Roark had just emerged from the guard room, energy revving his blood, when Alyss hailed him.

"I've learned something important," she called. "They have a battering ram and a catapult."

Her words doused the fire in his veins. What the devil had she been doing close enough to the walls to determine that? A stray arrow could have injured her. Or worse. His tone low and savage from unexpected fear, he demanded, "How do you know?"

She grasped his wrist, fingers digging into flesh. He could vow her hands trembled.

"I was helping some villagers store their belongings in the outer bailey when I heard a strange pounding. When I went to investigate, I saw soldiers working on something. And others were trimming branches from a tree they must have cut from the woods. What else would they use a tree for?"

"Battering ram," he agreed. "Get back to the hall. Can't you see the damned arrows falling all around? You could be killed."

"If you will listen, I have an idea."

"I know about the siege machine, and I have a plan for it. The rest will wait." A handful of arrows soared over the wall. "My lady, I am very serious. You need to be inside, away from danger."

Taking her by the shoulders, he turned her toward the keep, but she pulled away and faced him. She was unstoppable. He shook his head.

"After dark, send out a small party," she said. "When the time comes, we can attract attention to the other side of the wall. Come with me. I'll show you and explain."

Roark held back as she tried to move him. "I have it in hand. Leave the fighting to the warriors."

Alain joined them, trailed by Bernard and Sir Baldwin.

"We'll be ready come dark, captain," said Bernard, scratching the red bush on his chin. "If we leave from the back, we can sneak around before they notice us."

Alyss snapped a look then Roark, then Sir Baldwin, who nodded. "They'll have the postern gate guarded. We'll go through the dog gate, if you'll allow."

She paused only a moment. "Very well. It's the escape route for the castle. Only Baldwin and I know it. And you, now. But come, I want to show it to you." She dashed off without waiting for an answer.

"Her place is inside with the other women."

Roark's grumble reached Sir Baldwin.

The old knight sighed, a huge gust of resignation. "You won't convince her of that, I'm thinkin'. Lady Alyss has a better grasp of fightin' than most knights. Did you think *I* came up with all the tricks these past months?"

Roark couldn't believe his ears. "Are you telling me you allowed her to help you plan the fighting before?"

"No."

That was better. Roark was beginning to think his entire world was arse upward.

"I'm tellin' you she allowed me to help her plan."

A cleared throat and a snicker reminded Roark of the trio at this back. He swung around glaring, but the faces looked back innocently.

"It's not amusing," he insisted. "She's a woman. She can't understand battle."

"Puzzles," Sir Baldwin explained in his usual less-than-voluble manner. "She's always been good at'em."

She might be good at puzzles, but Roark knew battles, and he didn't need help from a woman, even one he couldn't seem to get out his mind.

He ate a quick midday meal of bread, cheese, and ale that Martha and some of the village women prepared for everyone. Leaving the hall, he encountered Alain.

"They're putting the catapult together," his friend reported. "Recall the stories about the fancy ones King Richard built on crusade. The trebuchets?"

Roark grunted. He had reached the foot of the steps when another volley of arrows came across. A cry and a shout signaled two hits. "The arrows may be a distraction while the siege engine's completed," he muttered, "but they're taking a toll."

It was late afternoon when a call sounded from the guard tower. "They be bringing it."

Alain rallied the bowmen who took aim at the men moving the tall structure, but the wood acted as a shield and most arrows missed their marks. Sounds of jeering came from the camp, but rather than demoralizing Chauvere's defenders, it angered them.

Not long after, the first boulder sailed over the outer wall and landed in the middle of the bailey. Chauvere archers picked off two of the soldiers moving the contraption back. Soon, another boulder cleared the wall, this one closer to a structure.

The second round of rocks was followed by a loud crack and clatter. "Somethin's wrong wi' the devil's arm," came a shout from the guard tower, using the term some of the archers had dubbed the catapult. Roark dashed up the steps to the guard tower in time to see soldiers pushing the siege machine to the west side of the open field, out of range for the castle's archers. The long wooden pole had broken.

****

Alyss wished her stubborn husband had allowed a moment to hear her idea, but she realized he'd made other concessions to her position here in the past days. Perhaps there was hope for him. Not that she wanted to rule the castle, she just wanted him to recognize that she was capable in her own right.

The memory of their night together nudged into her mind. He'd been gentle, tender, patient. Had that been the same man she dealt with this afternoon? If he left on the raid tonight before she could see him, she would tear him limb from limb. Darkness had fallen, time for the handful of soldiers to set out on this mystery plan of Roark's. She couldn't let him go with no words from her. What if... Pride be damned. Disregarding her vaunted calm and composure, she picked up her skirts and ran.

Reaching the small gate concealed at the back corner of the outer wall, she discovered the men ready to slip out. Just as she'd feared. Baldwin was there with Alain, Bernard, Roark, and two men-at-arms. Outside, the path from the side opening led around the corner of the wall. The gate itself was cleverly placed between the ledges of two large stones. Unless someone knew it existed, it was nearly invisible to the eye.

The rich hum of Roark's voice reached her in the moon-dappled darkness, and Alyss's heart skipped. The group listened to his instructions. This was the first time she had seen the redoubtable Alain so serious.

She slipped around the cluster of men to Roark, intending to give him a last piece of advice on navigating the path. He stopped speaking and looked at her, his expression shuttered. Alyss surprised herself when she went up on tiptoes and kissed his cheek. Whatever had possessed her to do that? She could feel the warmth of embarrassment surge up her neck and into her face.

Roark jerked his head down in surprise. He said nothing. She supposed he'd scold her for being there. Let him try. It's not as if she hadn't fought before. Of course, he didn't know that. Perhaps she should be pleased he tried to protect her, but she didn't want to stand behind him, she wanted to work beside him.

The men wore no mail, to cut down on noise. Alyss

knew the reason, but she still worried. They were so susceptible to injury. Alain, at least, had covered his fair hair with a hood.

Baldwin opened the gate just wide enough for each of the five to slip through. He had scarcely closed it when shouts and sounds of fighting arose. Discovered so soon? Fear bubbled like bile in Alyss's throat.

Archers on the wall had been warned not to shoot if trouble arose for fear of hitting their own men in the dark, so there would be no help there. Alyss grasped Baldwin's arm. She couldn't let Roark and the others face an unknown force alone.

She motioned to the half-dozen men-at-arms left guarding the inside gate. They snapped alert, grabbed their weapons. Clustered at the door, the soldiers waited as Baldwin threw the bolt.

Before he could open it, a quick three slaps sounded.

"Roark," Alyss whispered, tense as the door opened a crack, then wider. Bernard dragged an unconscious Alain, followed by the pair of staggering men-at-arms. All four were bleeding. Where was Roark?

Alyss ran to Alain's side. His head dripped blood.

"Take him to the hall," she ordered Bernard, then stopped him. "Where are you hurt?"

He shrugged his shoulder beneath a torn tunic sleeve. "I'll do, my lady."

She directed the other men inside where women were waiting to treat any injuries. When she turned, she saw Lady Isobel and Betts in the middle of the bailey. Betts's husband was one of the new men-at-arms who accompanied the knights.

Roark hadn't returned. No matter his orders, she wasn't about to let him fight out there all alone. Perhaps to die. Alyss grasped a long knife and hurried to the partially open door.

Before she could slip out, Baldwin jumped back. Roark stumbled in. The door slammed closed, and the heavy bolt shot.

Alyss flew to his side and slipped her arm around his waist. Blood covered his tunic, but she couldn't see where it came from. His squire, Ralf, appeared at his other side, taking the sword and offering support. Roark stopped, bracing himself on their shoulders.

"They were waiting for us," he panted. "We have a traitor."

Chapter Twenty-Two

After the men had their wounds treated, Roark gathered them in the solar to hear Alyss's idea. She'd been speechless when he asked her.

Attention centered on an old parchment spread across the table. Alyss bent over the rough map she had outlined and pointed to a spot with her quill.

"This spot, here, where the west and south walls meet. It's hidden from the front. No one will be watching the sides. We can knot rope around a merlon, and the men can reach the path from there. If they keep to the deeper shadow of the wall, they can slip over to the catapult."

It was a good plan. She looked at Roark eagerly. Not that she wanted his approval, not at all. She would, however, like for him to acknowledge that a woman could have a workable plan for defense. Roark pulled the map around to study it closer. He grunted, his lips thinned in concentration. Looking at Baldwin he said, "What about secret escapes from the castle? Any passages leading outside?"

Alyss spoke. "There is one which opens in front of the castle near the woods, just beyond Windom's camp." She made a tiny "x" on the map to show the exit.

Roark glared at her, then Baldwin. "Why wasn't I told of this? How can I protect you if you keep secrets?"

Baldwin had the grace to look shamefaced.

To Alain, Roark said, "I want guards posted at that passage as soon as we're finished here. Sir Baldwin will show you where it begins. How big is it? How many men can pass?"

"Narrow," Baldwin answered. "Room for one if he has a weapon; two, but no fighting room."

Roark scowled. "An escape passage wide enough for only one man?"

Striving to bring calmness back to the discussion, Alyss said, "No one knows of this passage except the family and Sir Baldwin. The opening is camouflaged on the outside. It would never be found unless someone knew where to look."

"Nevertheless," Roark muttered, still frowning.

Through lowered lashes, she peered at Roark—to find him looking at her, his face impassive. "How do you know the catapult has been moved or the location of the campfires around it, my lady?"

Caught off guard, Alyss felt a bit guilty. "I looked."

"Don't tell me you stood in full range of their arrows again." His gaze locked with hers.

Golden flakes gleamed in his dark eyes, the iridescent green chips hidden in the uncertain candlelight. Words she had planned to utter evaporated as she stared at the shadows flickering across his strong face.

Was that worry she saw? "You might trust me to have more sense than that."

He glanced at the rough map she'd devised, and she could swear a corner of his mouth curved up. "I'll consider it." To the others, he said, "You should all get some sleep. Dawn will be here mighty quick."

"Wait." The others turned back to face him. "Any idea who the traitor is?"

Silence. No one could offer a name. Only the people involved in the foray had known the entire plan.

Alyss considered the men before her. As far as she knew, only two people in the room were absolutely innocent—she and Baldwin. And Roark. Unlikely he'd betray all he had worked so hard to get.

That left Alain and the newcomers—Sir Bernard, Sir Nicholas, and Sir Rance. The last three arrived recently and, to think on it, conveniently—just a day before Windom's army appeared.

Bernard had been wounded earlier. But not badly. A cover, perhaps? She looked obliquely at her husband. He was watching her. Slowly, he shook his head. "I trust them with my life, and have many times."

How was it he could read her mind?

"None of us would betray Sir Roark, my lady," Sir Rance said quietly. "We followed him here because he's our captain. We want to be part of what he's building."

"It's normal you might suspect us, my lady," Bernard added. "We're strangers here, after all."

Alyss looked at each of them. After a time, she nodded. "If Sir Roark trusts you, then I shall. I have faith in his judgment."

Baldwin cleared his throat. "We can't know who it is right now, I'm thinkin'. Don't forget the villagers. Some here don't like change. Could be, plans were overheard without our knowin'."

Agreeing to question who and where possible, they

all adjourned to seek their beds except Baldwin, who returned to check defenses.

As Alyss carefully folded the precious parchment, Roark placed a hand on her wrist. "Show me where you looked at the camp."

Quiet greeted the pair when they reached the far corner of the outer wall, guards merely nodding when they passed. They climbed a little-used stairway, arriving at a spot sunk in deep shadow.

Moving right along the narrow battlement, Alyss drew up to the merlon, then eased her head around the side. There it was. The catapult had, indeed, been moved. Now it set back on the south side of the campsite, out of reach of Chauvere's crossbow bolts.

Roark's breath hissed through his teeth. She could feel the movement of the air on her cheek. He was close behind her—too close. His chest was hard against her arm as he peered around.

Her heart beat so loudly, the troops outside were bound to hear it. Tingles skittered across her shoulders and up her neck. Bit by bit she eased back into her husband's warmth.

"Don't expose yourself to danger again," Roark murmured. "Someone could see you up here and a well-placed arrow could—harm you."

"But I look quickly, and then I hide. I'm not stupid, husband."

He didn't answer. His arms slipped around her waist and held her snug while his big warrior's hands slid up her sides to the swell of her breasts, then around. She gasped as his fingers closed over her nipples.

His mouth touched her neck. Branding her skin, the tip of his tongue halted at her ear; he whispered, "Best get some rest. Morning is nearly here."

****

Outside their bedchamber Roark stopped, forcing himself to let Alyss enter alone. He disapproved when she placed herself in danger, haunting the walls, keeping watch on the movements outside. But he was learning not to forbid her to do anything. He had to admit, her quick analysis was valuable. If she were a man, Roark would praise her actions. If she were a man, he would punish her for disobeying orders. If she were a man, he wouldn't be frustrated by desire each time she was near.

In the doorway, Alyss turned a questioning look on him, but he shook his head and put away his turbulent thoughts.

"I'll sleep with the garrison tonight. Tomorrow we'll decide on a plan."

Alyss paused, opened her lips to speak. Roark swiftly kissed her, his tongue edging the inside of her upper lip. She gave a low moan when he turned away. As he retreated along the corridor, he heard the door close—forcefully—and the bolt thud.

A movement caught his eye near the top of the stairs. Halting, he lifted his head to look, to listen. Silence. He must be imagining things. Still, with the possibility of an informer in their midst, caution was needed. He slipped around the corner of the solar door and narrowed his gaze toward the shadows. Nothing. He sighed. An hour's sleep. That's what he needed.

What he needed was in the now-barred bedchamber behind him. Not tonight. Once the fight was over, he'd have ample time to sort the strands of feeling that wound inside him.

****

Red-streaked dawn was greeted with the *whoosh* of a rock clearing the wall and the answering *zunnng* of crossbow bolts seeking targets. The catapult had been repaired.

With distance adjustment by mid-morning, sailing rocks had found the walls, although the first ones did little damage.

The early promise of a bright, warm day faded as hours passed. By midday, clouds clotted the horizon like week-old cream. Occasionally, between the crash of rock against rock, distant thunder rumbled, a hungry belly too long without food. Injuries began to add up, and among the anxious, confined villagers, tempers sparked.

Rounding the corner of the keep, a running lad collided with one goodwife, sending bread and a cup of ale flying. Will apologized, but she shouted at him until Sir Baldwin strode up to demand what was going on. Taking the opportunity offered by the woman's indignant listing of his sins, the stable boy escaped and continued to race across the open bailey.

Standing at the entrance to the guard tower, Roark watched the youth head straight for him. God's eyelashes, the boy could run. Pulling up short in front of him, Will was out of breath, but obviously excited.

"I need to report, milord, quick, afore they make me go back," he gasped through his bobbing curls. "Though why they treat me like a baby, I don't know. As if I need watchin', with you around."

Roark had ordered the stable master to keep all his young helpers out of the way of danger, but Will wasn't taking the order kindly, it seemed.

"What is it you want to report, lad?"

"Don't you 'member, milord? You told me to keep an eye open whilst you and milady were occupied? I couldn't get away 'til now."

Roark searched his mind until he hit upon the day he had given the youngster a harmless task, to watch for anything suspicious.

Will grabbed Roark's hand and pulled him toward the guard room at the bottom of the tower. "Quick, afore someone sees us."

Inside the dim room, Will sidled up to Roark and pulled him down to reach his ear.

"I were with Cin last night. He were a bit restless and needed a snack. I saw somebody sneaking around. You know, walking close to the keep's wall, like he didn't want to be seen? I followed 'im inside, after everyone were asleep, and he went right up to milady's special room."

Lady Alyss's special room? "The solar, you mean?"

Will nodded. "That be the one. I lay down and acted like I was sleeping when he come back, and he went to the kitchen, but when I followed 'im, he was gone. Just gone."

Excitement had increased the volume of his voice. "He didn't come by me, and he didn't go out the kitchen door, 'cause it was still bolted inside."

Roark motioned for quiet. "Who was it?" he asked.

Will looked downcast. "Couldn't see a face, milord. He were all wrapped up and had something pulled over his head."

So Roark hadn't imagined things in the corridor last night. Damn, he should have investigated after all.

A small, sad voice floated upward. "I'm sorry, milord, that I lost 'im, but someone *were* there."

"I believe you, Will." Roark put his hand on a small shoulder. "You did very well, lad. I'm proud of you. But don't take chances like that. I wouldn't want a good man to be hurt."

The youngster lifted his head, looking proud and hopeful. "Thank you, milord."

Roark smiled. "Is there anything else you have to report?"

"Umm." Will looked away, the perfect picture of a boy trying not to lie. "Nothing important." He looked back, his eyes sparkling in the weak light. "Just gossip, Ma says." He chuckled. "Guess who sneaks away to the chapel ever chance she gets? Rose, milady's maid."

Not a great piece of gossip, Roark thought, although he wouldn't have pegged the girl as the religious type.

"She don't go to pray, neither. She meets Father Eudo. That is, she did afore the soldiers came."

Roark ruffled the boy's curls. "It's no crime to see a priest."

"Maybe not. But she don't just *sees* him, if you know what I mean. I watched 'em once, in the line of duty, 'a course. She was cryin', and he put his arm around her shoulders."

Before Roark could learn more, a shadow fell across the doorway and Alain stepped in.

"We have a problem."

Roark turned Will toward the door. "Thanks for your work. Go now. Keep Cin calm amid all this noise and have care for yourself."

The boy looked up in what Roark recognized as

hero worship.

"Yes, milord. And I'll keep my eyes and ears open just the same, won't I?"

As Will ran across the empty yard, Roark turned to Alain, his brows raised.

"You need to see this." Alain nodded toward outside.

Up on the battlement, Roark peered over the side. The large trimmed tree trunk had been mounted on a platform with wheels. Soldiers lined up on each side of the contraption. The battering ram Alyss had warned of.

Stepping back Roark checked the gates. All the boulders that had found their way over the walls were piled against them.

"Better get the archers ready." Alain had undoubtedly already given the order. For a moment, he considered his friend. Alain's bandage had slipped to one side, lending him a rakish air. Dried blood matted his blond hair.

Roark thought of all the years they had been together, from the day he had found the young smith's son walking along a road, belongings in a rough bag slung over a shoulder.

"Goin' t' make my way in London town," the burly fourteen-year-old had said. "Pa died. Smithin's not for me." Roark thought of himself at that age and asked Alain if he'd like to train as a squire. The young man subjected Roark to a lengthy scrutiny before nodding once. "Might give it a try." Over the years, through sickness, wars, feuds, tournaments; through drinking and wenching, they'd stood back-to-back.

Three years Roark's junior, Alain was like a brother—one who had refused knighthood until Roark forced it on him the year before. And still they had each other's backs.

Roark's voice roughened with emotion. "Get the bowmen in place, then come to the hall and get that bandage changed. We must plan for tonight."

Outside, the bombardment of stone had halted, and the catapult again moved to the west side of the field, beyond range of the castle arrows. Attention concentrated on the battering ram. Roark was confident the gate could hold for a while with the help of the archers, who efficiently picked off soldiers manning the huge log. Night would halt the fighting. He hoped.

He was glad Lord Paxton wanted the place in good shape, or alternate measures might be employed, such as fire. Well, it wasn't over yet.

Reaching the solar, Roark found turmoil.

"Did you take the map last night?" Alyss searched the sheets of the account books.

"It's gone?"

Voice tight, she said, "I left it on this table; it's not here now." Absently she tucked her hair behind an ear.

"That's what someone was after." Roark outlined his experience the night before and related what Will had told him.

"Narrows our options for tonight, doesn't it?" Alain swung through the open doorway with a clean bandage over one eye.

Roark looked at the people gathered in the room. "It might work to our advantage. My lady, you marked the passage exit, didn't you? Whoever has the map may think the attack will center there."

Alyss's eyes met his and brightened as she caught his meaning. "The element of surprise is with us," she said, breathlessly.

They spent the next hour refining the plan.

"Let's get started," Roark said at last. "One thing. Stay away from the wall, Alyss. I can't fight if I'm worried about you." Wrapped up in plans, he almost missed her surprised expression.

Leaving the solar, they met Father Eudo in the corridor. "Ah, there you are, Sir Roark. I've been asked to bring you out. It seems a problem has developed."

"The gates are holding?"

"Yes, yes. It's another situation, altogether. But I must ask if you have a plan to counter the threat at our gates."

A perfectly reasonable question—why did Roark object to it? Perhaps it was the smugness of the holy man, the arrogance with which he treated Lady Alyss, or perhaps it was the sharp, assessing gaze that frequently slid across his fox-like face.

"We have, Father," Roark answered. "We'll attend to the defense, you attend to the injured."

****

After a brief visit to the hall, Alyss made her way through the clusters of villagers' campsites to reassure her people, then slipped up to her bedchamber. Digging to the bottom of one of her chests, she came up with chausses and tunic she'd worn when training with Baldwin just a short few weeks ago. It seemed like another life. Replacing the small sword Baldwin ordered made just for her, she scooted the chest against the wall.

She slipped into the garments, then wound her braid around her head and stuffed a cap on. No one would mistake her for a man, but at least she could move freely, unhindered by skirts. The people were used to seeing her dressed so.

Darkness finally arrived, deepened by lingering clouds. Alyss made her way to the southwest corner of the wall where the men gathered. Two buckets, half-full of melted grease, sat nearby. She hunched down in the shadows, listening to Roark argue with Ralf in low-pitched voices.

"My lord, give me this chance," the youth pleaded. "I can carry the buckets; you and the others can fight."

"I won't have you in danger," Roark insisted. "Stay here."

"I'm your squire, now. It's my duty to watch your back." Then Ralf added softly, "My lord."

Roark considered for a moment, then gave an abrupt nod and motioned him to follow.

"Stay behind us. When the signal comes, I'll go down first. You lower the buckets to me. The rest of you follow, one by one."

Chapter Twenty-Three

Like stars from Hades' sky, campfires flared across the flat before the castle. A handful of soldiers clumped near a small one, not far from the catapult. His men waited for the signal. His men. Roark liked the sound. But they were more than his men, they were his friends.

When the knights turned up at Chauvere, Roark had been stunned. They gave up home and employment for the unknown of what he might provide. He wouldn't question it. And he wouldn't fail them.

At last, the plan went into action. Sounds of argument rose from the far battlement, attracting the attention of the other guards. Soon shouts grew louder. Roark could make out Sir Bernard's booming voice. Other scuffles erupted along the top of the wall, and in the midst of the staged furor, a large bundle sailed over the side.

On the ground, Windom's army took notice of the fights. Laughter rang out as attention centered on the commotion. A few soldiers drifted over to investigate the bundle, some shouting out raucous advice. The three guards posted near the catapult joined the group.

Roark gave the signal. He stepped into the sling, grasped the rope, and was lowered over the side of the wall. At the bottom, he tugged on the rope, which was drawn up and a bucket attached. He removed it when it reached ground, and the routine was repeated. The third, smaller bucket, covered with a piece of wet toweling, went down more slowly containing, as it did, two lighted candles in a low bowl.

Moving quickly, Ralf followed, then Rance, and Nicholas. Alain went last. At the top of the wall, Baldwin stood ready.

****

Alyss slipped up beside Baldwin. He acknowledged her presence with raised brows and a resigned shake of the head. She didn't respond, concentrating on the progress below.

Ralf, carrying a bucket of grease in each hand, walked carefully behind the four knights who were alert for discovery. Keeping to shadows, they made it to the base of the catapult. Roark took one bucket and rounded to the other side. He poured the grease along the wood while Ralf soaked the near side. Alain stood by, shielding with his body the faint glow coming from the candles.

They were about to set flame to the doused wood when a Windom soldier walked out of the darkness behind them, straightening his chausses.

He shouted and some half-dozen soldiers appeared from the shadows farther ahead. They advanced, brandishing weapons. Alyss could make out Roark as he threw his bucket at them and pulled free his sword.

Nicholas and Rance leaped in front of Ralf and Alain as they struggled to light the grease. It caught sluggishly. Alain threw his candle forward, on top of the now-slick base, and turned to the fighting.

Alyss couldn't understand what Roark called out, but Ralf, without weapon, started to run. A sword loomed, and he went down. Alyss gasped. Again, none of the men wore mail. They had gone in dark tunics and chausses only. They wouldn't have carried even light swords if Alyss hadn't insisted.

With speed and determination, the men fought their way toward the wall. Rance and Nicholas dragged Ralf, with Roark and Alain protecting them from behind. They reached the rope, looped the sling beneath the squire's arms, then turned to meet attackers.

Baldwin pulled Ralf up, but the dead weight proved difficult. Alyss leaped to his side, braced her feet on the wall, and towed. Once Ralf reached safety, Alyss unwrapped the sling and threw it down again. Her gaze followed it. They should have brought more ropes.

Rance and Nicholas didn't bother with the sling. Grasping the rope, they walked up the side of the wall, one ahead of the other, finding footholds in the rough stone.

Flames began to lick up from the base of the catapult, illuminating Roark and Alain, who held off the remaining attackers. Flames and sounds of fighting had captured the attention of more of Windom's soldiers. They flocked to the wooden structure, batting at the spreading blaze. Squinting, Alyss counted five fighters at the base of the wall.

In the confusion below, Alyss couldn't make out Roark. Where was he?

God protect him. If he gets hurt, I'll kill him.

There, they were at the sling. *Now. Climb.* Alyss held her breath. Alain popped over the side, blood covering his head again.

Roark should be next. Time dragged. He didn't appear. Alyss leaned over the edge, searching for him.

She couldn't locate any figures. She couldn't *see.*

She rounded on the three knights beside her. "How could you leave him?" she shouted. "What if he's captured? What if he's killed?"

They stared at her. What was wrong with them? Had they been struck dumb?

Then she realized. Dressed as she was, none of the knights knew the figure in men's clothing was her. Until she screamed at them.

Ralf struggled to his feet, blood dripping from his shoulder.

"Help him," Alyss ordered. When the others turned, she grabbed the rope and jumped over the side.

Halfway down, she realized this was not as easy as she remembered. As a child, she had followed Henry down a rope dangling from just this spot. It had been easy and great fun, never mind that her parents had scolded for putting herself in danger.

Finally, she neared the bottom. Attention of the Windom forces was centered on the fire, and no one watched the wall, thank the saints. She slipped into the darkness when she reached the ground, then moved toward the clusters of soldiers trying impotently to quell the spreading blaze.

Perhaps Roark had been captured and was being held. She had to find him. Darting from shadow to shadow, she moved closer. A noise at the left drew her attention. Not another soldier who had to answer nature's call. Did these men do nothing but relieve themselves? She knelt behind a bush and drew a dagger from her wrist sheath. Holding it low, she crept to the side.

A hand grabbed her left arm. A curse sounded in

her ear, and she was dragged around. By the rank odor of the man, Alyss knew it wasn't Roark. The action seemed to move very slowly as her attacker pulled her closer. He raised his sword. She swung upward with her dagger. It entered his neck as if she were carving a boar. She looked into his surprised eyes. She ducked under his arm as he fell, taking her along, and she heard the *thunk* of his head hitting a rock. He didn't move, but his heavy body pinned her legs.

Alyss lay stunned. She couldn't move. The odor of the soldier's body and blood clogged her breathing. And in an instant, the past swept back.

Jasper's heavy body pinned her to the floor. Alyss pushed at his shoulders, his chest, his sides, and her right hand brushed the handle of her father's knife beneath her skirt. She couldn't breathe—no air. His fetid odor was stifling.

As black spots swam before her eyes, her fingers curled around the hilt of the dagger.

He drew back slightly. Her vision cleared. She gulped a breath and eased the knife free of her skirts before he pressed down on her again.

Raising the dagger, she struck out. And connected.

With a roar of pain, the weight on her lifted, then disappeared. Rolling quickly to the side, she looked around.

Jasper sat on the floor against her father's bed, her father's short dagger protruding from his throat, a stream of blood trickling down his neck and chest, a look of surprise on his florid face. He was still very much alive.

The surprise turned to viciousness as he grabbed her ankle and tugged her toward him. She scrabbled for something to stop her slide, managed to get to her hands and one knee before a mighty jerk landed her on her stomach.

On his knees, he flipped her onto her back and pulled the thin blade from his neck. Alyss felt the blood on her before she saw it spurt from his wound. His eyes were wild with hatred and fury.

Suddenly, he collapsed. In a clatter of metal, Sir Baldwin burst into the room, his sword swinging, his sword connecting. But Jasper already lay still.

Blood. Alyss's front was soaked in it. She could feel the thick stickiness on her hands, her throat, in her hair. The metallic smell of it was so strong she could taste it.

She couldn't move. Perhaps, she thought, she was dead. No, she would not feel the awful weight on her if she were dead.

And then it was gone. Sir Baldwin knelt beside her, helped her to sit.

She clutched his arm and leaned her forehead against his shoulder. Looking down, she said irrelevantly, "I have ruined another gown."

Gasping, she came back to herself. Alyss had killed Sir Jasper of Windom. Just as she had killed the man above her now. But God's mercy, it had been their lives or hers, and she would not feel guilt any longer.

Finally wriggling free, she leaned over, hands on knees. The dagger protruded from the soldier's neck. She couldn't reach it. Grabbing his sword, Alyss turned toward the flames.

****

Roark stood panting at the top of the wall, where he had just pulled himself up. A gash in his side oozed blood, and his back hurt as if a brand had seared it. He looked around, counting heads.

"Everyone safe? Where's Ralf?"

"His arm," Rance said. "Being seen to."

"My lord," Baldwin broke in. "It's Lady Alyss. She's out there."

Roark looked at the man blankly. "Out where?"

"She sneaked up here, t' watch, and then—" the old knight choked.

"When you didn't come back, she went to find you," Nicholas explained. "We didn't know it was her at first. She was dressed in—well—like a lad. She screamed at us for leaving you behind. The next thing we knew, she just…disappeared."

"What in hell was she doing up here?" Roark roared. "Damned stubborn woman. Can't she ever listen? When I get my hands on her, I'll strangle her."

He grabbed the rope, but Alain stopped him. "You're hurt, my friend. Let me go."

Roark pushed him away and swung over the side. He'd gone but a few feet, when he felt the rope under him move. Looking down, he saw his wayward wife.

"Put your foot in the sling—the loop—and hold on," he shouted. "I'll bring you up."

Hands reached out to help him over the side, then Rance and Alain pulled. Roark shouldered his way in to add his strength. The rope fairly flew up the side of the stone, and they could hear an occasional, "Ouch," as she bumped against the rough surface.

When her head came into view, Roark grabbed her beneath the arms and dragged. Setting her on her feet, he saw the blood.

"Dear God." He ran his hands over her as he asked,

"Where are you hurt?"

"Not my blood." Alyss gulped for air.

It took a moment for Roark to realize she told the truth. When he did, he clutched her shoulders and shook her.

"What were you thinking?" he roared. "You could have died. Have you no sense?" With every word, his volume increased.

"Where were *you*?" Her voice rose to meet his. "You were supposed to come back with the rest. This is no time to be a hero, you are needed *here*. *I* need you, you great idiot."

Tears streamed down her cheeks as she struggled free. She punched him in the chest.

"Why didn't you come back?"

Roark's stomach clenched as he jerked Alyss into his arms. He pressed his cheek against her head, then reached up and flung off the rough cap. Caressing her freed hair, he wrapped her tightly in his other arm.

She could have been killed, taken from him, this stubborn woman. What had possessed her to drop into the midst of a battle, simply to search for him? Had she no trust in his ability as a warrior?

Roark didn't know whether to shake Alyss or to love her. At the moment, the problem was just to breathe, what with her arms clasped so tightly around the slash in his side. His chest actually tingled from the punch she'd delivered.

Who would have guessed the composed Lady Alyss was capable of such an outburst? Her stubbornness rivaled his own. God help him.

An acrid odor of burning wood lay on the night breeze that swirled thin smoke around them. Evidence of the successful mission. Along the battlement, knights hunkered and watched the catapult flame high. Slapping each other on the back, they chuckled, then laughed jubilantly.

Cheers could be heard on the other walls and from inside the bailey. Tomorrow would see the battle renewed. Tomorrow the battering ram must be dealt with. But tonight they'd celebrate.

All except the injured. Lifting his head, Roark caught Alain's eye. When his captain drew close, Roark said, "Take Ralf to the hall. I'll meet you there shortly."

Then he whispered to Alyss, "Come with me. You need to clean up."

He walked with her to their bedchamber but stopped at the door. "I'll send Lady Isobel to you with a bath. I must see to the men."

Alyss looked at him for the first time since their shouting match. Her eyes were stark and glassy with shock. Perhaps he should stay with her, but undoubtedly she would prefer the attentions of another woman.

He kissed her forehead. "I'll return when I can."

After he informed Lady Isobel that Alyss needed her, he made certain Ralf was not hurt seriously, praising the squire for his actions. Then he found Alain, Rance, Nicholas, and Baldwin, and motioned to the solar.

"Wait." Alain pointed to a bench. "Before you say a word, I'll look at your side."

Roark shook his head. "I'm fine." Alain ignored him. The slash wasn't as deep as the blood on his tunic threatened. Dipping a rag in a small bit of water, his friend cleaned it and located a strip of linen.

"Give it to me," Roark grumbled. The make-shift bandage tied, he led the small group up the steps.

Before anyone had a chance to speak, he closed the door and demanded, "Do any of you remember where the hidden passage exit was marked on the map?"

It took a moment before his question registered. Alain's eyes sparked. "To the south of the catapult."

"Did any of you see where our attackers came from? They came from the south, near where the opening was marked. They expected us there."

Nicholas frowned. "That doesn't make sense. If they knew a way into the castle, why not use it to attack?"

"Too slow, one at a time. Better to wait for us. If they could kill Sir Roark, the fight would be over," Alain said in realization.

"Lord Paxton is intent on taking Chauvere," Roark added. "A smart man would keep destruction to a minimum. People would be more likely to accept the change if death and damage were limited."

Baldwin snorted. "The bastard's mighty sure of himself, I'm thinkin'. Must have powerful allies."

"One of the most," Roark agreed.

Coughing slightly, Baldwin spoke again. "Not but a few men could make it through that passage, anyway. Mighty tight fit, narrow as it is."

"You know that outlet?"

"Long time since it's been used, but Lord Ulrich kept it ready for emergencies."

"Then whoever had the map took that way out. Who else knows about the escape route?

"Just the family, I'm thinkin'. The last time it was used—"

211

Roark closed in on Baldwin, his eyes narrowing. "What? What happened the last time it was used?"

Baldwin looked at his new lord. "Father Eudo took little Lady Evelynn out through it, before, when she went to St. Ursula's. I'd forgot that."

Roark said, "I think I'd better talk to the little priest."

But a search of the hall, where a holy man might be expected to offer prayers for the fighters, didn't produce Father Eudo. Nor could any of the people recall seeing him recently.

Outside the door of the deserted chapel, Roark and the others paused. "He will be found, don't worry," Roark told them. "For now, we go back."

Together the five circulated through both baileys and toured the walls. Roark congratulated the soldiers for their successful diversionary tactics.

"We scored a hit tonight thanks to all of you, but the fight's not over," he told the gathering in the outer bailey. "We've got hard days ahead. But if we keep our spirits up and our courage strong, we'll survive."

A woman's voice lifted from the back of the crowd. "And what'll we do for food, is what I'd like to know? Planting time's here, and with those men and horses out there trampling the pastures, we'll won't get crops in. Spirit and courage'll not feed us." The people swung around to look at the speaker, opening a path to her. Roark didn't recall meeting her.

"Food to eat and grain for crops can be bought," he answered, looking out over the men, women, and children clustered across the yard.

"And who'll be paying for that, I'd like to know? For I don't have coin, no, nor nothing to barter," the woman asked.

"I will," Roark said. Unwilling to argue with the woman, he moved on. "No one should worry about eating or about seed. It will be provided."

People moved away, a few shushing her, most ignoring her. Looking over his shoulder, Roark saw Father Eudo, the corners of his sharp eyes pulled down, take her arm. Where had the priest sprung from? Was he the one who had stolen the map?

"Now daughter, bitterness will get you nothing," the priest said in a comforting voice. "Our Lord will not allow His people to suffer. Come to the chapel and we will pray." Roark nodded to Rance, indicating the priest. Rance straightened and followed the holy man. He'd see Father Eudo held until Roark could question him. Satisfied, Roark turned his attention to Sir Baldwin and gave the order to alternate guard shifts for the night so everyone could have a chance to celebrate.

"They need this break," he said. "We both know tomorrow will be a challenge. Windom won't take this setback lightly. Now I'm for bed. We don't know what tomorrow will bring, men. We'd all best be ready."

He strode toward the hall and his bedchamber. The surge that came after battle still rushed through his veins as he ran up the stairs to his wife. Wife. Who knew the word would sound so good?

Perhaps she was asleep, exhausted by her experience. Not likely, not his warrior lady. A half-smile lifted this mouth. Perhaps a spirited wife wasn't so bad, after all.

Pushing open the door, he saw Alyss, dressed in a white smock, standing by the window. Her still-damp, hip-length hair swung loose. A round wooden bathing tub half-filled with water sat to the side of the room.

"I thought you'd be sleeping," he said.

She turned. "I'm not tired. I should be, but I feel—restless." She paced toward the table which held a tray. She poured two cups of ale.

"Men often get that way after battle." He took a cup, but promptly set it down again.

"Odd. I didn't feel that way. Before."

"You sure you're all right? No injuries?" Roark worried at her fretful pacing. "Tell me what happened tonight."

Still moving, she began to speak. Her voice was detached, as if describing someone else. Roark had to force himself not to grab and comfort her; he knew she needed to talk it out.

She stilled. "He was standing with a raised sword. I had my knife. All I could see was Jasper looming over me and I…swung my hand. He fell forward, and it was Jasper pinning me, his blood on my gown." Panic edged her voice. "For a moment, I didn't know where I was. Then I saw the fire, and I remembered. You were missing."

Alyss flew into Roark's arms. She reared back and landed a weak punch to his shoulder. "Don't *ever* do that again."

His fingers curled into her shoulders. "Don't *you* ever run off into the night, alone and unprotected." His low voice was fierce. "That's what I'm here for. To protect you. Don't you forget it."

His mouth descended on hers, and her reply became a sigh.

Chapter Twenty-Four

Desire surged through Alyss like water hurtling over rocks. Where had the anger got to? Her skin tingled, her body ached. Ached and itched. She nipped at Roark's upper lip; the tip of her tongue brushed the roof of his mouth.

He lifted his arms from her back, leaving her to clutch at his tunic. Her body, on tiptoes, staggered at the unexpected freedom.

He cradled her face; rough, callused fingers traced gently across her cheeks. Alyss pressed closer and sucked his lower lip into her mouth. She slid her hands up his shoulders, around his neck, and cupped the back of his head.

His arms encircled her again, lifting until her toes barely brushed the floor. His touch trailed down her back to her bottom. She shivered. His fingers slid inward and upward, and she gasped, giving his tongue full access to hers.

The thick hardness of him pushed against her belly, then lower. As if the contact triggered a magic lever, her legs eased apart, and he drew her hips into him.

He turned her toward the table. The tray with its pitcher and cups clattered to the floor as he lifted her onto the flat surface. Stepping between her knees, he fit himself to her.

Alyss heard moans in the quiet of the room—hers

soft, his guttural. Moving her hands down his back, running them over his buttocks, she felt the muscles flex.

She wanted that throbbing ridge against her core, inside her. Her hands trailed around the waist to the front of his chausses and slid inside his braies, to his rigid cock.

Her touch stilled at the softness of it, like a baby's skin, yet richer, deeper in texture, stretched around a metal rod. He went still, tense, nearly breathless.

She traced down the warm, throbbing hardness. Gasping, he bucked his hips. His fingers joined hers at his waist in a fight to free his ties. He jerked up her chemise and found her cleft.

In the space of a breath, her legs were wide, her knees lifted to his hips, and he was inside her. An instant of shared stillness at an overwhelming, silent, "yes," and then he pounded into her, holding her bottom in his big hands to protect her skin from the rough wood. She clung to his shoulders, moving with him, hips struggling for their own rhythm.

Her arms grew heavy, and she fell backward to lie on the table. He lifted and steadied her hips, plunging in and out, faster, deeper, until it seemed she could taste him in her throat.

A slight change of angle and she cried out. A tingling numbness spread up the inside of her legs. Placing her feet on the edge of the table, she lifted, and every pore in her body seemed to explode.

Silver stars sprayed rainbows against the midnight sky of her closed eyelids. Her ears rang. She couldn't breathe, but the suffocation was exquisite; then she gasped in quick, soft gulps.

With a hoarse groan, Roark jerked and Alyss felt the liquid warmth of his seed. He stood, head lowered, fists propped on the table on either side of her. Slowly, his ragged breathing eased. He looked up, their bodies still joined, and smiled.

That was the most spectacular event she had ever experienced. She didn't know what to say, so she merely smiled in return, reaching up to touch his dimpled cheek. He closed his eyes, took her hand, and kissed it.

****

A weight lay on his groin. Warmth cupped him, then began to knead gently. One eye open, Roark looked down in the thin, early light to find Alyss on her side, studying his body intently.

It responded, firming, lifting. She looked at him and smiled. "Fascinating," she murmured in a raspy, morning voice.

"Umm. Explore all you like."

Slowly she dragged her body up his and kissed him.

Hands on her waist, he had lifted her across his hips when shouts reached their ears. A pounding on the door sounded, followed by Alain's voice.

"You're needed. Fire arrows."

****

Throughout the day, men and women worked to extinguish the burning arrows that fell to earth. Containers of water set around the keep were emptied and refilled time after time. The range of the crossbow bolts wasn't great, but damage was real.

One arrow got lucky and found the roof of the wash house. The dry thatch went up in no time, although water was passed from hand to hand and tossed up. After a few minutes, attention turned to dousing neighboring roofs in an attempt to keep those structures safe.

Roark brushed soot and ashes from his face and shoulders, impervious to his reddened hands. In spite of the loss of the building, they had been lucky. So far.

"Thank God, the stables are out of reach," he muttered to himself.

Elsewhere, injuries added up, and two bowmen died as they picked off soldiers manning the battering ram. It, too, reached its target more frequently and with greater force as the day progressed.

Midday came, went. No one thought to eat except the children, who had been moved into the great hall for protection. Martha and the younger girls were challenged to find new ways to entertain them and keep them out of the way.

Bit by bit, the attack was wearing down Chauvere's defenders. Time for an alternate approach. God knew Roark had plenty of experience at alternate approaches. He found Alain by the front guard tower and pulled him inside the lower room.

"I'm going out alone tonight to talk to our neighbor. I want you to pick six men to stand guard inside the passage." He shook his head when Alain started to speak. "Just see to it. But keep it quiet."

As Roark made his way back to the hall, he saw Alyss on the outside steps and motioned to her. When she drew close, he took her arm and moved to a spot where they could not be overheard.

"Show me the entrance to the secret passage."

She looked at him suspiciously. "Why? Hasn't Sir

Alain told you?"

"He's busy. I want you to show me. I'm making use of it tonight." He saw her take a breath, and he shook his head.

"Don't argue. We don't have time."

With a pointed look, Alyss lifted her chin. Roark could feel an answering half-smile curve his lips at the unconscious gesture of resolve.

"All right. Come with me."

She led him to a storeroom next to the kitchen and opened the door…to find containers overturned, a trapdoor in the floor open, and Rose lying in a pool of blood.

Alyss dropped to her knees. "She's breathing."

Roark knelt across from her and gently turned the maid over. "A blow to the back of the head. She was surprised, looks like."

"Take her to the solar," Alyss said. "I'll get Lady Isobel."

Before long, the still-unconscious Rose lay on the cleared work table, high enough for Lady Isobel to tend the injuries. "Not as serious as it could have been," the lady said. "Move her to my bedchamber. I'll stay with her. You're both needed outside."

Roark was relieved the girl would be all right, but a greater issue worried him. He stopped Alyss at the bottom of the stairs. "Why would the passage door be open?"

Alyss rubbed her forehead. "I know of no reason. Or why Rose would be in the storeroom. Although I fear…"

She needn't name the fear. He had it too. But where would enemy soldiers have got to if they entered the castle through the secret tunnel? He'd neither seen nor heard any evidence of intruders.

At the concern in his wife's face, Roark snaked his arm around her shoulders and hugged her close. She leaned into the embrace, sliding both arms around his waist.

"Do you think—?"

"I think I'd better inform Alain. You tell Baldwin."

Roark stalked outside to find Alain on the wall with the archers. Windom's army scurried, trying to fire the battering ram. Damnation. If they managed to wedge it against the wooden gates... Bowmen were doing their best to pick off the soldiers, but the huge log had been rolled back, almost out of range.

A new threat couldn't have come at a worse time. Roark had no spare fighters to search for intruders who might have breached the castle.

****

Alyss lost no time in climbing the wall stairs for a better look. Windom's men were nourishing the incipient flames at the log. Foolish men. The fresh-cut tree was green and would take its own sweet time to blaze.

Nowhere did she see a mounted knight that could be Lord Paxton. With a quick count, she reckoned about a score and ten soldiers—mostly men-at-arms and bowmen—shifted around outside the walls. They were readying for something.

She prayed it wasn't an attack from the inside.

Then, in the distance, a movement caught her eye. Horsemen. And behind them, men on foot. A stray beam of setting sun glinted off what looked like a pike. Men-at-arms. Windom had reinforcements.

Before she could call out to Baldwin, Windom's archers sent up a round of arrows, then another, and a third, giving Chauvere's bowmen little chance to return the attack.

Bending low, Alyss made it to the steps. Baldwin reached her before she could descend.

"My lady, you should not—"

She lifted her hand. "Reinforcements."

He ducked around to peer out. "They're coming at a run. Be careful," he added, when she stood.

"Still too far off to count." Alyss squinted. "Wait. It looks like there's something waving. Can you make it out?"

"God's bones... I'm thinkin'... It's our men!" Baldwin bellowed. "Lady Lissey, it's our—" A bolt slammed into him. With a surprised grunt, he toppled back.

Alyss knelt at his side. The arrow had pierced the old man's mail and embedded in his chest.

"Baldwin. Baldwin, old friend." Alyss eased off his helmet and brushed back gray hair, wet with perspiration.

Tired eyes half-open, he whispered, "Godfrey's brought 'em home."

Chapter Twenty-Five

By the time Alyss summoned men to get the injured Baldwin below, the returning knights had descended on Windom's forces.

"Keep the gates closed until we get a signal," she shouted to the guards. Racing down the steps, she spied the injured Ralf trying to move one of the boulders propped against a gate and pointed up behind her.

"Our men are home. Watch for a sign before you raise the portcullis and open the gates." She turned toward the keep. "I'll find Sir Roark."

****

Roark led Alain and three others to the storeroom. "We found this open and a maid unconscious. No sign of Windom soldiers, but they may be hiding."

"Waiting for a main attack outside, to take us by surprise inside," Alain said.

Roark nodded. "Gather more men. We'll search the castle for intruders."

In the hall, a breathless Alyss caught him. "Sir Baldwin took a crossbow bolt in the chest. I must get Lady Isobel. And we have help!"

"What do you mean?"

"Our men are home." She ran before explaining.

But Roark understood. The Chauvere soldiers had arrived with Sir Godfrey. A surge of relief was soon tempered by concern. Could any among the returning troop betray him? No. This was no time for doubts. The trouble from Windom was far from ended.

"You're needed outside," he said to Alain. His friend had already dashed away.

A quick hunt through the upper level of the keep failed to uncover enemy fighters. Unless they'd managed to retreat to the tunnel as he searched, all was safe. Roark allowed himself a moment of relief before heading into the bailey and facing decisions about the attacking army.

"I want to see the men who surrendered," he called to Alain. "Where have you stashed them?

"The barracks," came the reply.

"Bring all but the archers outside." Archers had wrought the damage, inflicted the injuries and deaths. He'd deal with them later. Now, he wanted to talk with the men-at-arms, most of whom were likely pulled from the ranks of servants and villagers in the neighboring holding.

True, they had attacked Chauvere, and he had every right to punish them. He must establish his right as lord, and strength demanded respect. But to kill these soldiers who were little more than neighbors would not bring him the kind of respect he wanted.

He would take a chance. Beside him, Alain stood with sword at the ready. Roark motioned to lower the weapon.

"Soldiers of Windom, you have been captured in the act of attacking a peaceful neighbor. You know the punishment. Imprisonment or death."

Murmurs came from crowd gathered to watch the proceeding, and a young village woman pushed through. Perspiration gleamed on her angry face. "Ned.

What d'ye think ye be up to, attacking us like ye did?"

One of the soldiers stepped from among the prisoners. "Hush, now, Ertha. Keep out of men's work."

"How do you know this woman?" Roark asked.

"She be the daughter of m' mum's friend. We was friendly before the trouble began. Then we talked sometimes, a few days back, when I was watchin' the place."

"You were one of the guards camped in the woods?"

"That be right, m'lord."

"And did you visit with Ertha during that time?"

Ned's face turned red once more. "That I did, m'lord."

"Did she give you shelter?"

Realizing what giving shelter to the enemy might mean for his beloved, Ned blanched. "Oh, no, m'lord. She sent me off with a cuff to m' ear."

"Don't be lyin' to milord, now, Ned." Ertha turned to Roark. "I couldn't let 'em starve out there in the rain, milord, if ye recall how bad the weather were. I give 'em food."

Roark remembered those rainy nights vividly—he had spent them with Alyss.

Ertha's eyes shifted away guiltily. "It were wrong, I know. If ye mean to lock me up, milord, I'd like to tell Pa so's he won't worry I up and disappeared."

Ned couldn't let this pass. "No, now, m'lord, don't be blamin' her, not but what she be a stubborn one. And I didn't lie to ye. She did cuff m' ear."

"Ye deserved ever bit o' it," Ertha answered. Her eyes now glittered with tears. "Just think what yer ma would say to ye and yer friends, skulking around her old home. And I told ye I'd wed ye, even if both our lords do got goosedown fer brains."

A sound suspiciously like a laugh caught up in a cough came from Alain. Roark gazed at the young couple, then at the crowd. Be damned!

Providing food to a sweetheart from another holding was one thing; when the sweetheart was a guard left by the enemy, the action took on a different light. If he allowed the maid to escape with no punishment, the people might consider him weak. His glace caught Alyss's. Her expression looked suspiciously like a plea. Or perhaps they wouldn't.

The soldier was like many of those from Windom standing before him—honest men who had no choice but to obey their lord.

However, if the girl had provided her sweetheart food while he watched the castle, she could have as well provided information. That he wouldn't tolerate. But Roark didn't think the young woman was a plotter. She'd been too quick to admit to her earlier fault.

"Ertha," Roark asked, watching her closely, "did you give Ned information about the keep?"

Her shock was honest. "Milord, no! I never would."

He believed her. He only wished he had more experience at this kind of decision. But he must trust his own instinct from working with men. He hoped it proved correct.

He raised his voice so all could hear. "I have no quarrel with those of you who were simply following orders. You had no choice but to obey commands. This night, I lay claim to Windom Castle as my right. Your lord attacked me, and he was defeated."

The king might see it differently, but Roark didn't plan to mention it to him at the moment.

"Those of you who pledge to serve me as lord will be freed. Those who choose not to, will be given escort to Nottingham Castle in two days' time."

Raised voices nearly drowned Roark's last words. "You can think about your choice for the rest of the night."

"I don't need to think on it, milord," Ned said. "I'll serve ye, if ye mean to keep the peace and give us some rest."

"God bless ye, milord!" came a cry from the onlookers.

Roark held up his hand. When the crowd quieted, he continued. "Lady Alyss will determine punishment later for the lass who provided aid to the enemy guard."

Silence met that pronouncement.

"Think seriously of your choice tonight," he said to the prisoners. He nodded to Alain, who ushered the men back into the room where they were being held and set a pair of guards outside.

Right or wrong, his decision was made. Now, he should seek out the returning soldiers, but first he wanted to see Baldwin. Bile scorched his stomach. He hated to lose such a fine old fighter.

In the hall, Lady Isobel sat beside her husband's pallet, clutching his hand. "The bolt came out easily. He opened his eyes earlier," she said, her smile watery. "I think he's sleeping now."

"Take care of him," Roark said, then realized how useless that sounded.

"I need him up and around as soon as can be," he

added, his voice suspiciously gruff, and he cleared his throat. "Tell him we can't do without him here."

Isobel's cheeks were streaked with tears. "Thank you, my lord."

He moved through the hall, then into the bailey, looking into one face after another, but he didn't recognize the newly returned Chauvere soldiers. What a perfect opportunity for intruders to blend in.

As he worked his way to the outer yard, he caught sight of Alain trotting toward him. "You've got to see this," Alain called.

Inside in knights' quarters, a pallet had been slashed open, straw flung around. Nearby, a chest was turned upside down, its contents scattered across the floor. Knife scratches marred the inside of the lid, and one side had been torn apart.

"What's missing?" Roark's voice was tight.

"Nothing that I could see. It contains but a few clothes."

"But why carve up the top and side?" He and Alain realized immediately and spoke together. "The message."

"That's all it could be," Alain confirmed. "My bed, my chest. The only ones bothered."

Roark tapped the small leather pouch safely beneath his tunic.

"How could anyone have known?" Alain asked. Roark shook his head.

"Our traitor is not only sending messages, he's receiving them." And who but the priest had such access?

****

Alyss stood in the bailey, listening to Roark's

speech to the prisoners. At first she was surprised at his decision. On second thought, she admitted it was what she would have expected of a man who knew how to lead. This was the Roark who commanded loyalty from hardened knights who followed him across England.

Her attention was drawn to Father Eudo winding his way across the cluttered ground. His long brown robe flapped against his ankles; his sandals scuffed up tiny clods of dirt.

She went to meet him, impatient to learn where he'd been.

"Father, at last. Sir Baldwin is seriously injured. He needs you." Alyss nodded toward the keep. "And Rose is in my bedchamber. Someone struck her. She is unconscious."

The priest stopped abruptly. "Your maid is wounded? Rose is hurt?" His flat voice fluttered at the edges. His face leached to pasty gray. He ran toward the hall before Alyss could say another word.

"Sir Bernard needs you now," she called to his retreating back. "Father Eudo." He didn't heed her.

A warm tingle touched her neck as Roark appeared at her side. "Seen anyone you don't recognize?" he asked tightly.

With a shake of her head, she turned. "Father Eudo is behaving oddly. When I told him Rose was hurt, he seemed almost—afraid."

Roark looked furious. "I ordered that priest held. He may be the one providing information. Who released him?" Alyss had to run to keep up as he stalked toward the hall.

The bedchamber door stood open, and they could see the priest hovering at Rose's side. His hand gently brushed the hair from her forehead, avoiding the area where she'd been hit.

He gave no sign he heard them enter, but he said, "There was no reason for this. She wasn't a danger to anyone."

Alyss looked a question at Roark, who merely watched the priest. "Did you—"

A shuddering thud reverberated and a handful of men poured into the chamber through the open door.

"Get Alain." Roark shoved Alyss toward the corridor. The squeal of swords played a discordant song that followed her.

The clatter of fighting nearly obscured her shouts for help, but they were heard. The response was instantaneous. Boots thudded up the steps. Alyss ducked into the solar, reached beneath the table for the chest, and pulled it to her.

Roark was a warrior, but there were only so many men even he could handle at once. She intended to do her part. It was, after all, what Baldwin and Godfrey had trained her for this past year and more,

Inside the container lay a thin bundle. She tore off the rough cloth wrapped around her small sword. No room to use it in the crowded chamber. Grasping the hilt of her father's dagger that lay beside it, she raced back to the bedchamber.

The half-dozen invaders had formed a semi-circle to advance on Roark. When Alyss dashed through the door, an enemy swordsman halted his blow to gape at her. Her dagger caught him in the upper leg, and he fell.

One down. She stepped over that body and a second of Roark's victims so the doorway would be cleared for his men, who surged inside. Blocking a blow, Alyss turned on her toes to bring her blade across, a maneuver her lighter weight and smaller weapon made easy.

The next few seconds were a blur of clashing metal, spurting blood, grunts, and cries. The chamber became so full, it was difficult to keep track of who was who.

Then it was over. The enemy fighters were down. Alyss gasped and lowered her dagger. From the corner of her eye, she saw a wounded knight rise to his knees, his sword aimed at Roark's back. With a leap she was before him. A sharp pain in her side drew her eyes downward. Oh. The tip of a sword thrust through her gown into her flesh. In an instant, Roark loomed beside her, and the other man fell without a word.

Good. The pain was gone. No harm. Roark said something that she couldn't quite make out over the high whine in her ears. Perhaps she would sit. Just for a moment.

****

Roark caught Alyss as she collapsed, surprised she'd given way to shock. Then he felt the wetness on her side and pulled away his hand. It was sticky with blood. His roar could be heard in the bailey.

Chapter Twenty-Six

Roark lifted Alyss onto the bed. She was pale and still, and for the first time in his life, he felt real fear. "Get Lady Isobel." The words were a whisper.

Nicholas ran to carry out the order, while Alain and Bernard sifted through the downed soldiers. Two were dead, the other four wounded, and Alain set men to guard them.

Part of Roark's mind grasped all that, but his focus centered on Alyss. Tenderly, he turned her to the side where he eased red-soaked cloth from around the gash, blotting the blood with the hem of her skirt. The ugly wound looked deep.

He needed something to staunch the flow. The bolster. He stripped the linen covering off the pillow, folded it into a pad, and pressed it against the slash. He wanted to rant, to shout at her, to shake her for putting herself in danger yet again. What possessed his wife to dash into the midst of a sword fight carrying only a dagger? Whoever gave her that miniature weapon would answer to him.

Why did she lie so still? He'd never seen her so pale. She wouldn't dare leave him, now that he'd found her. His throat tightened. If she would just open her eyes, scold him, he'd count himself the luckiest of men.

"Alain, get Isobel up here," he roared, his heart throbbing with dread.

"She's on the way," Alain assured him.

Looking around, Roark eyed the prisoners. "Lock them in the...why in Satan's own Hades is there no dungeon in this place? Get them out of my sight before I throw them out the window."

Bernard jumped to obey.

Alain picked up Rose from where she lay beside Alyss. "We'll take the maid below, with the others. Lady Alyss needs room." Without a backward glance, Father Eudo, who'd cowered in a corner, followed.

Alone with Alyss, Roark brushed her hair from her face, tucked that damned stray strand behind her ear.

His lips on her forehead, he whispered, "Don't you dare die on me. I traveled hundreds of miles and all my life to find you, and I don't intend to lose you. I love you."

He drew back. Had he really said that? Was it true? Did he love her? Did he even know the meaning of the word? Right now, he only knew the twisting pain in his chest was not from a sword wound.

Lady Isobel rushed in, Martha the cook right behind carrying a basin of water and cloths. In seconds, he had been moved aside, the two women vowing to care for her well. He wanted to remain, but he knew he had to see to the new prisoners. Lord Paxton hadn't been among the group that burst through the passage. *Which means that Devil's spawn is still on the loose.*

Reluctantly consigning Alyss to the women's care, Roark stalked downstairs, each step feeding his determination to find the man and kill him, prince's favorite or no.

Less than an hour later, a dirty, battered knight, hands and feet bound, stood in the middle of the room.

He wore a look mighty close to a smirk. Roark had regained some of his temper, so refrained from knocking the expression into the man's bearded chin. He knew from another prisoner that Paxton was gone. He had ridden away when Chauvere's reinforcements arrived.

The knight in front of him, the leader of the fighters who barged into the bedchamber, had been saved for last to question. He had yet to open his mouth.

"Your commander left you to fight a losing battle while he escaped." Disdain oozed from Roark's voice. "What kind of man would do that?"

The other's jaw hardened, but still he didn't speak. "Sir Alain, what do you call a leader who deserts his men?"

Alain blew a derogatory sound from between his lips. "A coward, my lord."

That did it. "Hah. That's all you know about it," the knight said, his voice a swagger. "Lord Paxton didn't run. You'll find that out soon enough."

Roark and Alain exchanged a glance. As he paced around the prisoner, a mercenary like the others who had invaded the castle, Roark appeared to consider the answer.

"So your brave commander gave you the honor of attacking from inside and facing certain capture while he rode away untouched? Or did you badly misjudge what you would find here?"

Rounding on the bound knight, he stared into the man's eyes. "What will he do when he finds you failed?"

A look of discomfort passed over the prisoner's

face.

Roark changed tactics. "What's your name?"

No answer. Alain spoke. "One of the others called him Sir Claude."

Roark raised an eyebrow. "So, Sir Claude. You say your master didn't run from the fight. Then where did he go and why?"

The smirk returned. Cocking his head, the man replied, "You'll find out soon enough. When Lord Paxton gets back, you'll be leaving—one way or another."

A flick of the hand had Alain dragging the prisoner out the door.

"Wait." Roark walked to Sir Claude. "Why did you try to kill the maid, Rose?"

A look of disgust replaced the one of gloating. "What did she expect? Needed to keep her nose out of men's business. Just like the Lady Bitch I stopped earlier. A weak leader you are, letting a woman fight."

In an instant Sir Claude lay on the floor, howling as he cupped his smashed and bleeding nose. Roark stood over him, both fists clutched. Between clenched teeth he gritted, "Get the bastard out before I find my sword."

For the first time he could remember, he *wanted* to kill someone. How dare that rabble say a word against his darling girl. Struggling to regain control, he sat at a wobbly table in the guard chamber where the interrogations were being conducted. Another secure spot had been found for the remaining five mercenaries, all of whom had traveled with Lord Paxton from France. They would be dispatched to Nottingham. Sir Claude, however, would remain a guest here indefinitely.

None of the other attackers had information, although one said he'd heard Lord Paxton tell his squire to prepare for Nottingham.

Roark called for the smith and ordered chains attached to the walls in a storage room in the guard tower. There would be plenty of soldiers to keep watch, now the others had returned.

As he made his way back to the hall to check on Alyss, he passed several villagers leaving with their belongings. Tomorrow he'd visit to make sure they had what they needed. And tomorrow, repairs would get underway. But not tonight. Tonight, the people would celebrate victory and the return of their men. In spite of that, the walls were well supplied with guards. He wasn't chancing a surprise.

Alyss slept, Martha sitting nearby. "It wasn't so bad as it looked with all the blood." She said nodded toward the still figure. "Lady Isobel stitched the hole and give her something to drink. Now you're here, I'd best see to the kitchen."

Quiet settled around Roark; his shoulders slumped. His very bones ached as he dropped to the stool beside his wife. He should be lying there in her place. Her head was turned toward him. Absently, he traced his fingers across her forehead, around her ear. Her hair was smoothed away from her face; a sad smile tugged at his lips as he liberated a golden brown strand and draped it across her cheek in its usual flyaway place.

How had she come to mean so much to him in such a few short days? He'd never thought to feel this way about any woman, certainly not a lady. As the son of a freeman, he could not aspire to such heights. Even after achieving knighthood against all odds, he had been landless. He never had the resources to wed, and heiresses were seldom awarded to a man with no land or political connections.

In his dark nights of introspection, he had dreamed of marriage. Those dreams of a perfect future, of course, included a faceless but beautiful creature who would provide a comfortable keep, healthy sons, and never interfere with him.

Now he had a future brighter than any he had dared imagine. And a wife who was nothing like that compliant, agreeable, boring dream creature he must protect.

This wife defended him. She scaled castle walls, scolded, wielded daggers, took deadly injuries meant for him. She could stir him as no lover ever had simply by lying in the same bed or by smiling down the table during mealtime. He loved her touch, the light strokes that tingled across his skin until his body ached.

An unexpected warmth in his chest had Roark straightening. Moisture collected in the corners of his eyes. He sucked in a breath, brushed back the strand of hair from her face, and touched his lips to her warm cheek, to her blue-veined eyelids with their long, thick lashes. How had he ever thought her plain?

She was unlike any other woman he'd known, and despite his lack of fortune he'd known plenty. They seemed drawn to his rough looks, though he couldn't understand why, with his scarred face and prominent nose. Some ladies flocked to him as a tournament champion, enthralled at the idea of power. One daughter of a house where his troop once quartered slipped into his bed, whispering she'd heard he knew how to pleasure his partners. He hadn't disappointed her.

None of those lusty encounters matched the passionate nights he had made love with the woman lying motionless before him. Love? Was that this feeling of restlessness? Was love wanting to shake his woman? To turn her over his lap and swat her soft, shapely bottom? To raise her skirts and caress the smooth, rounded contours? To kiss her and laugh with her and always wake beside her? Was love never wanting to let her go?

Shifting on the stool, Roark adjusted himself, then realized where his thoughts had led. He grunted in disgust. His wife had nearly been killed because of him, and all he could do was lust for her. What kind of man was he?

Had he really said he loved her in a moment of weakness earlier? Perhaps she hadn't heard. His hand reached to check the bandage on her side, then dropped. He'd do better to leave her alone and let her heal without his constant presence. Yes, that's what he'd do.

Tomorrow morning, he would ride to Windom and claim it while Paxton was gone. By God, it was rightfully his, anyway. The fool had attacked Roark, then deserted his own men to certain capture. So what if the law didn't favor Roark? The king had other things on his mind right now. Once Roark was in possession of the castle, well, he'd face that battle when it came. He hadn't succeeded thus far by ignoring unexpected opportunity.

But Roark didn't leave the next morning. He couldn't bring himself to go while Alyss lay unconscious, so he helped with repairs to the wall and directed rebuilding. He consulted with villagers who'd begun to get the fields in shape again for planting.

Late on the second evening, Alyss opened her eyes, squeezed his hand that held hers, and asked in a whisper, "Shouldn't you be securing Windom?"

Huffing a laugh, he kissed her gently. His fierce wife would be fine. Warmth washed through him as she brought his fingers to her mouth.

Shortly after dawn the next day, Roark saw the well-guarded prisoners off to the sheriff at Nottingham. Then he, Bernard, Rance and ten soldiers headed west, leaving Bernard in charge.

****

How she hated inactivity. Walking slowly across the hall to check on Baldwin, Alyss longed to be at work in the solar, or outside, anywhere but here, doing nothing. Isobel and Bernard insisted she continue to rest, but this morning she simply descended the stairway. Very slowly and with pauses along the way. Her side was a little tight where the stitches marched, but dizziness no longer sent her staggering to a bench.

Roark had been gone for three days. There had been no word from him, and she prayed he had not found trouble at Windom. Guards who escorted the prisoners returned from Nottingham with a grim tale. The castle had refused to surrender, was under siege, and King Richard was expected any day. Unable to leave the captured fighters at the castle, the guards had turned them over to one of the captains, compliments of the Lord of Chauvere.

Baldwin's injuries were not healing as they ought, and Alyss worried. He had not been well enough to move to his own cottage; here, everyone could keep an eye on him.

Rose had recovered from what had turned out to be only a blow to the head. She told Alyss she couldn't remember anything, even what had drawn her from the hall to the passage.

Father Eudo checked on the maid often. The priest was hurrying from the kitchen with a basket when Alyss hailed him.

"I want to send a message to Lady Evie. Will you take it tomorrow after mass?"

"You must not worry about Lady Evelynn, my lady," Father Eudo said. "The convent is protected; no word could have reached it about the battles here. But now I must attend to your maid, Rose. She needs a good strong broth to gain strength."

He was right. Her sister was safe and would not have heard of the recent trouble here.

A commotion at the door drew her attention. It was Wat, one of the guards charged with delivering the prisoners. Alyss started toward him but the pull in her side slowed her step.

"Did something go wrong?" she asked.

"I must speak with ye, my lady," Wat said, his voice low. "Trouble may be comin'."

"What has occurred?

Wat cleared his throat. "That Lord Paxton. He's in Nottingham and tellin' ever'one ye were forced to marry and yer bein' held agin' yer will."

"He knows better."

"Well, my lady, it makes a good story with none there to dispute it. We said 'tweren't true, but most folks didn't listen."

Alyss drew in a breath. Surely no one would believe him. She probably should prepare for a trip to

Nottingham, but at the moment her head throbbed, and she couldn't think clearly. If only Roark were here.

Chapter Twenty-Seven

When Roark arrived two days later, Alyss met him at the gate. Her hands were clasped at her waist, but she couldn't contain her smile of welcome. Not because she'd missed him, not at all. She'd simply worried about the conditions he'd find at Windom. Oh, very well. She was happy to see him...home.

He dismounted wearily and pulled her to him. "You are well?" he murmured, his lips brushing her temple.

She slid her arms around his waist, reveling in a sense of comfort. "I am very well, now you are home."

"Sir Baldwin?"

"Better today. Are things settled at Windom?"

He nodded. "I left Bernard there with a few of the men. I'll send more tomorrow. They'll need supplies."

Alyss longed to stroke away the lines of exhaustion at each side of his mouth. The scar that slashed through his brow stood out in relief, and his cheeks seemed leaner. He needed rest—she would spare him the message from Nottingham for now.

The night candle had burned down two marks before he stumbled into the bedchamber and dropped beside her, his hair still damp. A soft groan issued from his lips as he stretched out and patted around until he found her hand. Grasping it, he murmured something unintelligible and promptly fell asleep.

Alyss eased her arm onto his chest. As the heat of his body enveloped her, apprehension of the past few days trickled away. His musky, spicy scent tingled through her and she sighed. She had missed this. She had missed *him*.

In the days of his absence, an old worry revived, only to be put to rest. For good, she told herself. None of the returning soldiers knew him. They recognized his name. Sir Roark was a formidable fighter and Cantleigh's former captain. Because of that, and because of Sir Godfrey's stories, they accepted the news that their lady had wed him. Truthfully, most seemed relieved to have a strong lord in control.

Why would soldiers know their commander's friends, Baldwin asked, and did it make a difference? What mattered was the way Roark behaved. He treated the servants, villagers, and castle garrison with consideration and fairness, all the while maintaining firmness and confidence. Her father would have approved. So did she.

The following morning, Alyss dressed in silence, and when Roark appeared in the hall, she'd begun arranging supplies for Windom. Shortly before the last meal of the day, the tower guard reported a lone rider approaching.

"Another visitor. We've seen more strangers this past fortnight than we did all last winter," Isobel muttered as she carried the word to Baldwin.

****

After verifying the horseman traveled alone, Roark returned to the hall. He recognized a royal messenger when the man walked through the door, flanked by Nicholas and Alain. With an oblique glance at Alyss,

Roark took a deep breath and shook off an unfamiliar sinking sensation. The time had come at last. Spurs clanking in the suddenly quiet hall, the messenger came forward holding a parchment from which dangled the king's seal. "Sir Roark of Stoddard?"

Roark nodded.

"King Richard directed me to deliver this message into your hand."

While Alyss called for food and drink, Roark made a pretense of reading. Eyebrow lifted in what he hoped was disinterest, he handed it to her. "I believe you might like to see this for yourself, my lady. And read it aloud for all to hear."

Alyss opened the sheet. "This is a summons 'to answer in the matter of marriage to Lady Alyss of Chauvere, a ward of the court.' We are both to appear immediately."

Gulping his ale, the messenger added, "I am to accompany you to Nottingham."

"The king has arrived?" Roark asked. "Was there a battle?"

A small smile flitted across the other man's stubbled face. "No need. After a bit of negotiation, the castle surrendered. The king has called up the Great Council to discuss what to do with the rebels."

Alyss appeared calm. She smiled brightly and directed him to the table. "If you have need of anything just ask, but now I must pack. It's been years since I visited at court. I assume there are many people who have gathered to be with our king?"

Roark jerked his head to Alain, and the two went through the kitchen, then outside. The odor of horses wafted on the westerly breeze. Roark gazed toward the stables where two lads cleaned stalls. "Do you think Richard still believes Lord Martin defended him?"

Alain shrugged.

"Bernard says not. And the king can't prove Sir Henry didn't give his sister over to my care. He won't deny the dying wish of one of his favorite knights."

A dog yapped in the distance. Faint voices of a man and woman arguing lifted over it. Finally Alain said, "Just remember what you've said before. The king needs money. Be careful."

"Don't worry. I've worked too hard to get this castle. No one will keep me from holding it. Not even the king."

"Lady Alyss?"

"She's my wife. No one will take her from me." Not until later did Roark realize that wasn't the question Alain asked.

****

The entourage for Nottingham left at dawn. For a distance Alyss rode in the cart Roark insisted she share with Rose, who would not be left behind.

"Don't go without me, milady," the maid had pleaded. "I'm well and I can serve ye. What will ye do without me?"

Alyss gave in with Isobel's assurance that the girl had recovered.

Late into the first day, Alyss deserted the hard, bumpy box on wheels. Roark didn't deny her the escape after she pointed out that riding her mare, Berry, could hardly be harder on her healing injury than bouncing around in the cart. He conceded after a short grumble.

She and Roark were never alone, and she found herself oddly quiet. An unusual sense of expectancy had troubled her since the night before; rather than anticipation, the sensation carried an air of foreboding. But whether the worry was for herself or her husband, she didn't know.

Although she spoke little to him, she was aware of his every movement. She knew when he galloped off to scout ahead, and she knew when he returned, whether or not she saw him. If she unexpectedly caught sight of him, her stomach lurched. When they rode together, she often had an overwhelming urge to reach out, touch his arm or his sword-callused hand.

The group made steady time in the unusual warmth of the March day. As the sun reached a point directly overhead, Alyss pulled her mare alongside Roark's black gelding.

"There's a cluster of trees ahead," she said, raising her voice to be heard above the clop of hooves, the creak of leather, and jangle of reins. "A good place to stop for nooning." She swiped at a drop of perspiration trickling down her cheek.

Roark nodded and called, "We'll break here."

Alyss smiled. "Thank you." Their gazes held, and she could see green and gold prisms glowing in his hazel eyes. The corner of his mouth finally quirked up. The breathlessness that seized her made her duck her head and touch her heels to the horse.

Reaching the cart, she pointed the driver toward the copse. Some coolness and rest would do them all good. Surely a stream ran near all those rich, green trees. Resisting the natural urge to gallop ahead, Alyss resigned herself to keeping the horse at a sedate trot.

****

Across the clearing where the camp had been set,

245

Alyss laughed with Ralf and James. The sound of her voice wrapped around Roark like a soft cloak. He draped his arms on his raised knees, a twig swinging from two fingers. Her attitude puzzled him. After he allowed her to ride, she became as reserved as when he'd arrived weeks earlier. And though he often felt her gaze on him, she seldom met his eyes.

After their nights together, he'd been certain they'd attained an understanding.

He switched the grass beside him with the twig. "Where are the rules to dealing with women? In a tournament, knights battle, winners collect ransom, and they walk away knowing the rules have been satisfied. That's simple." Roark scowled. "All was fine last night. Today, she's become as distant as a stranger again."

"I noticed. Any idea what's troubling her?"

Roark shook his head.

"The king might remark on the coolness between you."

"It's likely." Roark tossed the thin stick to the side. "Still, at court no one expects a husband and wife to show affection. All we must do is convince Richard that I fulfilled a vow made to her brother before he died. She wasn't a royal ward."

Alain pursed his lips. "But a beautiful rich lady satisfied in her marriage is a different creature from a beautiful rich lady who wants freedom to marry another. Isn't she?"

Roark didn't answer.

"You don't need to pretend a great love. But the two of you might at least look like you tolerate each other. Of course"—he stretched out his legs, crossed his ankles nonchalantly—"I've never been to court. You have. I'm probably wrong in thinking a dozen men will want to claim an heiress like Lady Alyss. Especially if they think she's unprotected by a husband who doesn't give a damn. Doesn't the king have knights that he owes? Ones he could award the lady to if he set aside your marriage?"

His friend had a point. Roark should make an effort to discover what was wrong. When the journey resumed sometime later, a hot, dusty—but determined—Roark helped Alyss into her saddle and ordered her to stay next to him. Damnation. He should have asked, not commanded. Roark wondered if he'd ever learn.

Then she turned to him, a smile teasing her lips and her brows raised.

"That is, ride next to me if you care to, for your safety," he ventured.

The sparkle in her eyes told him he'd been troubled over nothing earlier. He straightened his shoulders. Suddenly, facing the king seemed much less daunting.

****

The following day, travelers became more numerous the closer to Nottingham the party drew, and thoughts of court crowded Alyss's mind. Her last visit had been years before, but she doubted anything had changed. What would her husband make of that slick den of vipers? She peered at Roark. He sat easily in the saddle, but there was no doubt he was a man who commanded. He was a warrior. Determined. A man who got what he wanted. And he was handsome, in a rough, dangerous way. The kind of man who drew women.

Had he ever been to court? As if he read her mind,

he said, "You've been among these people before." It was a statement, not a question.

"Yes," she said. "Have you?"

He nodded, his gaze on the countryside. "A few times with Lord Martin."

"Did you have a woman there?" Alyss gasped. Where on earth had that question come from?

"You must not ask those things." His voice was firm and he frowned, but she had the oddest feeling he was amused. "That's not proper for a wife."

She realized, again, that she knew next to nothing about him. "Have you been married before?"

"Of course not. And ladies do not discuss their husbands' women."

"So you did have one there."

Roark looked uncomfortable. "No."

"I should tell you," Alyss said conversationally, "no matter the reason, we are wed. I expect you to be faithful." She might entertain an occasional doubt about him, but he'd best not stray. He was hers.

She cut a glance his way. Rather than angry, she could vow, he looked pleased.

About mid-afternoon, encampments around Nottingham appeared. Apart from the guards who passed them through, their arrival at the castle went unnoticed. Finally, a few servants scurried up to assist. One assigned Roark and Alyss a bedchamber. After their belongings were unloaded, Alain took the other knights and men-at-arms to find quarters. James, an old hand at the process as Sir Henry's former page, accompanied them importantly while explaining the "rules" of "court behavior."

Alyss looked around, dismayed at their tiny square

room. It bore slight resemblance to the comfortable chamber she occupied on her last visit with the royal family, when Richard received the crown. At least the bed was large enough—in truth, it dominated the space. Beside her Roark stood, hands on hips, eyes narrowed.

"I think so many lords are here, this is best we can expect," she said.

His lips quirked, and he turned away from the bed. "You don't want to know what I think." He started for the door.

"You'll be careful?"

He turned and lifted the undamaged eyebrow. "The only danger is if I don't find the garderobe soon."

She snorted with surprised laughter at his unexpected humor, then inhaled deeply. Her shoulders eased. She hadn't realized how tightly she'd been strung. The sense of foreboding had lessened, so perhaps she'd just been nervous about the outcome of the trip. Now began the wait to see King Richard. Depending on his mood, he could summon them before the evening meal or a week from now.

The call didn't come that afternoon. It was just as well, because Roark had not returned by the time Alyss prepared for the meal. Perhaps he was seeing to the men. More likely, he had tracked down acquaintances. Rose helped her unpack then don a gown left over from her last visit to court. No doubt it was out of fashion, but she didn't care. It was one of her favorites. An admirer once said the deep blue brought out golden highlights in her hair and warmed the faint glow of her skin.

Smoothing the skirt, Alyss smiled gently. "I wore this to King Richard's coronation."

"Ye look beautiful, milady," Rose said. "Ye look so…"

"'Old' is the word you're searching for," Alyss said with a chuckle.

"She's right. You *are* beautiful." The deep voice filled the small chamber and her stomach dipped. She whirled to see Roark leaning against the side of the door, his hair in disarray.

"Ah, I am not." Alyss wished he would not flatter her. She knew her face was ordinary.

His dark brow lifted. "Must you always contradict me? Wives have been beaten for arguing with husbands. You do know that, don't you, beautiful lady? The church requires a husband to control his wife. For your own sake, the good priests say."

Poised for a sharp retort, she noticed the teasing light in his eyes and relaxed. He'd been drinking. Perhaps he had already found some friends.

"You'd best hurry to change. A page will be here soon to direct us to the hall."

"Will you help me, then, wife?" He reached for the hem of his tunic as Rose, uttering a squeak, ran from the room.

So he could be playful, as well as charming. That could be dangerous. Alyss caught herself before she smiled and handed him a fresh tunic. When he reached for it, she gasped. His knuckles were bloodied.

"What happened?" She grasped his hands and pushed him to sit on the edge of the bed.

Releasing her, he ran his fingers through his disordered hair. "Someone hit me in the head as I returned from the stables. He didn't land a solid blow, or it might have knocked me senseless."

Alyss's breathy groan interrupted him.

"I'm fine. Don't worry." Roark caught her hand. "While I was down, whoever it was took a knife to the leather around my neck. James heard the noise and shouted, but I got hold of the packet before the man ran. All he got was the cord."

Alyss's face tightened. "That knife could have found your throat." She shook her head against a buzzing in her ears.

"It could have found my back, first. Sit. You look pale as snow." With one arm around her waist, he pulled her to sit beside him.

She struggled free. "I'm fine. But you..." The thought of what might have happened to him threatened to make her retch.

"Whoever it is doesn't want me dead. He just wants the message."

Catching her breath, Alyss fought for her usual calmness. Blast the man. Since he had popped into her life, she'd lost her calm all too frequently.

She nodded. "No doubt a dead lord would raise too many questions."

"I'm not a lord," Roark reminded her. "But I think you're right about the problems my death would raise right now."

"What is this message you're protecting? It can't be worth your life."

He pulled the parchment from the leather packet. "This was found on Lord Martin's body."

Alyss's brows drew together as she reached for it. She recognized it as the one he'd been reading days earlier. "What does it say?"

Clasping her soft hand in his scarred fist, he smiled

grimly. "I don't know."

"May I read it?"

He handed over the message.

She read it quickly then shook her head. "It looks like a promise to pay for delivery of one stray donkey. There are letters and numbers across the bottom: '3 M 3 T.'"

Alyss looked up. "No signature. It makes no sense."

Frowning, she reread the note. "Why would anyone keep a message about a lost donkey? Are you certain this is the same one he carried? Could someone have switched the contents of the packet? Tell me what happened."

Grimly, Roark recounted finding it after the battle and the lengths he'd gone to protect it since then. "Before Alain's quarters were searched, I took it, and the bag hasn't been out of my sight since. You're the only other one to see the parchment."

Spreading it out, she read the words again. "A stray donkey. What would a donkey mean? An ass?"

Her gaze flicked to Roark. He had a wicked light in his eyes. "I've heard the king's brother has a grim humor," he said. "Could it be? What are those numbers? 3 M, 3 T."

She turned the puzzle over in her mind. "That doesn't stand for any coin I know. Three men? Three days? M could stand for Monday. It could stand for matins. Three matins, three Mondays?"

Roark stilled. "Three days. M—not matins, Mainz. Three Mainz. We were attacked three days out of Mainz. What's the next? T—Time? Terce! The ambush was before midday."

Roark fisted and unfisted his hands as he paced. Alyss could feel the leashed energy surrounding him.

"You took this from Lord Martin's body?" She gasped, at last realizing the import of his words. "But you said he was guarding the king, that he died defending the king. Why would your lord have a message predicting the attack if he were loyal?"

"That is the question Alain and I have asked these last weeks."

"He was a traitor! Did you know?"

He swung around. "Never! Not until that day. I swore loyalty to the king when I was knighted. I would never betray England." His face was dark as his gaze caught hers.

"But you also swore to your lord."

With a growl, he swung away, and Alyss could feel his anguish. Her words tormented him. But why…and then she realized. "You were forced to choose between two vows, two loyalties."

"I've told you enough." He faced her again and reached for the parchment.

She whipped it away, holding up her other hand. "Who would want it?"

"The one who wrote it." Hands propped on hips, Roark looked at the low ceiling and huffed out a breath.

"This note has no name to it. It could prove treason. As long as you carry it, you're in danger."

He shook his head at her and crossed his arms. "There is no other place."

"Then," she smiled, "we'll give them something else."

"What?"

"A different message. We'll write another note to

replace this one. You can leave the packet where it will be found—not around your neck, mind you—and the problem is solved. The author of this one"—she waved the original—"can't complain or he'll admit he's to blame." Alyss tamped down excitement as her mind laid out the plan.

Roark grabbed her in a hug, then set her away from him, an expression of wonder on his face. He winked. "You're a deceitful wench, wife."

Chapter Twenty-Eight

At her husband's teasing compliment, Alyss pressed her arms to her sides and smiled, as giddy as that girl she hadn't been in years. "It will work. Oh. I have no parchment nor ink." She started toward the door, but Roark stopped her.

"I'll send James and say we want to send word home."

He reached for the door, reminding her of his raw knuckles. She went to the small table beside her chest where a pitcher and basin stood.

When he returned with the writing supplies, she advanced on him, holding a dampened cloth. "Your hand."

She grabbed it before he realized her intent and dabbed at the scrapes. With a noisy sigh, she turned his head and ran her hand up the back of it. He winced as her fingers nudged the knot the blow had raised.

A void opened in her stomach, and she choked. "You've blood in your hair. Let me wash it out."

****

Roark pulled away, plucked the cloth from her grasp, and tossed it toward the table. "I'm fine."

He damned well wouldn't be if she didn't stop touching him. The bump on his head wasn't even a discomfort, and his knuckles had fared worse just scraping against his own mail.

255

What really bothered him was the caress of her breath against his face, the stroke of her fingertips against his scalp. He considered if his wife was willing to minister to the real needs he felt. Likely not with the evening meal so near.

Pity she'd noticed the scrapes. He hadn't intended to say anything about the attack, hadn't wanted to alarm her. But looking at Alyss now, he didn't face the kind of alarm he had anticipated.

What he saw was resolve. He took up the damp cloth. "Let me finish while you compose your message."

She moved the pitcher and water to the floor and bent over the table. The scratch of her writing filled the small chamber while he cleaned the blood from his hair and hands.

When she finished, he reached for the missive. "I'll keep this until I decide where to place it."

"I don't want you putting yourself in danger any longer." Alyss stood with arms crossed, the folded parchment dangling from her fingers.

"Not for long. Now, what did you write?"

She opened it. "My darling. I have been sleepless these past nights, looking toward the time I am in your arms again. Come to me when you can."

He looked at her incredulously. "That's a love note."

She smiled. "Yes. What a romantic man, your lord, to carry his wife's parting words close to his heart."

A short laugh greeted her words. "You can lay odds it wouldn't have been from his wife."

The two letters were exchanged. Alyss took the original, turned her back to Roark, and lifted her skirt.

"I'll just keep this in my pocket," she explained over her shoulder. "A lady should have a hiding place on her person."

She swung around, patting her side where the skirt of the gown covered the pocket tied over her smock. "There. No one will know I'm wearing it."

He didn't like involving her in the danger, but when he said so, she laughed. "What risk? No one will be running hands down my body."

Taking her in his arms, he proved her wrong. "Just your husband," he whispered.

As she lifted her head for a kiss, a scratch sounded at the door. She smiled. "Time to eat."

Soon, Alyss stood close to Roark at the entrance to the hall and surveyed the crowded tables. The page had informed them the king would not be dining with everyone tonight. Some important information required his attention, the youth said confidentially. Before he left, he looked up at Roark, wide-eyed.

"Sir? My brother fought you in a tournament last year," he said in awe. "He said you were faster 'n the runs." He paused, mouth open, when he realized what he said.

Roark's laugh boomed across the hall, and the boy flushed red. Crimson tinged even his ears as he turned and raced toward the kitchens.

The laugh caught the attention of a few of the diners. One man rose, came toward them, and grabbed Roark's hand.

"God's blood, man. Back from the dead, are you?"

Roark withstood the friendly pounding on his back for a moment, then smiled.

Alyss felt her stomach flutter at the sight of his

dimple. Would she ever grow used to it?

A change came over his face when he smiled. He glowed with energy.

The conversation washed over her as the man, Sir Something or other, led the way to his table. They were scarcely seated when the knight said to Roark, "I heard your lord and many of his men were all killed defending the king. Tell us the story. How did you survive?"

****

Food appeared in front of them; a page poured wine. Roark sipped it and busied himself with the contents of the trencher while he considered his friend's words.

Sir Martin, a hero for defending the king? So the story is still about? If that was the explanation circulating, he must be careful how he answered. Roark chose to postpone a reply.

"I'll gladly tell you the tale. But tomorrow. Tonight, we've just arrived, and my wife is weary."

The word 'wife' popped from mouth to mouth and the attention turned to Alyss. When Roark introduced her, the conversation quieted, and a few of the couples exchanged glances. Although politeness required they all continue dining, every one of the group hung on the words as the knight who had hailed Roark said, "So this is the Lady of Chauvere, and you're the rascal of a mercenary who has stolen the heiress from the hands of Prince John's choice.

"Man, you've been the topic of conversation for days, although we didn't know it was you. More than a few bets ride on the outcome of the mystery man's audience with the king. Now that the mystery is solved,

I might wager a few coins, myself."

Glancing at Alyss, Roark saw her pale face was lowered. When she raised her head and met his gaze, light glittered in her eyes, and he was warned. He may have known her for a few sennights only, but *that* look he was well acquainted with. It meant trouble

Lifting her chin higher, she opened her mouth. Before she could utter a word, Roark grabbed her by the waist and hugged her.

"No stealing here," he said, then kissed her quickly. Pink flushed her cheeks as she tried to pull away. Roark held her tighter. Chuckles and titters sounded down the benches as he winked at his fellows.

One of the women leaned forward with a friendly smile. "I'm Lady Gwen, Sir Orlo's wife, if he'd but introduce us. But then, he's a man. Yours is a story we would all like to hear. You must join us in the ladies' solar tomorrow."

Lady Gwen looked at the garrulous man at her side. "I believe a hunt is planned for the men?" He nodded, and she turned to Alyss again. "Then we ladies must entertain ourselves." Roark was glad when Alyss smiled and inclined her head in agreement.

****

The invitation from the ladies surprised Alyss. Their friendly overture seemed sincere, although clearly they hoped to share gossip of her recent wedding to this friend of their husbands'.

Still fighting embarrassment from Roark's quick kiss, Alyss glanced away—and stilled. There, three tables ahead, his wheat-gold beard trimmed closely, his moustache curling gently beneath his thin nose, sat Gareth, the man she had once thought to marry.

A fragile-looking lady clung to his arm while he fed her a bite of meat. She looked at him adoringly. His wife, Lady Lucinda, undoubtedly. In the years since their broken betrothal, Alyss had not seen Gareth, and the pain of his betrayal had faded. Yet she sometimes wondered what she'd do if she saw him again.

She watched the couple dispassionately and realized she felt…nothing. Gareth looked so young, even with his beard, which as a fifteen-year-old she had once found dashing. Not at all like the scarred and battle-hardened man at Alyss's side. Her husband.

The word revolved in her mind. Husband. Looking again at Gareth, she couldn't imagine him in that role. How would he have handled Lord Paxton? How would he have handled her in bed? Her face burned, and she shook her head. What a foolish child she had been to mourn his loss for so long. Was it possible to thank God for ignoring her fervent, youthful, prayers?

****

Roark sensed the moment Alyss spotted someone she knew. Tension radiated from her, although she did not move. He scanned the diners but didn't see anyone remarkable, unless… His eyes returned to a couple seated at the end of a table in front of them. A blond man and a black-haired lady. Somehow Roark knew they were the source of his wife's anxiety.

Just as surely, Roark knew this was the man who jilted Alyss. Too pretty, with his oily beard and moustache and red- and blue-trimmed green tunic. Weak. He could never have handled the spirited, strong-minded woman at Roark's side. She would lead him around by that silly hair on his chin. Alyss should consider herself lucky she wasn't wasted on the posturing peacock.

Conversation at their table involved him again, and by the time the meal was over, musicians were tuning their instruments. The evening was early by court standards, but Roark was tired. Leaning to Alyss, he asked if she would like to retire. She nodded.

Arriving at their tiny chamber in silence, he paused. If Alyss were upset, Roark couldn't detect it, but he had learned his wife was adept at concealing her feelings.

He couldn't resist saying, "That was the man you were to marry."

Alyss looked at her hands, then lifted her chin and met his eyes. She knew exactly whom he meant.

"Yes. Their family had the manor north of Chauvere. Our families visited often. It was always understood he and I would marry. Our parents were friends until Gareth's father died and his mother remarried. Then…Gareth wed elsewhere."

"You would have been miserable living with him."

She smiled. "I'm not miserable living with you?"

He swept her into his arms and deposited her on the bed, coming down beside her. "You are not."

The king did not send for them the following day. Roark went hunting with his friends, and Alyss joined the ladies in the solar. Nervous about the meeting, she found they were eager to include her in their gossip and, to her surprise, patiently gave her time to relax before deluging her with questions about the marriage.

They kept her chuckling with their wry observations on people gathered for the court and council meeting, and by the time the ladies parted to dress for the banquet, Alyss felt she had made friends.

She smiled at the thought. She'd not had a female friend her own age since Katherine in their childhood.

When she returned to their chamber, she noticed Roark's fresh tunic missing. The hunt had ended, then. He must be with the men. Rose wasn't present either. Well, she could make do as she always did at home. Raising the lid of the chest where her gowns were stored, Alyss paused. The saffron wool was not on top. She was certain she placed it there that morning, because she planned to wear it later. There it was, under the blue. Her slippers were missing, as well. No, they were arranged neatly on the floor at the side. Just where Alyss always left them, except this morning she hadn't removed them from the chest. Something wasn't right.

She dug deeper. No other items were out of place, but Alyss couldn't shake the feeling her things had been disturbed. Had they been searched? Impossible. Why and by whom? Perhaps Rose had rearranged the gowns. But the maid knew Alyss organized her own belongings.

I must be more tired than I thought. Next, I'll be imagining a plot against me.

Alyss managed to reach the ties of her gown, but she really could use help to arrange the blasted braids. She was trying to pin one in place when Rose appeared.

"Oh, milady! I be sorry. I were talking with the other maids and didn't mind the time. Then I got lost in the hallways again." Avoiding Alyss's eye, she took the brush and finished securing the braids.

Rose was lying. Alyss had no idea why, but she could tell by the way the girl acted. "Rose, did you look for anything in my chest today?"

"Oh, no, milady." The maid scrunched her face in

262

concentration but didn't look up. "I know ye like to do all that yourself. I'd never."

Alyss wasn't convinced, but since nothing was missing, she let it drop. Perhaps she'd been mistaken after all.

Roark sent a page, asking her to meet him in the hall. She arrived first and was looking over the tables when a wave caught her eye. Lady Gwen signaled to places beside her, and Alyss wound through the crowd.

"Hello, Lady Alyss." Lady Gwen reached both hands toward her. "Such excitement! Quite a mystery, isn't it? The king being called out of council, then jumping on his horse and riding away, all his guards scrambling around, trying to catch up to him. Have you heard anything?"

The king, gone? What about their hearing? And why hadn't Roark come to her? Alyss shook her head. "I don't know what's happened."

"Oh, my dear, neither does anyone else, but what does that matter? Gossip and speculation are much more entertaining." Lady Gwen giggled. "Not that I gossip, mind. Come, sit. My husband went looking for yours when he heard. They're bound to be here soon."

Alyss greeted the other ladies. Talk around the room quieted slightly as servants brought in food and people found their spots at table.

It wasn't long before Roark and his friends arrived. He slid in beside her and sent a searching glance before turning to the platter of roasted venison being passed around.

The men had discovered little of substance about the king's departure, but they did verify the tale. The king rode away without a word to anyone. What would that mean for them now? Alyss hardly touched the food and soon excused herself, pleading a headache. Surely Roark would understand.

She had nearly reached the door when a group late for the meal rushed through, one colliding with her.

A soft voice reached her ears. "Oh, my, I beg your pardon, my lady. I was not watching."

A man from the group stepped forward and drew the other lady to his side. "Are you all right, my dear?"

Alyss stood speechless. Gareth and Lucinda. He stared at Alyss for a moment before recognition registered. Then he smiled.

"Alyss! Lady Alyss. How good to see you. It's been so long." Guilt flashed across his face, as if he recalled the reason why. "Ah. Yes."

He drew the other lady forward. "Lady Alyss, this is my wife, Lady Lucinda. My dear, this is my childhood friend, Lady Alyss of Chauvere."

Lady Lucinda smiled, and a look of gentle sweetness filled her dark eyes. "I am so happy to meet you." Her smile faded, then, as if recognizing the name, and she added, "Oh. I...I." Her eyes went to Gareth, who looked decidedly uncomfortable.

Confronted with the surprise meeting, Alyss paused, not certain what to say. But before she could answer, an arm clasped her waist. She looked up in relief to see Roark. He glared at the couple in front of them. Laughter bubbled up in her throat at his dark expression. He was demonstrating his possession. Subduing a chuckle, Alyss smiled calmly and introduced her husband.

A look of relief crossed Gareth's face. "I am happy for you, Alyss," he said. "We heard you might be married, but I didn't realize you had arrived yet. I wish you God's blessing."

Roark spoke before Alyss could answer.

"Yes. I'm fortunate other men were blind to her beauty and charm." With his hand in the small of her back, he firmly pushed her out the door.

"That was rude," she whispered when they gained the corridor.

"Saying what I thought of him would have been ruder."

They walked in silence until they reached the bedchamber. Rose wasn't there.

Roark closed the door and kept his voice low. "I told everyone I needed to consult with my wife. A convenient way to escape talk at the table. Are you all right?"

Alyss turned in his embrace. She smiled and touched his jaw. "More than all right."

Rising on tip toe, she kissed him.

It was well into the night when a knock sounded. Groaning, Roark rolled out of bed, paused to pull the sheet across Alyss's nakedness, then opened the door a crack. Ralf leaned forward and murmured. "The king has returned. There's quite a commotion in the stables. Seems he's had some word that's upset him, and he's ordered four guards to watch for a wagon that's coming behind."

Alyss had awakened when Roark returned to bed. "We'd best be ready," he told her. "It won't be long now."

Chapter Twenty-Nine

The summons came later that day, an order to appear the following morning after breaking fast. Alyss fought for her usual calm as she handed Roark the heavy parchment, so different from the lighter one still concealed in the pocket hidden beneath her gown. But her heart raced, and a deep breath hissed as she sucked air past the constriction in her throat. Her hand shook.

"He will see us tomorrow," she repeated. It was all she could say. Her mind buzzed.

Roark nodded. "I'll tell the men. We should be ready to leave quickly."

Pacing the small chamber, Alyss tried to imagine what might be required of her when they met the king. Scenes from the past weeks moved through her mind, but she couldn't seem to focus on one thing.

What should she say if Richard asked her about the wedding? She had, after all, consented to wed Henry's friend. And if he inquired about Sir Jasper's death? Her heart pounded.

By the time Rose arrived, Alyss felt in control once again. "Tomorrow while Sir Roark and I are with the king, please pack," she told the maid. "We'll leave as soon as possible."

A look of surprise passed over Rose's face. "So soon, milady? Then if ye don't need me no more tonight, I'd best gather some supplies."

Nodding, Alyss sent her off.

****

That evening, Roark again visited his men. They were ready to depart at a moment's notice. Thinking of the information he'd learned since their arrival, he wondered whether his plans would succeed after all. He'd learned that Lord Paxton had gained the ear of the king, and Richard was loyal to those he allowed into his favor. How Windom's lord had managed that feat in such a few short days, Roark wouldn't venture to guess.

Stories going around at court featured Paxton in a heroic role during the attack on the king. Those tales were false. Roark knew Paxton had not been among the knights defending the king. If Paxton had fought that foggy morning along the Rhine, it hadn't been for Richard.

The man had his motives: he wanted Alyss and Chauvere. They belonged to Roark. At last he had what he'd always dreamed of, and he would never surrender them. He pictured Chauvere, golden against the morning sun, its village sprawled below, surrounded by rich crop land. His.

Paxton. The dog had kept himself scarce since Roark's arrival in Nottingham. Not once in three days had the man shown himself at a meal or other function. Laying plans, was he? Roark had one or two of his own.

Since his parents' death, he had fought every day. He'd fought to survive, to advance, to achieve his dream. And Roark would fight to protect every particle of what he'd gained.

That included Alyss. His stride slowed, and he thought of her. Quiet little caterpillar that had turned into a butterfly before his eyes. A snort of laughter escaped. Wrong comparisons. No sluggish caterpillar ever wielded a knife like Alyss. No gentle butterfly could flay a man with angry words.

But her soft smiles when she woke beside him soothed his heart. Alyss was still a mystery in many ways, but she came to Roark at night without fear now, her desire unfurling. The two of them had yet to explore all the hidden paths of love.

Love. Was that the emotion that filled him when he thought of her? All he knew of love between a man and woman was what he remembered of his parents. Love had never been a part of the encounters he'd experienced with women. Desire, the relief of boredom, these he knew.

Did he love Alyss? He recalled the fear he'd felt when she was hurt. The thought hit him: if he lost Chauvere, he would lose her. His muscles tightened as if he'd been dealt a blow to the gut.

Why had he not realized that before? What a fool he'd been. With all the worry about the land, he'd taken for granted that Alyss would be with him. She would not be.

Roark stopped in the darkness. No Alyss? His mind refused to grasp the thought. Impossible. A great, gaping hole opened inside him, and for the first time in nearly two decades, he felt lost.

Distracted, Roark did not hear the slight swish behind. The ground came up to meet him before he finally felt a searing pain in his back. He lay still while a thin form bent over his body and fumbled at the cord around his neck.

He brought his foot up behind the assailant and

hooked the figure's legs; the shadow stumbled. Roark staggered up, grabbed a handful of cloak, and pulled the figure backward. In a matter of seconds, he had subdued and dragged the smaller person into the light from a nearby torch.

"Rose."

His wife's maid glared at him in fear.

"It's been you?"

The maid averted her head, her mouth a tight line.

"You fed information to Windom," Roark accused. "You betrayed me and your lady. Why?"

"No. Milady would have been safe. It were only…"

"What did he promise you?" he demanded. Shock of the blow to his back began to wear off, and his vision wavered. He clutched the maid's wrist with fingers that tingled cold. He'd had worse injuries—the knife on the ground was small—but he needed to get Rose to their chamber before anyone came upon them.

"My lord? Sir Roark?" Ralf's voice floated above the buzzing in Roark's ears.

"Get Sir Alain. Now." Rose seemed unaware of his weakness and stood, eyes widened as if realizing what lay before her.

"You had help." Roark's voice sounded far away to his own ears. "You couldn't have done all this on your own. Who?"

He was beginning to tire and blackness oozed in from the edges of his eyes. Grasping his sword, he straightened. He couldn't afford to lose consciousness.

Almost immediately, he heard his friend's voice. "I'm here. I was coming to tell you… What's this, then?"

"Get me to Alyss," Roark said, handing Rose off to Alain. "Bring her along."

The small group made its way toward a door to the inside. Alain trained his sword on the maid while Ralf walked on Roark's right. They were passing through the watery light of a flickering torch when Roark heard a *zizz*, a groan, and the sound of a body hitting the ground. He turned to see Rose lying facedown, an arrow protruding from her shoulder.

****

A few minutes later in Lord Paxton's quarters, Sir Roland scowled. "I almost had him tonight, but for the interference of another. You didn't tell me the maid was still looking for the package."

Paxton was furious. "She's not. You told me you could do the job."

"And I would have, if not for the bungling of that stupid cow. She stabbed him in the back but failed to down him."

"I told her to leave off interfering. Our other informer could handle what needed done at the castle. He'd been channeling information to Windom long before I got there. He doesn't dare stop now." Sir Roland plopped down on a bench. "So?"

"Find a way to get to her before she reveals anything."

Sir Roland smirked. "An arrow fortunately found her as Sir Roark's men returned her to their quarters."

With raised brows, Lord Paxton turned. His fine, dark moustache curved up with his smile. "A man of foresight. I approve. Just don't forget whose vision you follow."

****

Alyss answered the knock at the bedchamber door to find Ralf supporting her husband. Roark dropped onto the end of a bench facing the wall opposite the bed. She pushed down the fear pulsing through her body. Surely he wasn't hurt badly or he wouldn't be walking.

"Bring warm water from the kitchen," she ordered Ralf, ignoring a commotion behind her.

She bit her lip against a moan when she saw the blood matting Roark's back. Grasping the fabric of his tunic she tugged. When he grunted, she held out her hand for his knife. Gently she sliced the soft, russet-colored wool away from the wound. By the time she reached his shirt, the cool blade was trembling. She paused to renew her grip on the handle and glanced at him.

He looked at her over his shoulder and winked in reassurance. Alyss caught her bottom lip between her teeth, handed him the knife, then ripped the linen.

"Careful. That was my last shirt."

She kissed his cheek and tried to smile through her tears. "I'll sew more for you," she murmured. "What happened?"

He inclined his head toward the bed behind her and Alyss turned. She hadn't realized anyone lay there. "Rose! The arrow— How…"

She looked at Roark, then back to the still body of her maid. Her mouth fell open. "No. It isn't possible."

"Either the bowman missed me, or he didn't want the girl to tell what she knew," Roark said.

Her thoughts swirled—and her mind, which always managed to clearly arrange order in chaos, froze. For a moment she stood unmoving before her thoughts came together. Rose must be examined, but after she knew the extent of Roark's injury. Oh, where was Ralf with the warm water? *Cool will have to do*. She grabbed the pitcher on the nightstand and poured water into the mazer.

As she cleaned the stab wound in Roark's back, Alain returned with a footman. "We'll take your maid to the servant's quarters. A healer will see to her there."

Rose had regained consciousness and begun to moan.

"Stay with her please, Sir Alain," Alyss said. "I'll be there soon."

"Too dangerous. Whoever shot her may decide to finish the job if he learns she survived," Roark put in. "I'll go when you've patched me up."

She didn't like her husband taking on such a task while he was hurt, but she knew by now once he'd set his mind on something, he wouldn't be moved.

After she'd bandaged Roark's back, kissed him, ordered him to be careful, then kissed him again, she sent him on his way. She'd begun packing a chest when she heard a commotion in the corridor. As she rose, the door swung open, and a brown blur hurtled toward her.

"Alyss!" The blur threw itself into Alyss's arms. "I'm so glad to see you."

"Evie?" Alyss drew back to stare at her weeping sister. "What has happened? How have you come here? Is Father Eudo with you?"

The girl buried her face in Alyss's shoulder and locked her arms around Alyss's waist.

Before Alyss could speak again, the priest stepped into the chamber, a frown twisting his thin face. "My lady, I'm sorry to have arrived in this way. I didn't know whether your appeal to the king had been successful, and I thought Chauvere might hold some danger for her."

"You made the right decision, Father. But why did you take her from the convent?"

Evie pulled away, sniffing, her eyes red and swollen. "Oh, Alyss, a fire. It was horrible.

"Sister Mary put me in a storage cellar and everything burned and I couldn't find her afterward and Father Eudo made me come away. So many of the buildings were gone and the smell was awful…"

Alyss placed her arms around the girl and glanced at the priest.

"The fire started in the kitchen and spread to other buildings," he explained. "Only the stone chapel escaped. A message reached me the next day, and I went immediately."

"He made me leave before I found Sister Mary," Evie mumbled, dragging her sleeve across her face.

His gaze held Alyss's. "Not all of the nuns had been accounted for, but some likely ran into the woods nearby. They may not have felt it was safe to return yet."

The unspoken message was clear. Several of the women had perished in the blaze, and Evie's missing friend likely was one.

Evie's breathing had calmed. "I didn't want to be alone at Chauvere. I wanted to be with you."

"You did exactly the right thing." Alyss hugged her sister. "And Father, you've arrived at a perfect time. Rose has been injured. I know you'll be a comfort to her. I'll have someone show you where she's resting."

The priest's face paled. "Let me see her right

away."

****

Roark remained with the maid until the healer finished. He knew Alyss would want a full report on the girl, and he wanted a chance to question her. Rose had refused to look at him the entire time, choosing to stare at the wall instead. Before he could demand she explain, he heard voices at his back and turned.

Father Eudo? What had brought Chauvere's priest here? The man ignored him as he rushed past.

"Oh, my daughter, what have you done?" When Father Eudo approached Rose's cot, the maid turned her head.

"Father, I be sorry." Tears rolled down her face. "I were trying to help."

He brushed the tears from her cheeks. "This is why I asked you not to interfere. That man was never to be trusted."

Roark frowned. Something about the conversation sounded suspicious. He strode forward, questions filling his mind.

The maid grasped Father Eudo's hand. "He'll do what he threatened. You got to leave. Where will you go?"

Roark interrupted. "Tell me what happened, Rose." The maid flinched at his low, commanding tone, and closed her eyes. Roark turned to the priest. "Father Eudo, why must you leave? And who threatened you?"

The priest's face crumpled. He stared at his and Rose's clasped hands but didn't speak.

Roark's hard gaze moved to the girl. "Rose..." The girl's face paled even more, but she opened her eyes.

In a faint voice she said, "He threatened to tell the

church about Da—Father."

"Why?" Roark cast a puzzled glance to the priest then back to Rose.

She raised their clasped hands. "He's not a priest. He was but he's not. And if the church finds out, they'll do bad things to him."

Father Eudo shook his head, then sighed quietly. "I was asked to leave the church when the bishop found out about my family."

No wonder the man feared discovery. Pretending to be a priest after being tossed out of the priesthood carried serious penalties. "How?" Roark asked.

Rose patted the priest's hand. "When Ma died, I sent word, and Da—Father—came to see me."

"I had been quite fond of her mother when we were young, before I went for the church. I didn't think anyone knew of our vows. They'd been so long ago.

"But someone in their village told the bishop," Father Eudo said. "So I took my daughter and we traveled north."

"But how did you come to be at Chauvere posing as a priest?"

"In our journey, I heard of the fever there that took the priest and many of the people. It seemed God led us to this place. I presented myself to Lord Ulrich and told him I had been a priest in the south. He invited me to stay."

"You didn't mention you were no longer a priest?" Roark asked.

"How should I deny God's plan? My daughter had waited for me a distance away and later came to the castle for work. When Lady Alyss learned Rose had been orphaned, she welcomed her at once. No one was harmed by our small deception."

"Except all those who looked to you for the sacraments. But how does this end in your being threatened and Rose's being shot?"

"The last knight to be awarded Windom—"

"That was Sir Jasper?" Roark interrupted.

"Yes. When he arrived, his household included a priest who knew me from the old life. The priest told Sir Jasper my story, and he demanded my assistance. If I refused to help him, he threatened to inform against me."

"When Sir Jasper died?"

"I thought all would be right again. Until the new lord came. The priest told him as well, but I refused to help again. I was through with betraying the people who trusted me."

"But it didn't stop. You—"

"It weren't Da's fault." Rose's weak voice interrupted Roark. "That Paxton told me if'n I didn't give him information, he'd see Da was taken away and never heard from again. But he promised no one would be hurt at home."

The more Roark heard, the more he struggled with his anger. But if he raised his voice, the girl might stop talking. "What did he want you to do?"

"At first I tried to see the wall wasn't repaired fast," she said. "Then he wanted me to find some kind of writing for him. He said you had it, but when I asked Da, he told me he'd take care of it."

Roark looked at the priest. "It was you who searched Sir Alain's chest." The man hung his head. "What about the attacks on me tonight and earlier?"

"Tonight was the only time I done anything," Rose

insisted. "He was mad and said to leave off trying. I'd failed, and he said he'd see Da paid for it. I…I tried one last time, so's Da would be free."

The tale sounded too impossible not to be true. "At home, how did his orders come to you?"

"Sir Roland. After you made him leave, he went to Windom. He'd come to the village and find me when there was word from the new lord."

The priest faced Roark at last. "Will you give me a little more time with my daughter before you take me away?"

"Father, I have no intention of taking you anywhere. If you are here when I return after tomorrow, I will make a decision."

Alyss needed to hear the news. Roark swiped a hand across his face and headed back to her bedchamber. Perhaps afterward, he would rest. He had a feeling he'd need every drop of strength for tomorrow's meeting with the king.

Alyss's raised voice from his chamber reached him down the hall. Panic pushed him into a run. If Paxton had moved against her, Roark would kill the man and to Hades with the king.

He burst through the open doorway to find a young woman—a girl, really—clutched in his wife's arms. Alyss smiled at him through tears.

"It's my sister. This is Evie."

Chapter Thirty

The next day, Alyss smoothed the back of Roark's deep blue tunic, borrowed from Sir Orlo. It fit over the bandage on his back. Thankfully, the wound had been high enough to avoid serious damage. She'd worried about him much of the night, when her thoughts hadn't been centered on the duplicitous priest. And Rose. How could Alyss have been so mistaken in anyone?

Overnight, Roark had bedded down in the barracks with the men, leaving Evie to share Alyss's bed. This morning, he'd arrived to collect her for the audience with the king. The exhausted Evie still slept, watched over by a maid Lady Gwen insisted upon sending.

"Ready?" Roark asked.

Alyss smiled ruefully. "No. But let us go." She slid her hand into Roark's and squeezed. "Are you certain you're well enough?"

"I've suffered much worse injuries," he said.

In the corridor they met their escort.

Once they arrived in the antechamber to Richard's reception room, Alyss and Roark waited. The page who accompanied them disappeared immediately. Roark had been quiet throughout the delay, throwing glances her way when he thought she didn't notice.

At least the small anteroom was private. The two of them didn't have to endure sly glances of others waiting hopefully for a word with Richard.

When the door at last opened, Alyss's stomach sank and her palms began to itch; she clasped her hands together. Side by side, she and Roark walked into the crowded chamber. By all the saints, was every person in Nottingham stuffed into the room?

She sank in curtsy. From the corner of her lowered eyes, she saw Roark bow. She wanted to whisper "lower," blast the man.

"Well, well. Lady Alyss. It has been years since we met." King Richard smiled, and she relaxed slightly. He seemed in good humor. "I was sorry to hear that your father had died. Every ruler should have the loyal support of a man like Lord Ulrich."

She summoned up a smile. "Thank you, Sire. He loved your grace as he loved your father."

"No, no. Not so formal, dear lady. Your family and ours are closely bound by love and loyalty. I speak of your brother, Sir Henry, now. When I heard he had fallen in the monstrous attack against me, I was deeply affected. More than a good friend and loyal knight, your brother. One might say we grew up together. But no greater love has any man than to lay down his life for a friend, I believe Our Blessed Lord said."

Her throat constricted, Alyss fought tears. The king's words were touching, but in that analytic corner of her mind, she thought Richard's tone was bland. *He doesn't sound sad.* She looked up to find the king's assessing gaze directed at Roark, although he continued to speak to her.

"That brings us to the reason you are here. Another of the brave knights who fought beside me has brought a serious matter to my attention."

Only then did Alyss notice Lord Paxton standing in

a group of courtiers behind the king. When Richard beckoned, Paxton moved to his side. With one look at him, she lost her nervousness and felt an urge that had become much too familiar. She wanted to hit him with the heaviest object she could find.

****

Roark spotted the damned traitor the moment he and Alyss stepped into the packed chamber. His gaze darted to the men around the king, weighing their expressions, noting any weapons. In another glance he assessed the room, marked the doors and windows, gauged potential exit routes. A pathway, there, where only women clustered, would lead them to a narrow opening, perhaps to a corridor. If only he'd been allowed to keep his sword. But he would make do.

Satisfied he had mapped the best emergency path, he listened as Richard talked with Alyss, but when the king fixed his gaze on him, Roark came alert. He caught the reference to Paxton and watched the man ooze forward. *Brave knight, my arse.* Roark could feel his lip curl.

"It has long been accepted that widows and other unmarried ladies without a man to protect them should come under the supervision of the crown. We help them find worthy lords to wed, strong and loyal fighters to watch over them and their holdings."

Roark grew more tense with every foolish, stilted word out of the royal mouth. This was his king, he reminded himself, the man he chose over Lord Martin when the die was thrown that fateful day, the ruler he had sworn to uphold and protect with his life.

Remembering that, Roark swallowed his ire and let King Richard speak.

"We hear that once your brother died, you wed Sir Roark of Stoddard, late captain of the guard with Lord Martin of Cantleigh. Lord Paxton has challenged the marriage. His people at Chauvere tell him you were forced to wed."

His mild tone hardened. "Now, my lady, what say you?"

Alyss looked at her clasped hands, her lips compressed as she thought.

"Sire, I don't quite understand the challenge," she said. "Is it that I wed without permission because I was orphaned and alone and, thus, a ward of the court? Or is it because I was forced into the marriage against my will?"

Roark caught the shadow of a smile around the king's mouth before Richard nodded. "Good questions, my lady Alyss. What say you, Lord Paxton? Which of these two things do you challenge?"

Without blinking, Paxton stepped forward. "Indeed, Sire, as you say, good questions. Before I answer, I must admit to something and pray for your understanding."

With an expression that combined contriteness and craftiness, he said, "Prince John, whose holding in Nottinghamshire contains Windom and Chauvere, had granted me the lordship of Windom when he learned it was open. That was before I knew of the prince's perfidy in plotting against you, which was uncovered so recently.

"When I learned of my good fortune, it was my desire to further a natural connection between Lady Alyss of Chauvere, sister to your trusted knight, Sir Henry."

By this point in Paxton's performance, he had broadened his delivery to include the surrounding lords and ladies, who listened avidly.

"When I arrived to press my suit, I was met with armed soldiers and the news that her brave brother was dead, and she had been forced to wed some mercenary who had arrived the day before. Naturally, I was concerned for her."

During the speech, the king studied both Alyss and Roark, and Roark realized Richard had heard this story before. Of course he had, or he wouldn't have brought them here, now.

Richard spoke then. "And this mercenary was Sir Roark of Stoddard?"

Paxton threw a smug look at Roark. "Yes. The priest himself told me that Lady Alyss was all but dragged to the hall where the ceremony was ordered under threat of death."

"As the good father is not here, we will continue," the king announced. "Lord Paxton, you have confessed your ill-advised alliance with my poor brother privately, and I have accepted your explanation."

Richard turned his forceful attention to Alyss. "So, my lady. Be so kind as to tell us the tale of your marriage."

Alyss lifted her chin and smiled. Roark sensed the tension that coiled inside her, but she drew calmness around her like a cloak.

"Certainly, Sire. At Chauvere, we were awaiting the return of my brother, who was among those chosen to escort you home. We still mourned my father, Lord Ulrich, who died in an attack on the castle only weeks before, carried out by Jasper of Windom. Sir Jasper also died that day." She took a deep breath.

"Sir Roark of Stoddard arrived to tell us that my brother had fallen while protecting you. He informed me that Henry had consigned me and my people to his care. As his dear friend, Sir Roark accepted that charge." She turned to look at Roark, then faced the king again.

"I was never orphaned. Henry had arranged a marriage for me before his death, and I agreed to it."

Lord Paxton stepped forward and started to speak, but Richard held up his hand for silence.

"You did agree, then? You were not forced?"

Alyss smiled. "I was angry at the man. He demanded the ceremony be held at once. I had no time to prepare." She appealed to the women, who were hanging on every word. "I had to marry in my oldest gown."

Murmurs swelled around the room as ladies reacted in sympathy.

If the situation weren't so serious, Roark would have laughed. Alyss was as good as Paxton at performing for an audience. Yet he was concerned. This was her chance to tell the king she had been forced, to nullify his claim on her. In spite of their recent accord, he found himself braced for her answer.

"So, then, Lady Alyss. You say this man," he nodded to Roark, "told you he was a friend of Sir Henry's and your brother arranged the marriage?"

For the first time, Alyss looked uncomfortable. "In a manner of speaking."

Richard nodded. "You say you agreed to wed? You were not forced?"

She was prevented from answering the same

question again when the guard returned and whispered to the king. Darkness shuttered the light of enjoyment in Richard's eyes as he looked at Roark.

Stepping closer to Richard she said, "My lord husband is a knight, Sire, and he is honest. His word is true."

Roark wanted to smile, to shout, but he struggled to keep his expression blank. She loved him. She loved him, or she would never support him in such a way. But his elation proved short-lived. *If she knew the truth, she would never speak to me again.* No, she would likely finish the job on his back the maid started the night before.

Richard considered Alyss, his gaze filled with speculation. He turned quickly.

"Sir Roark of Stoddard." His voice boomed. "I know of you." The complete switch in the king's attitude startled the crowd; whispered conjectures flew around the room. "You were Martin of Cantleigh's captain for many years. A tournament champion in Normandy and France. God's legs, sir, you could have hired yourself out to the highest bidder. But you were content to remain with the man who, what say you, raised you up from your village's dirt?"

The mutters in the room stopped cold. This gossip was too good to miss. Roark didn't blame the people. He could tell by the king's attitude that this day wouldn't end well for him, one way or the other.

He would not be coerced. "You are correct, Sire. My father was a miller, a free man, respected for his honesty. He taught me that a man is known for his word. I gave mine to Lord Martin."

Roark sought Alyss's gaze, hoping she would

understand, but the silence brought his attention back to the king. Richard looked him in the eyes. "And would you ever break your sworn word?"

Roark held the king's gaze. "Only if a higher vow commanded it."

Something flickered in Richard's eyes, and Roark was as certain as if the words had been shouted—he knew. The king knew Lord Martin had betrayed him. And he knew Roark was Cantleigh's captain. Roark listened for the accusations, the condemnations. He'd wagered all and now he'd lost. No land. No wife. An odd chill enveloped him: no Alyss. Roark couldn't face her. He stared straight ahead; pain clamped his heart like a vise.

How convoluted life was. The land he had thought worth anything, even honor, even betrayal of a woman, was worth nothing. The woman he'd considered a liability was worth everything. He had lost it all now. And it didn't matter. All that mattered was Alyss.

King Richard rose abruptly. His counselors clustered, and his guards rushed over. His face was grim when he waved to Roark and Alyss "I'll see you both in my private chambers."

Alyss looked dazed at the sudden turn of events, but she took Roark's arm and they moved forward, hemmed by guards. His muscles flexed at her touch, and he covered her fingers with his own. After a quick word from the king, Lord Paxton joined them.

The much smaller party entered a lavish chamber. Richard threw himself into a cushioned chair in front of the hearth where a small fire blazed.

He took a goblet from an attendant and drank. With a sigh, he looked at the handful of people in front of him.

"Now," he said wearily. "Let's get to the truth of this. I've learned that Lord Martin of Cantleigh was a party to the attack against me on the way to Cologne. I believe I know who is at the heart of it, and evidence will show I am right. I have already stripped Cantleigh's lands and titles and given them to another."

Roark's head jerked. Martin's son, Geoffrey, would suffer for his father's sins, and him just a squire. And Lady Elinor, blameless in it all, where would she go?

Motioning to Roark, King Richard said, "In another situation, I might salute your initiative. I like a man who can turn misfortune into fortune. Escaping to England with such a story, persuading Lady Alyss you were sincere. Shows determination. However, attempting to kill the king makes you a traitor."

Alyss gasped. Her face had gone white. She knew the punishment for traitors. Roark wanted to hold her, but the king still spoke.

"Well? Well? What have you to say for yourself?"

Roark refused to make excuses. But he would say the truth as he knew it. About the attempt on the king's life, at least.

"Sire, I had no knowledge of any plans to attack you."

Richard started up straight in the chair. "Hah. But you were his loyal captain. When your lord rode into battle, you followed, am I right?"

Silence stretched.

"I am right," Richard answered himself.

Alyss's soft voice broke the quiet. Her wide blue eyes pleaded.

"I believe him," she said. "I, too, wondered at his story. But I have come to understand his goodness, his honor. His men respect him and follow him. Sire, Sir Roark loves England. He would never try to harm his king. He isn't capable of that treachery. My brother would never have befriended such a man."

Lord Paxton slid forward a step. "I think I can prove Sir Roark did have knowledge of the attack, Sire." Attention in the small room went immediately to him.

"Show me this proof and let's be done with it." Richard sounded weary.

"Ask Sir Roark to remove the packet from around his neck. I believe you'll find what you want inside. A note warning him of the attempt on your person—the day, the time of the attack." Paxton's smile at Roark was filled with malice, but he was careful not to let the king see.

Roark didn't show surprise. He'd identified Paxton's hand behind the attempts to get the message. He had come from Prince John to begin with. But how had John known Roark possessed the note? Unless Paxton had seen Roark take it from Lord Martin's body. That would explain Paxton's knowledge of the battle that day.

With a deep breath, Roark pulled the cord over his head and handed Richard the pouch. The parchment crackled in the silence as the king unfolded it. Roark didn't dare look at Alyss.

Richard looked up, his expression fierce. "This is evidence of Sir Roark's guilt? A love note? Easy enough to see a woman's hand has written it. Lady Alyss?"

287

She nodded. "I did send it to my husband while he was at Windom, after Lord Paxton's attack. Shall I write something so you can compare?"

The smirk was wiped from Lord Paxton's face. "It can't be." The king flung out the parchment in his hand toward the other man.

Paxton ignored it, but he spoke. "They exchanged it. But I have other proof. One of Chauvere's former knights and the son of one of your loyal barons."

The king nodded to a guard who left with Lord Paxton.

Alyss moved close to Roark. "Do you know who it is?" She slipped her hand into his.

He watched the door as he shook his head. Roark recognized the knight immediately when he entered. The one he had ejected from Chauvere that first day.

"Sir Roland." Alyss also recognized him. "What have you to say about this?"

"My lady," Roland bowed to her. "I was there when he came. I saw how he coerced you, how he threatened your people if you refused. And when I challenged him, he forced me to leave. After hearing about his reputation, I believe I'm lucky he did not kill me, as well."

He stepped toward her, lowering his voice. "I had no choice but to leave you in his power; I feared for my own life if I remained."

Looking perplexed, Alyss shook her head. "Sir Baldwin told me you were discharged for insubordination, for refusing a direct command. He said you behaved in an unknightly manner."

King Richard had settled back into the chair and was calmly observing the interplay.

Roark had enough. "Yes, I forced you to leave, and made sure you were gone. You refused to show respect for your captain, Sir Baldwin, and you refused a direct command from your lord. That proved you untrustworthy. No soldier wants to serve beside a knight who can't be trusted. I have more respect for my men than to ask them to do so."

"Well, well. This does seem damning. Sir Roark, the word of your own man condemns you. My dear Lady Alyss, you have suffered needlessly at the hands of the rogue. Freedom will seem sweet."

Tears were trickling down Alyss's face as she grasped Roark's hand. "He is innocent, Sire."

Roark's throat thickened with love, with regret.

The king shook his head. "You were fooled, my dear. Taken in by lies. Before I pass sentence, you should know the rest. But for that, we must take a short walk."

He led them through a door into an adjoining chamber, where a figure lay on a heavily gilded oaken bed. The king motioned her forward. Reaching the side, she looked down and gasped. "Henry! Dear God, Henry." Roark shook free of the guards and leaped forward to catch her before she hit the floor.

Chapter Thirty-One

Sir Henry swung his legs to the side of the bed and sat, carefully balancing his bound left arm. Linen wrapped his chest where healing wounds peeked around the edges.

"You're alive." Alyss's ears rang and black spots danced before her eyes. Her beloved brother lived. Her knees must have given way because Roark was suddenly at her side, holding her close. She shook off the faintness and struggled to her feet, brushing away the strange dampness on her cheeks. "Thanks be to God and all his angels."

She sat next to Henry but didn't hug him. He was bandaged everywhere, and she feared her touch would cause him pain. He smiled and enfolded her hand in his. It was rough, warm.

"I'll live," he said, "although it wasn't certain for a good while." He moved her to his right side and slid that arm around her waist.

It felt warm. Comfortable. Her throat clogged. She hiccupped. *Thank you, God, for answered prayers.*

"I want to know everything that has happened," he said. "But first I want to see this man who says he's my friend."

Alyss turned to Roark, suddenly aware of a tension in Henry's grip. She glanced at Roark. He stared at her brother, his face no longer blank. In his eyes, a look of—resolve?

Henry shook his head. "I think I would recall a man I asked to marry my sister. This knight is not familiar."

That couldn't be correct. She frowned. "But you must have done so. All the things he knew about you, about us. How could he have discovered them otherwise?"

Stepping to Henry's other side, the king placed his hand on Henry's shoulder. "That's all we need to know, my friend. You and your sister can be private now. Then you will rest. I'll return later."

Panic hit Alyss, and she pulled away from Henry. "No. No, wait. You can't just leave the question at this. Henry, perhaps your injuries have made you forget. Look at him again. Even James said you knew Sir Roark."

Scrambling to recall what exactly James had said, she stilled. James said Roark had told him. And Godfrey.

"Sir Godfrey knows. Henry, James said Sir Godfrey told him you and Sir Roark were friends."

Henry continued to hold Roark's gaze. "I know who Sir Roark of Stoddard is. I've watched him fight at tournaments." His voice rang in the now-quiet chamber. "But we've never met."

****

Roark felt...numb, disconnected to reality. As if he stood outside himself and observed the surroundings. Henry was lucid; anyone could see it. Nothing would be gained by drawing out the play. He watched Alyss as he said, "Sir Henry is right. He and I have never met."

His wife went pale. Numbness gave way to an odd

pain in his chest. Her eyes widened, and her lips compressed in a look of betrayal. He *had* betrayed her trust and, perhaps, her love, although she'd never said the words. Just as well, the way things had worked out.

The king clapped his hands once, a final gesture as he said, "Another problem solved today. Guards, take Sir Roark to the dungeon."

This was happening too quickly. Roark needed to talk with Alyss, to tell her he was sorry, to explain. What would he say? That he'd lied to her, taken advantage of her, all so he could have her land? That the land didn't matter now? That he loved her?

Nothing would be changed by his words. Yet her pale face, her huge, tragic eyes made him long to take her in his arms and tell her he hadn't lied about everything. Not about his feelings for her.

But he'd never confessed his feelings. He'd only just recognized them himself. No, it was better this way. She would be free at last, and she would forget him.

An iron grip brought Roark around. Over his shoulder, he cast one last glance at Alyss. She still looked stunned, lost. He shot a look at Sir Henry, who frowned back.

Roark turned; the talk at the bed resumed. He had been shoved to the door when the king called, "Wait. Bring him back."

Throwing off the guards' hands, Roark straightened. Sir Henry stood and motioned him forward.

"Something about you is familiar. When you turned your head, I thought... Turn to the side again." To the guard, he ordered, "Pull back his hair."

Roark looked at the wall, avoiding Alyss.

"The profile. I know it. It was you. You shouted the warning." Henry turned to the king. "The shout alerted us to your danger. It came from a knight who'd lost his helmet but fought like a fiend. He rode a dark horse with white mane and tail." He nodded to Roark. "It *was* you."

"Is this true?" the king asked.

"Yes." Alyss's voice rang out.

"Impossible," Lord Paxton insisted, his tone a bit less certain then before. "Another lie."

No one paid him heed.

Roark and Henry stared at each other, then Henry did a strange thing. He lifted his right arm in a brief salute, just as the two had done on the battlefield that day. Roark nodded once.

From the corner of his eye, he saw Alyss stride toward him. Turning, he waited for her to reach his side. But instead of moving into his outstretched arm, she shoved past him and raced away.

He heard the king give orders for Paxton and Roland to leave, promising to deal with them later. Soon only he and Sir Henry remained in the chamber. And Richard.

The king sighed gustily. "What shall we do with you, Sir Roark?"

Roark turned. He didn't much care right now. "Do what you will, Sire."

"Hmmm. Let me see if I understand. You pledged your service to Lord Martin and kept that pledge faithfully for many years, rising to the position of captain of his troops. Yet he did not include you in his plans for my attack, and when you saw his intent, you called out a warning for me. Do I have that correct?"

"You have, Sire. None of our men were part of the plan. Only three were with him, and all hired while we waited for your release. I don't know why I was left out."

"Perhaps he did not trust you to kill your king."

Roark inclined his head. "I wouldn't have." He didn't mention the challenge of making the decision. Or the sense of betrayal he'd felt.

Richard glanced at Sir Henry, then back to Roark. "I have something of a problem. There is a large holding near here, and no one to take charge. The last two lords who did so proved unreliable. I believe it would be in good hands with you. Would you swear allegiance to me and take on Windom?"

Breath left Roark's lungs, and he couldn't seem to draw in more. The king was offering him Windom? Was his dream at last to be realized? Would Alyss be content to live there, close to her family?

Alyss. His heart sank. She wouldn't be with him. She hated him, and he couldn't blame her. Not the way he'd deceived her. She must believe he'd made a fool of her.

"Sire," he managed to get out. "I will always swear allegiance to you." He paused. "But I can't accept. Now that my wife—that is, Lady Alyss—is free to find a proper husband—"

"Are you casting my sister aside?" Sir Henry demanded, struggling to rise.

"Never. But I lied to the lady, tricked her into marriage. She would never have agreed otherwise. If that is not enough to release her, the priest who blessed the vows is an imposter."

Neither of the other two spoke. Then Henry said, "Isn't there an old way to marry—the couple vows they are wed to each other and it is done?"

For a moment, Roark knew hope. Then he shook his head. "Your sister is too fine a lady to trap in that way. I will set her free to find someone she prefers."

"If you think my sister doesn't care for you, you must be blind."

Roark ignored him. "You can see to the proper documents, Sire. And the bishop is sure to agree."

The king pursed his mouth. "Are you certain you won't reconsider? I need two strong barons in the shire."

A baron? Richard offered him a title? Roark's emotions had been on such a ride today, the thought left him numb. Then he realized—he couldn't accept and live near Alyss. Watch as she found another, wed, had children. Without him.

"I am grateful for the honor, Sire, but I cannot."

"Then what are your plans?" Henry asked.

"If King Richard has room in his army for another sword, I'll serve him in that way."

"Damn fool idea if you ask me," Henry muttered. "You make me tired. Go away." With that, he lay back.

The king merely nodded at Roark and turned away.

He'd been dismissed. What had he expected? At least he was free. The word sent a pain stabbing through his middle. He'd tell Alyss she was free as well. Then he'd leave.

****

The hour was late when Alyss reached their quarters. Explanations were still being made to the king, but she had no heart for it. She'd been to the

chapel to thank God for Henry's safe return, and she'd
see her brother tomorrow, but now she wanted to be
alone. Evie was with Lady Gwen, so there was time.

She had to try to make sense of what she'd learned.
For the last hour she'd felt frozen, moving without
thinking, reciting prayers dutifully. At last, she felt
pain. It was all she felt.

He had betrayed her. Roark had lied to her from the
first breath. Not one word from his mouth had been the
truth. All he had wanted was what he thought was
hers—Chauvere. Land and power.

He had lied when he said Henry sent him. He had
lied about wanting her. He had lied when he called her
beautiful. She'd believed it all. Oh, she should have
listened to her head, not her foolish heart. After all the
years she'd spent fortifying her pride, telling herself she
was useful and taking steps to ensure it would be
enough to guarantee a place at Chauvere no matter
what, she had allowed herself to be duped by a
handsome face and figure.

His face was not handsome, and his figure… That
tiny rational corner of her mind reminded her that his
figure was, indeed, handsome. And his face was beyond
handsome. It was compelling, strong, commanding.
And in secret moments, sad, showing his vulnerability.
Thinking of him made her stomach flip and her body
warm all over.

No. He was not worthy of her love. Love? Dear
God. She did not love him. He had used her, lied to her.
Pain radiated in her chest.

She had defended him to the king, to everyone.
What a fool she'd been. To have believed anything he
told her, allowed him to lead her like a lamb. How easy

it had been for him. He must have laughed at her so often. Arms folded across her stomach, she lay curled on the bed. She couldn't even cry.

But the worst of it—they were wed. How would they continue life together? They could not. She could not.

What was she to do? Enter a convent? No. She had no calling for that life, and she wouldn't shut herself away as if what happened were her fault. It was him. He would have to go.

How would she face him until then?

Hours later Alyss lay awake. She'd missed the midday meal, and she probably should see to her sister. But Lady Gwen had insisted on having Evie join her for the day. Perhaps she would wait. As for Roark, she needn't have worried what to say to him. He hadn't returned. On her back staring at the ceiling, she couldn't repress a satiric smile. Her darling husband must be having as difficult a time as she, adjusting to his changed status. With Henry alive, Roark no longer had a right to Chauvere. He wouldn't want to stay.

Of course he had risked his life for her and her people, but he thought they were his. He'd worked alongside the villagers to repair the walls, prepare for planting. He organized and trained the soldiers into a fighting unit.

He'd held her when she finally came to terms with Jasper's attack, had gently introduced her to desire, teased and encouraged her, consulted and deferred to her at times when her knowledge of castle life and business exceeded his—which was often. But he was learning. Soon he would be able to administer it all, except for the books.

She had even planned to teach him to read. No longer. She rubbed her chest. Could a heart actually hurt?

She'd thought he had developed tender feelings for her, that it was just difficult for him to speak of it. He had been alone so long. She glimpsed his pain and loneliness at times, the way he held himself apart, not from arrogance, but as if he thought himself undeserving of friendship or love.

It was an act, an elaborate plan, a take-over without violence. Roark of Stoddard had been very good at it, just as men said he was good at fighting. And Alyss thought she had been a strategist. She should have known; she should have suspected. There were clues, but she had refused to see them.

Would her small dower manor be enough for him? Perhaps she would insist Henry take it back; then there would be no place for them to go. How would Roark like living with Henry? That is, if she could forgive him enough to remain.

Where had that thought come from? She would never forgive him.

Perhaps he would leave, he and his small troop of men—hire themselves out. Alyss would give him her blessings. If she never saw him again, she wouldn't care. Long ago she resigned herself to remaining alone. She could do so again.

But that was before she had known Roark's touch. Felt herself blooming and flying and bursting with love. Oh! That word again. She did not love the lying betrayer. Unshed tears burned her throat, her nose, her eyes. Finally giving up, she turned to her side and cried herself to sleep.

Alyss awoke when someone sat on the side of the bed. Roark. How dare he show his face to her after his hideous deception. She brushed the hair from her eyes, glared at him, then turned away. She couldn't bring herself to look at her husband. Betrayer.

Neither spoke until finally he said, "Alyss, it may be hard for you to understand—"

"No." She turned to him. "I will never understand. Why? It was all a lie. You never cared for anything but the land, the castle. Look at you now. You have nothing, nothing but a wife. Will it make you happy to know my marriage portion is a small manor to the north? You'll have your land after all, just not on the scale you planned."

"That's not what I wanted—"

"I don't care what you wanted. Go away."

****

Roark stood outside the closed door. She would never forgive him. Why should she? He had lied and manipulated his way into her life, taking control of all she held dear. How she must hate him. The confidence in herself would be dead now, like a blossom in the snow. But she would get over it; she would rediscover those qualities that made her his Alyss. His beautiful wife. The loveliest woman he would ever know.

Perhaps when she learned what he'd done, she would forgive herself for believing in him. He couldn't stay. Not now. He had nothing to offer her except freedom, and he'd give her that. Another man would come along, some lord who would value her. But no one would value her as he did.

Roark hadn't realized just how much he cared for Alyss until today, when he saw the devastation in her face at his confession. He had crushed the woman he loved. He loved Alyss. He'd never told her, and now she would never know. She could never forgive him; he wasn't sure he could forgive himself.

For so long, only land had mattered. It meant he had achieved a place for himself. Ironically, now that he could have land, it wasn't important. Only Alyss was important, her happiness. Roark would ask Alain and the others if they'd like to join him in Normandy. The king was headed there in a few weeks. There'd be fighting enough for all, and who knew what fate might grant them?

Free Alyss, leave her with her heart intact and her own place. He wouldn't take it, for then she would never believe he did so from love of her, not love of power. Swallowing hard, he pressed his hand flat on the door, then walked away.

****

Much too soon, knocking awoke Alyss. A servant reported that Alyss's maid and the priest who had been with her last night had disappeared. No one had seen them leave, but a search had found no trace of either. Evie returned shortly after the evening meal, and Alyss told her what had happened.

Alyss cried herself to sleep again.

The next morning, she awoke calm. Nothing to be gained by more tears. She had responsibilities that didn't stop for broken hearts. She asked to see Henry. She got King Richard as well. The king announced he would leave Nottingham to work his way back to Westminster for a wearing of the crown. She shot a glance at Richard. His way of reminding the people he remained king? Perhaps after years of imprisonment, he might need to reassure himself, as well.

He was distracted, jovial, and intense, all at once. He ordered Henry to rest and recover, but advised him to get home immediately.

"You'll have your hands full, getting acquainted with duties as a new baron and lord of Chauvere. Who knows? When you've recovered, you might join me for a few battles? Perhaps Lady Alyss would like to travel south soon, to visit my mother."

His look assessed her. "You won't have trouble finding a husband, if you've a mind for that."

Her smile was bitter. "I have a husband, if you recall, Sire."

"No longer. What? He didn't inform you?"

A wave of cold fear swept over Alyss. "What do you mean?"

Richard stood, feet apart, hands on his hips. "Sir Roark confessed he had coerced you into marriage. Tricked, threatened, and lied, his words were, then forced you to wed under threat to your people. The bishop was duly impressed at the confession. I believe your annulment will arrive soon."

Alyss sat. Her clasped fingers were white at the knuckles. "But I told you yesterday I'd been willing."

"And he explained why you still feared his anger. He is a bully, obviously. You're better free of him." He slapped his hands together. "The man was too stubborn for his own good. Off to sell his sword, no doubt."

Staring at her fists in her lap, Alyss pushed down a turbulent stomach. Roark had left her, now that she didn't possess Chauvere. A small holding wasn't enough for him. She wasn't enough for him. Her teeth clenched the inside of her bottom lip. She refused to weep in front of the king.

Instead, after thanking Richard for his generosity, Alyss excused herself to pack for home. Wielding a stick to help his limp, Henry walked with her to the door of the chamber.

"You'll be glad to see the last of that seducer, won't you?"

She prayed her face didn't betray her thoughts, but she knew he was perceptive.

"Surely you don't love the lying rogue?"

She snorted a reply.

"I thought not. He's better gone from here. But I can't understand why he turned down the king's reward."

Alyss inclined her head in question.

"Alyss, your husband refused the king's gift for saving his life on the field that day. Richard offered him Windom and a barony."

She gasped and turned to Henry, nearly knocking him over. "King Richard offered Roark Windom, and he refused? Why would he do that?"

"Why do *you* think?"

"That he did not love me enough to stay for a smaller place."

"I believe he loved you too much. He asked that I tell you he was sorry. He never meant to hurt you. He said he gives you the one thing that will make you happy. Freedom."

"Then he's really gone?" Alyss couldn't believe it.

"He left early this morning. He wanted to collect his belongings at Chauvere before you returned home."

Alyss's hurt washed away in a tide of anger.

"God sear his stubborn hide. He was too much the

coward to tell me he loved me last night. Cut off his nose to spite his face. More likely, he misses the thrill of battle and doesn't want a family tied 'round his neck. We shall certainly see. He'll not get off the hook so easily as that. Henry, see to Evie. She's here." She jerked open the door and threw a glance toward the king as she stepped through. "Don't award Windom elsewhere, Sire. It's taken."

The door was nearly closed when her head appeared around the edge. "And don't let the bishop send his report. It's not needed."

King Richard laughed as she rushed out the door. "She'll catch up to him by nightfall. How do you like the idea of Lord Roark of Windom as a brother-in-law?"

Sir Henry smiled. "I'll like having a warrior on my western border even more."

Nodding, the king pursed his mouth. "And I'll like having two strong barons I can trust holding a good portion of the eastern midlands. I've worries enough in Lincolnshire."

"Can you trust Lord Roark?"

"He swore allegiance to me and to England. I can trust that."

****

Alyss, still wearing the same saffron gown, caught up with Roark long before dark.

"Why did you leave without telling me?" were the first words out of her mouth as she pulled her exhausted mare alongside his gelding.

He stopped the horse and leaned forward on both hands, stretching the muscles in his back and shoulders much as he had the first time she saw him. She had thought him arrogant and demanding then.

Her opinion had changed over the weeks. Those faults had become strengths, along with his good qualities, the most important of which was his reason for leaving.

"You refused the king's offer of Windom." Her tone was incredulous. "How could you?"

Roark looked at her for a long, silent moment. "Why are you here?"

"Don't change the subject," Alyss said. "Why did you turn down Windom?"

He sighed. "Don't you think it would be awkward living so close to the man who deceived you, forced you into marriage?"

"And that's another thing. How could you say I was forced?"

"You wed me, believing a lie."

"Do you love me?" Alyss demanded angrily.

Her fierceness brought a look of sadness. "I'm not sure I know the meaning of the word."

Remembering his anger at the risks she took, his tenderness, the soft glow of his eyes when he looked at her, Alyss was sure he did know in his heart. How could she make him say it?

"Then why did you release me? Windom is a fine holding. We could make it better, stronger. We could make it home."

"You'll be better off without me." Roark's voice was soft.

"Let me understand," Alyss said. "Before you knew me, you were willing to use any kind of deception to wed me for my inheritance? But now that you have a chance to become a baron with your own land, you refuse because you don't want to hurt me?"

Roark weighed the words, then nodded.

"That's because you love me," she announced.

Shaking his head, he countered, "You could never forgive me."

"How do you know?" Her sigh was exasperated. "You didn't ask."

His good brow arched. "Then you—love—me?"

"This damn and blasted dress was not made for riding, and I've had to relieve myself for hours, yet I sit here arguing with you. Of course I love you, you great fool."

Tears coursed down her cheeks, and Roark smiled, his dimple winking. As usual, Alyss's stomach flipped at the sight.

Before she knew it, he'd pulled her from the saddle. He caught the wayward strand of hair, tucked it behind her ear, and when he kissed her, all her discomforts vanished.

"Will you marry me?" she whispered, running a finger down the side of his strong nose, outlining his beautiful lips.

He smiled at her tenderly. "I'm sorry, my lady, but I've decided to keep the wife I have." He nipped at her fingers. "She's a terrible nag, but I don't want to live without her."

"You've forgotten. Father Eudo wasn't really a priest," she said as he smoothed tears from her cheeks.

His dimple appeared once more. "Then you'll have the pleasure of wedding me all over again."

Chapter Thirty-Two

Windom Castle
April 1195

A muffled scream drifted from the lord's bedchamber, and the servants gathered in the hall at Windom Castle fell silent. They wouldn't have dared slack their duties had their mistress not been otherwise occupied. Their master certainly made no effort to send them about their chores.

Roark stood at the bottom of the stairs, arms across his chest, lips between his teeth. He didn't care what the servants did. With every sound from above, he winced. He'd never imagined giving birth would be so painful for the father. The thought of his darling Alyss in such agony made him want to shout and stomp and take all that pain on himself.

Alyss's young sister, Evie, stood at his side, hands clasped before her mouth, tears streaming down her cheeks. "Will she be all right?"

"Don't you worry none. 'Twon't be long now," declared Betts, the wife of Chauvere's miller. She had accompanied Evie and Lady Isobel to Windom four days earlier to help with Alyss's confinement. "Lady Alyss has handled this with her usual efficiency. Why, the pains didn't start 'til this morning, and here she's near the end."

Roark turned to scowl at Betts. When another extended moan carried down, he shuddered and dropped his arms. "That's all," he grumbled and stormed up the steps.

Betts called, "My lord, men don't belong at a birthing."

Roark didn't bother to answer but flung open the door. Alyss clutched the arms of the birthing chair Lady Isobel had brought along. Perspiration dripped from his wife's face as the moan subsided.

The two maids squealed and ran to stand in front of Alyss, blocking her from his sight. Lady Isobel glanced over and shook her head. "You must leave, Lord Roark. This is no place for—"

Alyss gasped. "Thank God you're here. I need your hand. Let him remain."

Roark rushed to her side and wrapped one muscled arm around her shoulders, pressing a heartfelt kiss on her forehead. Fear trapped in his throat made his voice harsh. "I have you, my love. What can I do?"

She leaned her head against his chest. "You've already done it some months ago."

"How can you make light of your pain?"

Turning to look at him, she smiled. "But it's...wonderful...happy time." She gasped and grabbed his hand. "Another."

He almost winced. Giving birth certainly had increased her grip. He held her tightly as she cried out.

Lady Isobel threw a length of linen across Alyss's lap until all Roark saw was white fabric. She knelt in front of the chair.

Before he could order his thoughts, Isobel and the maids were talking at the same time, and Alyss gasped and slumped. Fear gripped him. What was wrong? Why had she collapsed?

Then a sharp wail rang out, and Alyss lifted her head, her hand still gripping his.

"Congratulations my lady, my lord. You have a daughter."

Later that evening, Roark sat at Alyss's bedside, their first child lying between them. They had agreed on the name of Juliana.

Alyss gave him a worried look. "Do you mind very much she isn't a boy?"

He lowered his head and kissed Alyss. "I love you..." Then the baby. "I love both my girls. I can't think of anything better than a daughter with her mother's courage and spirit. But I'll need reinforcements in the household. We will have to work on getting a brother for her."

And so they did.

A word about the author…

Award-winning author Barbara Bettis can't recall a time she didn't love adventures of daring heroes and plucky heroines.

Retired from careers in journalism and college teaching (English and Journalism), she now edits and creates her own tales featuring heroines to die for—and heroes to live for.

http://www.barbarabettis.blogspot.com

CPSIA information can be obtained
at www.ICGtesting.com
Printed in the USA
LVHW011025281019
635533LV00019B/990/P

9 781509 225477